Paul Radford's Private War

A Novel

By

Joel B. Reed

ISBN: 1-4107-3519-2 (e-book)
ISBN: 1-4107-3518-4 (Paperback)

Library of Congress Control Number: 2003091893

This book is printed on acid free paper.

Printed in the United States of America
Bloomington, IN

1stBooks – rev. 04/15/03

This is an original work of fiction. No character presented here represents any flesh and blood person, living or dead. The events reported never happened except those major historical events mentioned, such as the attack on Pearl Harbor. Yet, these could have been real people living out real events in the real world as we know it, and that is what makes the storyteller's craft. I hope this tale gives you as much pleasure in the reading and it does me in the writing. Peace be with you.

JBR
Woonsocket, South Dakota

...tragedy lies not in the conflict between good and evil, the divine and the diabolical, but in the conflict between different kinds of good and value--between the love of God and the love of men, the love of one's country and of one's nearest and dearest..... The life of love is full of such conflicts. The most terrible thing is to have to sacrifice one kind of love for the sake of another.

Nicholas Berdyaev, The Destiny of Man

Introit. Casualties of War

The letter slipped mostly unread from his fingers. While the first lines brought a smile of joy, with the words that followed came an icy claw, closing around his belly. Quickly he scanned the rest, hoping against all reason he was mistaken. Then he reread the words that could not be denied once more. There was more, but those simple words said it all. He sat there in shock, all blood drained from his face, too stunned to move, to even weep. Then his body took over. A strangled gasp escaped as the body forced him to breathe.

Another officer passing in the hallway heard him and looked in. The lieutenant looked like he'd been shot. Then he saw the letter lying on the floor. "What's the matter, son?" a gravely voice asked gently. "Bad news from home?"

The lieutenant looked up and saw it was the admiral who had spoken, who was looking at him with obvious concern. Forgetting all military etiquette he simply nodded and said, "Yes, sir, the very worst. I just lost my wife and my daughter." His voice was too quiet, too calm, as if he were speaking from a great distance.

"Jesus," the admiral said gently. "I'm sorry son. What took them from you?"

"The war, sir," the lieutenant answered, pulling himself together. When he spoke his voice was an icy whisper, almost a curse. "The war and the frigging politicians who caused it. That's who took them, sir." Though his voice was calm, cold fires of ancient rage burned in his eyes.

"Easy, son," the admiral said. "I know you've had a hell of a shock, but that kind of talk can get you in deep trouble."

"With all due respect to you, personally, sir," the other responded in the same quiet voice, "I really don't care. They took the one thing in this world I really cared for." He paused, then looked the admiral in the eye. "If you took me out and had me shot, I'd consider it a favor."

The admiral looked at him thoughtfully, then said, "I don't think you really mean that, son, but if you do, I have a better way to die."

"I'm listening, sir," the lieutenant replied. Suddenly he remembered his manners, jumping to his feet, snapping a belated salute. "I beg the admiral's pardon," he added.

"Not now, son," the Admiral told him, returning the salute. "Come see me next week if you feel the same way next then. It's unlikely that whoever takes this mission will ever come back."

"Thank you, sir," the young man told him. "I'll see you next week."

The admiral nodded and started to turn away. Then he turned back. "You're not up for a Section 8 are you, Lieutenant? I don't need a loose cannon on my deck."

"Check my record, admiral," came the reply. "I won't disappoint you."

The admiral nodded. "Very well. As you were. What's your name, Lieutenant?"

"Radford, sir. Paul Radford."

Jesus, the admiral thought as he walked away, reflecting on Radford's icy calm and the way he banked his rage. *I'd hate to have that young man after me.*

1. Stranded In Pisco

When war came Paul Radford was asleep in the arms of Rosario Martinez. Not that this was cause for envy, or so it was thought, for Rosario was considered ugly as sin, though she was not. Scarcely over five feet tall, she weighed over a hundred and fifty pounds and poverty had left her little to cover her mass but a shapeless faded dress pieced together from other garments. She wore no makeup and few bothered to give her a second look. Those who did were struck by the quiet simplicity of her features and the soft beauty of her complexion. Those with eyes to see beyond the surface, and the patience to look, were often startled by the depth of intelligence revealed behind her eyes in unguarded moments. Yet, there was little reason to give Rosario a second look, nor to watch her for any length of time, for she had little to hold one's attention. Nor did she seek it. With no family or land or wealth, and no social position, her only apparent possession was a painful shyness many took for stupidity. "Ah, Rosario," they would say. "Yes, poor Rosario! God was angry the day she was born." Then they would smile and add the second half of the jibe, "Yet, surely, she must be God's child. She's too ugly for the Devil!"

One exception to this opinion was Juan Emiliano Calderon de Vega, the parish priest from whom Rosario made a small living keeping the rectory clean and the padre fed. For this she was given her meals, a small quiet house on the church grounds used many years before as a cloister, and the leisure to pursue the basket weaving which took up much of her day. Occasionally she was also given the little money the padre could share on those rare occasions when there was a surplus. Yet Rosario never asked for more than she was given and mostly kept to herself, quietly tending the flower gardens around her house, weaving her baskets, and serving the padre with unmasked devotion. From time to time she went to the market to sell the beautiful, intricate baskets she wove, yet she never insisted on a higher price than the buyer first offered.

This was taken as a further sign of her stupidity, and only their fear of the old priest kept the vendors' greed within bounds when they bought up her baskets to resell at other markets. Even then it was only when Padre Juan quietly let it be known Rosario was under his protection that they treated her fairly. For many of the old people believed Juan Emiliano, now known as Father Juan, once rode with Pancho Villa, the famous bandit far to the north, long before he became a padre. What they did not know was there were many weeks when these baskets were what allowed the good padre and his housekeeper to eat.

The beautiful baskets were what first brought Paul Radford into their lives. An impulse took him to the market one day to look for gifts to send home to his family Christmas. While the holiday was still many, many weeks away, shipping was a slow business, and sent even now, their presents might not arrive before Easter, if then. Nor would his mother permit them to be opened if they arrived early, despite the pleadings of her husband and younger children. Only on Christmas morning, when the sun was officially up and their traditional cinnamon ring baking in the oven, did she take her chair and signal it was time for the children to distribute gifts from under the tree.

While Radford had nothing in particular in mind, he wanted something very special for his mother. She liked native things, beautiful, exotic things from far off places and different peoples, so he was watching for something native and durable enough to survive the handling of surface shipping.

As he walked through the city, though, market he was discouraged by most of what he saw and put off by the barely masked contempt of the merchants. Yet, as he was about to leave he spotted one of Rosario's baskets being carried by an old man, and when he asked where he might find another like it, the man smiled and pointed toward the end of a long, narrow alley. "See Rosario," the old man said in Quecha, jerking a thumb over his shoulder as he laughed. "Such a beautiful name," he added, shaking his head sadly as he walked away.

Paul Radford was puzzled, not understanding exactly what the old man had said. Yet he made his way down the narrow alley in the direction the old fellow pointed until he came to a small plaza surrounded by open stalls. Against one end of the plaza he saw a young woman talking to a tall, rather severe looking priest and surrounded by a number of the beautiful baskets. What caught his attention, however, was not the baskets. It was the beauty of her face as she talked to the old man, a gentle beauty made more radiant by her obvious love for him, and the gentleness of his manner when he spoke to her. When she looked his direction as Paul approached, their eyes met for a long moment before she smiled and dropped her gaze.

"Buenas dias, senorita. Buenas dias, padre." Paul Radford's Spanish was almost flawless as he greeted them the traditional way. Yet no one could mistake him for a native. For one thing, he was far too tall. At just over six feet, his lanky frame stood a full head above most natives. Nor did his fair complexion or the auburn hair above clear blue eyes speak of anything but Gaelic descent. Among the short, dusky people of the village, Radford stood out like an ancient Celtic warrior, one who was smiling at the moment.

Yet it was not just his looks which marked the young man as a stranger. The months he had spent prowling the backcountry of Peru had subtly changed his inflection, adding bits of Quecha to his speech, as well as local idiom. Even so, the words he spoke rolled off his tongue in a way unique to the borderlands between Texas and Mexico. Though his choice of words was far more educated than the normal patios of Tex-Mex, those with ears to hear, like Father Juan Calderon, knew this was a Tejano. Nor was the old man's memory of Tejanos altogether pleasant.

"Buenas dias, senor," the old man responded, somewhat severely as he looked around. Rosario's response was barely audible.

"These are beautiful baskets," Radford continued in Spanish. "Do they came from around here?"

The old man gave him a frosty smile. "Yes, they do. As a matter of fact, they come from my house. Do you like them?"

Paul was confused. "Oh. Well, yes, I do. So you are the one who makes them?" He glanced at Rosario. "I thought...." His voice trailed off.

"Ah! You thought that just because she is a woman, Rosario must have made them. Shame on you for thinking a priest can't do anything useful."

Radford held up his hands in apology. "Oh, I beg your pardon. That's what I did think. I mean that she made them, not.... I'm sorry, I didn't know," he added lamely.

"Padre!" Rosario's voice was full of reproach her smile denied. "Shame on you. Shame on you for telling such a lie!"

The old priest laughed, startling Radford. "A lie? Rosario, I haven't told a lie in days. Well, maybe hours," he added in response to her skeptical look.

"No, but you let him believe one. Shame on you!" She turned to Paul and said, "He's a shameless tease. I'm the one who makes the baskets. I'm his housekeeper." She glared at the old man. "I ought to feed him boiled lizard for supper."

"That was breakfast," the old padre protested.

"And breakfast tomorrow, too, if you don't watch your tongue!" She turned to Radford and started to say something. Again their eyes met. Suddenly Rosario became aware how bold she was speaking in front of a stranger and lapsed into silence. A deep flush spread up her neck.

Paul Radford did not know what to say and the awkward silence was broken by the old man. "Ah," he nodded. When the two looked at him he spoke to Paul. "So you like the baskets, no?"

"Very much so," the younger man answered, glad to be back on safe ground. "I've not seen anything like them around here."

"No, and you won't," the padre told him. "Most of the merchants around here import cheap trash from the interior. Very little is produced here and most of that is very poor quality."

Radford looked at Rosario. "You do excellent work. How much do you ask for them?"

The young woman murmured an answer so soft Radford could barely hear her voice. When she repeated it, he could not believe he had heard right. "That seems very little money for such good work," he observed. "Each of them must take several hours to make."

Rosario shrugged and the old priest looked down. Paul looked from one to the other, then said, "Well, I'll take four." He pointed out his choices. Rosario carefully stacked them together and picked up the money he laid down.

"Oh, senor, you've given me too much!" she said, trying to hand back part of the money. The young man had tripled the figure she asked.

"No," said Radford. "That's only part of what they're really worth. I insist. Please."

4

The old priest frowned. "Thank you, senor," he said. "I appreciate the thought, but we do not take charity. Not for ourselves."

"I understand, padre," Radford grinned, "but I have my pride, too. If I cheated an artist I'd have to go to confession and put it in the poor box, and the priest would get it. This way I cut out the middle man."

The old priest looked at him for a long, solemn moment. Paul Radford found the directness of the man's gaze unsettling. He suspected he had trespassed a boundary few were invited to cross and cursed himself for his mistake. Then, satisfied at whatever he'd seen within Radford's soul, the padre nodded and smiled. "Yes, there is that. Shameless people, these priests." He paused, then asked, "Will you allow us to feed you, then?"

Radford nodded and smiled. "Gladly. You are very gracious and I would be honored. Would you allow me to bring something?"

"No, you really must be our guest."

Paul Radford looked at Rosario, then back at the old man and grinned. "I know guests are not supposed to be picky about what their host serves, but are you sure? I've never had boiled lizard."

The padre laughed. "I think perhaps with a guest coming I could talk her into fried cactus."

"Marvelous! Let me bring some cheap wine to choke it down."

As the banter went on, Rosario said nothing. She had never seen the old priest warm so quickly to someone. As for Radford.... She looked at him out of the corner of her eye. Even while he was engaged with the old man, she knew he was acutely aware of her presence. She did not know what to make of this. No one had paid much attention to her before, except the priest, nor paid her such a high compliment on her work. Yet she was aware her work was superior to everything she'd seen, and she knew he meant what he said. She also knew he was interested in her, too, as a man. Why this might be, she could not comprehend, but she found herself happy it was so. And she found herself unsettled in a pleasant sort of way. It was enough, she decided, a gift from God. Quickly she said a brief prayer of thanks to Our Lady of Mercy, which was a prayer of fear and trembling, as well. Then she began to plan the feast she would set before this strange young man.

That evening Paul Radford arrived at the rectory a good half hour early. This was not his intent, but somehow it worked out that way. For one thing, his shopping took very little time. The choice of wine in town was rather limited, but he had found some which might pass for a fair burgundy. To this he added a bottle of the very best brandy to be had and a liter of a local *sangria* he liked. Having spent a half hour at all this he found himself with two hours to kill and returned to his room to wash and change his shirt. Then he decided to change his trousers, too, and to clean his shoes. Tramping around the mountain trails had left them well broken in and quite comfortable, but they were far beyond shining by then. So he scraped off the remaining smudges of dried mud from his last trek and applied fresh oil to the seasoned leather, making it dark, almost coffee brown. Glancing at his watch lying at an odd angle on the table he misread the time and panicked, and when the old padre opened the door, Paul Radford was still breathing heavily.

The old priest glanced at him quickly and pulled him inside, glancing quickly down the street as he closed the door. "What's wrong, my friend?" he asked, concerned. "Was someone chasing you?"

"No, padre," Radford answered, confused. "At least not that I was aware of. I was afraid I was going to be late."

"Late?" the old man asked, as if trying to remember a long forgotten concept. He glanced at the clock on the wall. It showed twenty-five minutes to seven. "Did I tell you the wrong time?"

"No, you said seven-thirty," Radford responded. "Your clock must be slow." He dug into a pocket for his watch. It, too, said twenty-five minutes until seven. He felt a deep flush spread up his neck.

"Ah," said the old priest, smiling. "Then you do us the honor of being early. Come in and sit down. I'll tell Rosario you are here." Pausing at the doorway he asked, "Could I offer you a beer?"

Radford remembered his manners. "Please," he said, holding out his parcel. "That would be very good. Here's something to go with dinner."

"Well, thank you," the old man replied, opening the bag of liquor. "Hey, sangria for our dinner! Rosario will really like that. And, my goodness, brandy for an old man after. What a delight to have a civilized guest for a change. What we get here mostly are visiting bishops and other pests." He took out the bottle of burgundy and glanced at Radford before setting it on the table. "I do not wish to offend you, Paul," he said, "but I don't wish you to go blind, either. I'll talk to Blas about this tomorrow. He should know better than to sell you this! He promised me he would stop."

Radford was at a loss. "I don't understand."

"A local...racket, I think you Americans call them. Blas's cousin in Buenos Aires works as a wine steward at a very good restaurant. He saves the bottles for Blas and he fills them with the very cheapest red wine. Then he adds a shot of cheap bourbon and sells them at import prices. Very few people have the palate to tell the difference." He shook his head sadly. "If it were only that I would let it pass. Blas has five children to feed and things are not good for him. I found out his cousin told him adding a shot of solvent would give it a kick and Blas didn't know any better. One of his customers almost died."

Paul Radford shook his head. "Are you sure? I looked at the seal quite carefully. It didn't look like it had been altered."

"Not altered, but duplicated," the priest chuckled. "When it comes to such things Blas is a real artist." He pointed to a corner of the wax seal where the color was slightly faded. "See, he didn't get it exactly right here, but still, it's very good. He's truly and artist. With the same effort turned to honest work...." he shrugged. "The sad thing is, Blas makes so little at it. He brings in nickels and dimes and daydreams of millions. His petty larceny gives him no peace."

"Who was that?" Radford asked.

"Who was what?" the padre asked, not comprehending.

"Who was that you quoted just then?"

"Oh, 'nickels and dimes and daydreams?" the old man asked, almost shyly. Radford nodded and the padre laughed and tapped his chest. "I was quoting Calderon. Juan Emiliano Calderon. Me."

"I'll drink to that!" Radford hinted, grinning and raising his hand as if it held a glass.

"Then we'd better get us something to drink!" the old man replied, shouting for Rosario to bring their *cervesa*.

The supper which followed was a marvelous affair. Paul Radford had not eaten so well in months and when the meal was done he found himself stuffed. With the beer, Rosario brought them a delicate appetizer cooked in batter and served with a spicy sauce which only sharpened Paul's appetite. This was followed by the main course, three types of meat rubbed with special spices and cooked over a low fire, black beans topped with a blend of chiles and avocados and flavored with lime and a light blend of pepper and other spices, and a rather strange dish which tasted like yams. All this was served with Rosario's own flat bread and sangria. Once again the spicy sauce appeared and Radford followed the others' lead of dipping pieces of the meat into the sauce. Never had he imagined beef and chicken and pork could taste so good. Then, having completely conquered the two men with the main course, Rosario brought forth her *coup de grace*, a dessert she'd learned from watching a cook from central Mexico.

"Oh, no," groaned the old padre. "Prepare to surrender, my friend. She's set out the *flan*."

As the three of them sat in the courtyard of the rectory later on, Radford shook his head. "I simply don't understand it," he said.

"What don't you understand?" asked the priest. He was having trouble keeping his eyes open.

"How you eat so well and stay so spare."

The old man chuckled. "I've wondered that myself. Rosario is such a marvelous cook." He smiled to see her blush. "Even with cactus and lizard." She giggled. "To be honest, though, we don't eat so well except when we have special company." He grinned a wicked grin. "When the bishop comes it's cactus and lizard, burned and greasy. It doesn't do to encourage them to visit." Rosario rolled her eyes and shook her head, as if asking God to forgive his priest these lies. He smiled and went on and Paul had the thought this was a game the old man and his house keeper played, one almost domestic in its intimacy. "However, from the feast we just ate tonight, I'd say we had very special company."

Rosario flushed and suddenly remembered something she's left undone in the kitchen. She fled, murmuring a quiet apology, and the padre grinned ruefully. "I really shouldn't tease her like that. She's a marvelous young woman and I don't know what I'd do without her here. Especially in the last three years."

"Is she..." Radford started to ask if Rosario was the old man's daughter, a normal question in most circumstances. Then he realized what an awkward question this was to ask a priest.

"Is she what?" the padre asked, frowning.

"I mean are you...related?" Radford stammered.

The old man glanced sharply at him. "No, young man, we are not. Rosario is neither my wife or my daughter nor my mistress."

Seeing the other's embarrassment, he relented. "Forgive me, my friend. She and I are very close and we have had to deal with some very sharp tongues. "He nodded and continued. "But understand this, too. Were I twenty years younger I would seriously consider leaving the priesthood and taking her for my wife. That's how dear she is to me. As it is, she is simply my housekeeper and I am her...protector." He shrugged.

There was a long, difficult silence. Then the padre reached out and patted Radford's arm. "I really do beg your pardon, Paul. Please forgive me. Rosario and I have been together eight years now, almost nine. She was only twelve or thirteen when she first came to town, an orphan no one wanted, including me, I am ashamed to say. For almost a year she kept alive by what she could steal from the market and by the money she could make as the lowest scullion. Or being exploited for pleasure by the trash. I didn't know about this right away, but I should have guessed."

The old man paused, then looked at Radford for a long moment. Coming to a decision he went on. "Then one of the dock workers thought he was dying and called me to make confession and I found out. I did not break the seal of the confession, but I threatened to curse the man instead of absolve him unless he told me who she was and where they were keeping her." He shrugged. "Maybe God will hold that against me, but I don't think so. The man was nowhere near death. Not that that would have mattered either way, and maybe that was my sin. I was very angry."

The old padre sighed and nodded. "I think I was mostly angry at myself for turning a blind eye to things I knew were happening in this place. Especially when I went and took her out. The animals! What they did to her!" He looked up and Radford was startled at the intensity of rage in the old man's eyes. "Never have I wanted to kill so badly as at that moment I found her! Not even in Mexico with all the evil things I saw there. Yet by the grace of God I did not kill them. I did not even curse them. Yet I could have, gladly, and I think they knew it. I even had a pistol with me and I ached for them to give me the least excuse to use it. But they wisely did not. So, instead of killing anyone, I simply took Rosario out of there and brought her here. I intended to let her recover for a while before finding a school or convent which would take her. She has been here ever since."

As the old man looked at Radford his eyes filled with tears. "Do you know what she told me? About a year after I brought her here she told me she was glad I had not killed them. Mostly for my sake, but also for theirs. I think that was when I stopped planning to send her away. How many men are given the grace of an angel?"

Once again, silence descended on the two men. This time, however, the silence was different, almost gentle, even though Paul Radford felt totally helpless before the old man's grief. Desperately he searched for words of comfort, yet nothing came. And since there was nothing he could say, he said nothing. After a while he simply reached out and gently laid his hand on he old man's shoulder. When he did, the old priest raised his head and looked into his eyes a long while. There was no way he could avoid the intensity of the old man's gaze and Radford felt as if the very deepest parts of his soul were laid bare before the man's demanding eyes.

"My friend," the padre said, nodding, "You have the most remarkable gift for getting people to tell you things. I have never, ever told anyone any of this. I hope by all I hold that is holy that you will respect my confidence in you. Not so much for me as for the sake of Rosario."

"Of course," Radford replied. "Of course I will. For your sake and hers. Forgive me for prying. Perhaps I should leave."

"No," said the old padre smiling. "Not at all. That would be wrong. You did not pry. I simply confessed that which has been a burden to my soul a long while. It is I who should apologize for burdening you with my sorrows. I should have sought out a confessor long ago. I simply did not want to forgive, and it was not my place to condemn. I was not their victim."

Paul Radford started to say something, then stopped. "What?" the old man demanded.

"Nothing. it was just a passing thought. I don't know why I had it."

"Perhaps an angel whispered in your ear," the padre replied. Radford glanced up and saw the other man was not joking. "Please," the priest implored. "Tell me."

"I don't know why I thought this," the other replied. "What struck me as you spoke is that in one sense, you were their victim, too. I mean, you couldn't forgive them when Rosario did. So it's almost like you've been their prisoner for all these years."

"Jesus, Mary and Joseph," the old man breathed softly, crossing himself as he spoke. Then he chuckled. "Those who think God does not have a sense of humor are wrong. He knew I was too proud to go to another priest to confess, so he sent you."

"I wish I could absolve you," the young man replied. "But I'm not even Catholic."

"That doesn't seem to matter," the padre answered softly. "You have absolved me. The burden is gone. *Gracias a Dios*."

There was nothing more to say and the two men sat is silence a long, long while. With the high walls which enclosed the patio, nothing could be seen outside the courtyard. Yet the night sounds of the town bedding down filtered across the glass embedded on top of the walls and through the leaves of the overhanging vines planted to give shade against the noonday sun. Several streets down Radford could hear a dog barking and from a cantina in the next square he could hear faint strains from a string band. Down by the harbor there were occasional shouts of direction as a crew noisily loaded a cargo ship, and inside the rectory there were faint traces of Rosario's progress as she went about her work cleaning the kitchen and preparing for the next day. For some reason this gave him an odd sense of intimacy, as if he would sense her awareness not only of his presence, but also of his awareness of hers. Then he heard her come out into the courtyard and felt, rather than saw, her seat herself quietly between himself and the padre. For a long while he sat very still, absorbing this comforting sense of her presence and the subtle textures of her smell. Of oil and spice and corn, and of woman.

When the old man spoke again, it startled Paul Radford, though the old man's voice was so soft he almost missed what he was saying to Rosario, "...is really a most remarkable young man. We have sat here for over an hour now and I've only heard him move twice. Once was when you came out a while ago. So I know he isn't dead. He isn't asleep, is he?"

Rosario tittered softly and Radford yawned and stretched. "No, not quite. I was just listening to the night. It's much quieter in this part of town."

"Tonight it's quiet," the priest answered. "Come fiesta and you might think there was a war on."

The young man nodded. "It's hard to believe there is one going on, isn't it? Back home that's most of the news these days, even though America is not involved. Here it seems a long way off."

The padre shrugged. "Yet, but your country is involved. Or so I understand. Your president seems to be aligning himself with the English." He nodded. "Fortunately, we are not involved too much here." Then he added, almost to himself. "Yet it seems it's not as far away as one might imagine..."

When Radford glanced up sharply, the old man shook his head. "Not tonight, Paul, if you don't mind. That's a long conversation and right now I think I need to drag these old bones off to bed. Would you mind Rosario seeing you out when you leave?"

The younger man jumped to his feet. "I think I need to be going, too. This has been a marvelous evening and I don't want to wear out my welcome."

Calderon smiled. "You would have to work very hard to do that. I do hope you will come back and please, don't wait for an invitation," he grinned. "Of course, if you drop in unexpected you may have to eat boiled cactus. Maybe even lizard."

"Padre!" Rosario protested, then turned to Radford. "Thank you for the sangria. I hope you will come back to visit." Then she dropped her eyes and lapsed into self conscious silence. It was the longest speech she'd made all night.

As the days became weeks and then months, Paul Radford became an integral part of the lives of Rosario and the good padre. While his work often took him out into the high mountains of the interior, whenever he was in town he spent almost every evening in their company. The second time he came to visit they began the habit of making *paseo*, taking a leisurely stroll through the town after supper.

As they walked that evening the old man passed on stories of the town and its history, as well as tidbits of gossip about the inhabitants. At his suggestion, they saved serious talk for the secure comfort of the courtyard where they often talked late into the evening. There they covered many subjects, but often Calderon spoke at length of the war which was raging across Europe and Asia and how it touched on the lives of everyone, even there in the remote areas of South America. "Even here," he said that first evening they spoke of the war. "Even here in Pisco, who no one has ever heard of before. Even right here you'd be surprised to know how active the Germans are."

"What are they after?" Paul asked. "Guano from the islands?"

"Yes, but not just the guano," the padre answered. "Although they do want the nitrate for their explosives, they're after more than that. You know what I'm talking about. You've been up in the mountains. You've seen the mines. There are minerals here they need for the war."

"Oil, too," Radford nodded. "Or so I think. I think there may be as much oil down here as there is in Texas. Not around here, maybe, but further north. Venezuela." He started to say something more, then stopped himself.

"I've heard rumors of that," the priest nodded. "That's why you are here isn't it?" The pained look on his friend's face gave him the answer and he hurried on. "No, don't say anything you are not supposed to talk about. Please."

A look of gratitude on the young man's face confirmed what Juan Calderon suspected and he changed the subject. "We have talked of this before, but I don't see how America can remain neutral much longer. Sooner or later you will have to get involved."

"You're probably right but I hope it doesn't happen soon," Radford nodded. "I like it here."

"You think you would have to go home then?"

"Almost for sure," the younger man answered soberly. "I hold a reserve commission in the Navy and I imagine they'll call me up right away if we go to war." He saw a look of disappointment flit across the face of his friend. "I don't want to go, padre, but I'll have to if they call. That's what I promised and I have to honor my word."

"I know, my son. I know," the old priest murmured sadly. "I know the choices of war." He lapsed into silence and the two men sat quietly a long time. Neither of them noticed the startled look which passed Rosario's face as she heard them speak of these things. Quietly, so quietly, neither man looked her way, she got up and went into the kitchen where she wept in silence alone, not knowing why she wept, but only that a deep sense of grief had come over her as they talked. Slipping quietly from a side door of the rectory, she crossed a smaller courtyard to a small chapel behind the church. There she lit a candle to the Virgin, the Holy Mother. The price of a candle would cost her almost as much as she got for one of her baskets but still she lit a candle for the sake of this strange young man who dropped so unexpectedly into their lives, this young man she was coming to love.

As Radford's visits became more frequent, it was not long until Rosario began to come out of her shyness around Paul. Soon she was laughing and teasing with the two men and in the days and weeks and months which followed a gentle closeness grew among the three of them. So much so that when Paul was absent for any length of time, Juan Calderon found himself looking forward to the young man's return as much as Rosario obviously did. Yet no word of this was ever spoken between them and close as they were, it was as if the subject of the young *norteamericano* was too intimate for either to broach. Nor did Paul and Calderon speak again of Rosario, except in a very light and casual way.

Then one evening after supper, Rosario asked the padre if he would mind if Paul walked her to the market to get some things she needed the following day. There had been trouble in the market the night before when a couple of *borachones* got into a drunken brawl which caused a great deal of damage to several of the *tiendas*. The miscreants were in jail but she would feel better if the young man came along. Not that she expected trouble, but one never knew.

Without thinking, padre Juan started to offer to come along, too. Yet Rosario caught his eye with hers and a look passed between them. The offer died on his lips. "Do you mind if I don't come along?" he asked. "There's something I wanted to look up in my books, but give us a moment together, chica."

Rosario smiled and nodded. When she left to get her shawl the old priest came and stood directly in front of Paul Radford. He looked deep into the other man's eyes and said quietly, "Be very gentle with her Paul." When Radford tried to protest Calderon shook his head and said, "No, listen to me, please. You are not the first man she has had, but you are the first man she has loved. So, please, be gentle with her. You have my blessing." Then, before the astonished Radford could speak he added, "And for God's sake, man, don't leave her with a child."

"We haven't..."

"I know you haven't. You've been quite honorable." The old man grinned. "You have been too honorable for her liking, most likely. Not that she hasn't respected you for it."

"Look, Juan. To me she is beautiful. She is one of the most beautiful souls I have ever know. I would do nothing to hurt her. Never." There was no mistaking that the young man meant what he said.

"I know," the old priest sighed. "You would never willingly do anything to hurt her. Nor would you do anything wittingly, knowing it would hurt her. But, Paul, she is a woman. God made her to find great joy and fulfillment in the arms of a man. This is a good and joyful thing God has given you both. Each other. So take joy in it, but be careful."

"Padre, I'd never take advantage of her!" Radford protested, almost indignant.

"Jesus, Mary and Joseph," the old man muttered, imploring the heavens to translate. "Have you heard nothing I have said? She is a woman. She will offer herself to you soon. I know this will happen as surely as I know the sun will rise tomorrow. Will you accept her gift in the spirit it is given or will you refuse it and shame her to the core of her being?"

"I'll ask her to marry me," Radford insisted. "Tonight."

Again the old priest signed. "My dear friend, you are a most honorable man. I respect you for it greatly. Yet for a moment talk to *me*. Talk to Juan Calderon, the old bandit, and not the padre. Talk to me like two men who know how wicked this world can be. Think about what you have just proposed. What would happen to Rosario if she were crazy enough to consent and marry you?"

"Well, there might be some problems with immigration, but I think if were married it could be worked out. We'd get the process started right away and after my work is done here we'd go back home and raise family."

"Where, in Texas? Do you think your family would accept a wife who looks like a Mexican? In Texas? Would your friends?"

"Well, if they wanted to stay my friends, they'd damn well have to." Radford's jaw set in defiance.

"And what of your children? Do you think you could protect them from what they would hear on the school yard? Or on the street? Do you really want that?"

The old man saw his words sink in. Paul Radford opened his mouth as if to reply, but the weight of the old man's words stopped him. He wanted to argue it made no difference, but there was no answer to the truth Calderon had uttered. Within his own heart he knew the old man was right. The only heritage he could offer a child of such a marriage was a curse.

Then the moment was lost. Rosario returned with her market basket and a cane and handed them to Radford. Sensing something amiss in the silence, she stopped, looking from one man to the other in question, but neither showed any sign of what had just passed.

It was the padre who broke the uneasiness. "That's for the dogs," he explained, pointing to the cane with a chuckle. "Those with two legs and those with four."

"Padre!" Rosario scolded, but she laughed uneasily.

Paul Radford laughed, too, smiling reassurance as he took the basket and followed Rosario out the door. Yet his laughter was hollow and as he left, the young man looked back at Juan Calderon. There was an anguish in his eyes which made the padre almost regret his words. It was a look he had seen often in the faces of children orphaned and in the eyes young men coming out of their first encounter with war. It was the look of innocence betrayed.

2. Other Voices

The war in Europe was much closer than either Radford or the old priest imagined. Even though the United States was not officially in the war yet, there was intense competition for the rich resources of the largely undeveloped South American continent. Nor did the Axis have any illusions that were the US to come into the war, they would find themselves the enemy. Though some might dismiss the US as a very capable manufacturer of razor blades, others understood the potential of America as an adversary and word was quietly sent out to keep track of the activities of American civilians wherever the Fatherland might find its interest in natural resources challenged.

This was certainly true one morning several weeks after Radford and the old priest first spoke of the war. The tall man in black livery driving the long Mercedes touring car looked stern, even grim as the car made its way through narrow gates into the embassy compound. At the doors of the embassy itself, guards snapped to attention expecting the arrival of an unannounced dignitary or someone else of importance, but when the car stopped at the curb it was Rott, one of the embassy drivers, who got out.

Rott was known as the driver for the commercial attaché, but he kept to himself and little else was known about him. All efforts to engage him in normal conversation or to get past his indifferent reserve simply failed, and this indifference to the forms of common civility offended the guards. Yet even their resentment, expressed in subtle ways, was of no concern to Rott. The man dealt with immediate business with a minimum of words and refused to respond to anything else. Conversational gambits and direct personal questions were ignored, as one might ignore the buzzing of the many flies, and the snub was resented by the embassy guards, who considered themselves the elite among the common folk of the service staff.

Even so, none dared to challenge the man or openly express their feelings, for Rott was said to be well connected. Only one man challenged him, and then only once, and he soon regretted it. When Rott ignored the guard's greeting, the man turned to the other guard and whispered loudly, "Never mind old Rott. He speaks only to

Schwartz, and Schwartz, only to God." There was no response from Rott, except that he turned and gave both guards a long, cold stare. The next morning they found themselves on latrine duty for a month, and the lesson was not lost on the others.

Yet there was more to the guards' fear of Rott than simple fear of his connections. They were afraid of the man himself, afraid for their physical safety. For while Rott was slight of stature and walked with a limp, his silence carried a tangible air of brooding menace only a fool would ignore. Nor did the butt of what was obviously a Luger service pistol protruding from the black holster at his belt leave much doubt as to his duties. Such weapons were carried by officers and a privileged few civilians, and though Rott's clothing was cut like a uniform and he wore the high black boots of cavalry, he was clearly not in military service. The fact that his livery was cut along the lines of the corporal's uniform worn by the *Fuhrer* himself. This being black, rather than Hitler's customary brown, only added to the air of threat the man carried into every space he entered.

This particular morning one of the guards was new, having arrived from Germany only the day before. Not only was he new, but he was also very young and one of the relatively few casualties of the invasion of France. At the end of his convalescence the assignment to embassy duty came like a gift from the gods and the young man was anxious to stay as far as he could from the European front. So as Rott crossed the pavement and approached the embassy doors the young guard barred his way.

"Halt!" the guard commanded. "Identify yourself and state your business!"

Rott stopped and blinked as if he were dreaming. "You're new," he snapped. "I'm Rott. Driver for Schwartz." He started to push past the young man.

"Papers!" demanded the guard, blocking Rott's way and pushing him back with his rifle.

Rott looked at the other guard who nervously cleared his throat and said, "It's all right, Johan. He's who he said he is."

"I said 'papers'!" insisted the young guard, pushing Rott back again with his rifle. Suddenly he found himself pinned flat against the wall, choking from the arm Rott had across his throat. Something sharp was pricking his stomach and he rolled his eyes down to see the blade of a long thin knife sticking through his tunic just above his belt buckle. When he looked over Rott's shoulder, mutely calling for help the other guard stood stock still and shook his head in warning.

The quiet whisper of Rott's words was terrifying as he stared into the guard's eyes six inches away. "Look, you useless piece of dog crap, I don't have time for your smart assed military foolishness right now. Understand?" When the young soldier nodded he found himself on the pavement as fast as he had been pinned to the wall. Rott was nowhere in sight.

"Here, Johan," said the older guard with sympathy and he helped the other man to his feet. "Someone should have warned you about Rott."

When Rott entered the spacious office on the second floor of the embassy, Schwartz was at the window overlooking the courtyard. "Helmut, Helmut," he said, shaking his head sadly. "You really must stop frightening the help." He chuckled.

Rott smiled, an act most of the embassy staff would have found more terrifying than his habitual glower. "I do beg your pardon, Jergen," he murmured so quietly the other could barely hear. "Fresh assholes are sometimes more than I can resist."

The other nodded. "And we have to keep the others on their toes, as well. Good work!"

"Thank you, sir," Rott replied. Alone with Schwartz the man was relaxed, looked almost human. Nor was this something of which he was unaware. While Schwartz outranked him by two grades, the two men were almost exactly the same age and graduated from the same officer's class many years before. There Rott had been the squad leader until the harshness of his discipline alarmed the school staff and he was replaced with the more political Schwartz. Yet Schwartz wisely sought out the man he replaced and became his friend, covering for Rott's excesses of violence on several occasions. Nor was his effort unrewarded. Rott was as tough as tank armor, mentally more than physically, and there was nothing in the way of dirty work he was not willing to do. In fact, he found that the dirtier the job, the more Rott enjoyed it.

More than this, it was Schwartz who was the cause of Rott's limp, something he never forgot. For it was Rott, early in the Polish campaign, who had violently pushed Schwartz aside, not only taking the bullet the Polish soldier fired at Schwartz, but killing the man with his pistol even as he fell. The wound was so bad Rott was mustered out, but Schwartz went to bat and had him permanently assigned as his orderly. When his wife once asked in intimate pillow talk why he kept this constant shadow he replied, "Rott? My dear, some people have guardian angels. I have Rott to keep me safe." Then he made a joke he later shared with his driver, who appreciated the compliment. "Rott? *Liebschen*, he is my Rotweiller."

Today Schwartz seated himself behind his desk and waved his guardian into a chair. "So, Helmut, what did you find out?"

"Either a great deal or not much at all. The questions he's asking could be legitimate questions any geologist would ask. Those that are not about geology could be simple curiosity, or not. So far, they are too general to be of much use to intelligence."

"Unless the other side is ignorant and just fishing." Schwartz pointed out.

"Yes, but the man is a trained anthropologist, too. Our people in New York confirm he was three years at Columbia earning his doctorate." Rott reminded him.

"In anthropology, not geology," the other argued.

"They do go together in a way," Rott said. "He was studying geology in Texas first, which is what I suspect led to anthropology. His original interest was archaeology, actually. Three years is a long time to spend just to develop cover."

"Too long or too short," Schwartz agreed. "Too long for quick cover, and too short for deep. But what if they recruited him later on? After all, he is working in one of his fields of expertise."

"That could be the case," Rott agreed, "but I don't think it is. From everything we can gather, the time he spent working in Texas was legitimate enough. Texas is where much of their oil is." Rott held up his hand and shook his head as the other started to speak. "I know. He claims to be looking for rare minerals and bauxite, but when it comes to training a geologist is apparently a geologist. At the first level the training is very general and the switch later on to archaeology seems logical enough."

"Too, logical," the other pointed out. "And the languages?"

Rott laughed aloud. There was genuine humor in his voice and few would have believed the change which took place in the man when he was alone with Schwartz. "Jergen, this is a real switch. Usually I am the one who is the devil's advocate. What's eating at you?"

Schwartz shook his head. "I really don't know. I just have an uneasy feeling about this man. You are perfectly right, you know. In all likelihood he is exactly what he seems. It all fits together very well without fitting too well. And yet...." He shrugged. "It smells."

"Well, your nose must be better than mine on this. If he is an agent he has the best cover I have ever seen." He made a face. "I think even to sleeping with that fat whore."

The other nodded. "Hmm. Yes. Maybe he uses a sack." They both chuckled. He thought for a moment. "Maybe she is part of his cover. Where does the old priest fit in?"

"Nowhere, I think," Rott answered. "He is part of the local scenery. He's been here for twenty years or more. If Radford's an agent he either has the old man fooled or has recruited him. My information is that the old man is no fool, but Radford might be who he seems to be."

The other nodded. "The old man impresses me as a hard one to fool, too. What else do you know about the priest?"

"He's a man from nowhere," Rott frowned. "He showed up out of the north one day speaking with a Mexican accent, but nothing is really known about him. The stories about him riding with Pancho Villa cannot be verified, although he is about the right age. Had he not been here for twenty years I would be very suspicious of him."

Schwartz nodded. "Yes, his age is right and he had been here long enough for deep cover. But why would someone bury an agent in Pisco twenty years ago? And who would think to do it then?"

"Unless they planned to move him somewhere else when the time came?" the other responded. "But the question is would they have done so at the end of the last war? Or who would have done so? Even the communists were just getting started. Their concern was Russia."

Schwartz began pacing the room. "Yes, it all fits together on the face of it. All the little details we have fit together well. Yet they could fit together in any number of patterns. There could be a dozen different explanations. To be safe, I think we have to assume the worst. So assuming Radford is an agent and the old man is working with him, what do you propose we do?"

Rott shrugged. "For now, nothing. The risk of drawing attention to Pisco is greater than the risk of Radford being an agent. The evidence is that he is not, in which case we need to do nothing. Or that he is and is remaining very low to the ground, in which case, we need to keep an eye on him. Yet we have been watching now him for six months and there has been no indication of contact with anyone but the embassy and the old man. To be certain he poses no risk, we would arrange a convenient accident, but that might be too great a risk without solid evidence."

Schwartz nodded. "I agree. Yet even waiting for him to make his move has its hazards. So continue watching him and if you see something suspicious, eliminate him at once. You don't need to consult with me. Naturally, it would be better if it looked like an accident, but the main thing is to take him out. He must not find out what we are doing here."

Rott nodded and rose to leave. "Very well," he said. "Consider it done."

Schwartz's voice stopped him just short of the door. "On the other hand, Helmut, it occurs to me the man does wander around some rather wild country, doesn't he? If one of those wild tribes were to kill him, who would be the wiser? An arrow works as well as a bullet, and even better for our purpose."

The man in black didn't bother to answer. His cold grin said it all and without another word he left the room. Not a minute later he was driving out of the embassy compound in a military scout car, fully loaded and equipped for a long time in the back country. His plans had been laid for a long time and the food and weapons he would need were long since prepared. Now the man the embassy guards called *Schwartz Tot*, Black Death, behind his back had what he wanted. Marching orders.

Some seven to eight thousand miles to the north and west of Lima, the Commander slipped out of his jacket and hung it on the coat rack by the window, rolling up his sleeves and loosening his tie. The day was warm already and he raised the sash, propping it up with a short stick lying there for just this purpose. Pausing a moment, he glanced out over the dry, dusty hills that surrounded his command and sighed. It was good to be back. As bad as the heat and the dust could be around these parts, to him it was paradise compared to the political jungle commonly called the District of Columbia.

Hearing a soft tap on the bulkhead behind him, the Commander turned back to see his Number Two standing in passageway and nodded for the other to come in and have a seat. Out here he was the man in charge of an operational command and while there was no question who was the boss, to an outsider his unit might appear very lax by military standards. Most of the time his men wore fatigues or dressed like civilians and normal military courtesy was discouraged. That was the nature of the mission, but if one looked beyond the obvious, there was no mistaking this for anything but a well disciplined unit. With equipment and other areas where it mattered, there was no tolerance for sloppiness, and the entire command ran like a Swiss railway.

"Good morning, Alex," the Commander said, offering the other a hand and smiling before taking his seat behind the desk. "I see the place didn't go to the dogs without me."

The other smiled back, a sign of genuine affection few others ever saw. Among the men of the command group it was said, and only half in jest, that in the mind of the Lieutenant, the Commander spoke for God and White was his prophet. Among his peers, White was known as the Iceman for his unswerving advocacy of simple solutions to geopolitical problems. "Why don't we just shoot the son-of-a-bitches?" he once asked, referring to the leaders of the German Reich and the Soviet Republic. "That would save us all a lot of grief." When asked if he, himself, would be willing to lead the team on what would surely be a suicidal mission, White shrugged and answered. "Of course. Why not? We all have to die sometime."

Yet there was an entirely different side to Alex White he revealed to only a few and Commander Rudd was one of them. "It was a close shave, Eric," White drawled, making a sour face, "but somehow we managed. We had to hang the cook, but what the hell." Alex shrugged. "Not much else to do on a Saturday night around here."

"Not anything to do around here come Saturday night," another voice broke in from the open doorway. A tall, thin man entered the room without invitation and folded himself into the chair beside the

Executive Officer. "Hell, this week there weren't even any delivery trucks to watch unload." He nodded soberly. "On the other hand, we did have some excitement here the night after you left." When the Commander glanced up sharply, but the thin man waved away his concern. "It was a full moon and someone spotted a couple of jack rabbits fornicating on the runway." He frowned. "At least, that's what I think they were doing. Been so long I couldn't be sure, but it looked familiar."

Even the taciturn Alex chuckled. Among the younger men in the unit Denis Blieu, third in the chain of command, had the reputation of being a ladies' man, even within the monastic conditions of the camp. Just how he came about the reputation was something of a mystery to anyone who had never seen him in mixed company, for Blieu was not a handsome man. While his clothing hung well from his tall frame, at first he appeared ungainly, and the wheat-straw hair which even a crew cut could not tame gave him the semblance of a disheveled stork.

Yet, like a stork, when Blieu moved, it was with incredible grace. And despite homely features, his remarkably blue eyes and radiant smile were like a magnet to the fairer sex. On one occasion, the first and only time the Senator brought along any of his staff when he visited the post, there was a minor alarm when the Senator's secretary mysteriously vanished for more than an hour until she reappeared on Blieu's arm looking somewhat distracted. Thanking Blieu for helping her find her way back from the library, she rejoined the Senator's party, giving rise to a long look between Eric Rudd and his second officer. The library was just down the corridor from Blieu's quarters.

Nor was Eric Rudd's concern out of place. The Senator's good will was essential. As a matter of official fact, this command did not exist. Completely clandestine, it was the brain child of the Senator and an equally concerned group of senior military staff. On the books it was carried as a remote area testing facility, quickly shortened to RAT-Fac in military jargon, one run as a cooperative project between the Army Signal Corps and the Department of the Navy. Since the Navy provided most of the funding, the camp was also designated an advanced Marine Corps training area. This meant most of the men in Rudd's command were Marines detached from various units for special duty, including Captain Denis Blieu. Yet, this did not prove to be the problem it might, for Rudd held the respect of Blieu and his leathernecks. Whenever they were in the field training, more often than not they'd find Commander Rudd right there with them, often leading the vanguard and humping it out with all the rest.

Blieu fished out a pack of cigarettes, raised his eyebrows. Rudd nodded and passed an ash tray across the desk, leaning back and wiping the weariness from his eyes.

"Tough flight?" Blieu asked, offering the pack to Alex, who shook his head.

"Very," Rudd answered, shaking his head. "It was all I could do to keep from kicking the pilot out the hatch and taking the stick myself." He let out a deep breath. "Come to find out, the dumb bastard just graduated from flight school last month and wasn't checked out for rough weather."

"Why didn't he fly around?" Blieu asked. "There wasn't a full storm front. Just area cells."

"That's what I wanted to know," Rudd answered. "Apparently no one ever told him not to fly into a line of thunderheads, especially in light aircraft over high mountains." Shaking his head, he shrugged it off. "What I need is a good cup of coffee. Anything else?" He grinned at Blieu. "Other than jackrabbits?"

"Not here," Blieu reported. "We got in some new equipment to check out but they forgot to put in the manuals when they shipped it. SNAFU. It was that system we were looking for last week."

"How long before we get them?" Rudd asked. "I want to get that stuff up and running."

"Oh, it already is, Jack," Blieu told him, grinning. "We had it going the afternoon it arrived. The way the manuals are usually written, they probably saved us time leaving them out."

"I should have known before I asked," Rudd said, smiling. Early in his association with Blieu he quickly found out there was nothing electric or mechanical his chief engineer could not only dismantle and put back together again, but usually improve in doing so. The way he discovered this was when Blieu borrowed his prized Leica one day and returned it the next, mentioning out a couple of things Rudd knew needed repair. Yet Rudd discovered these ailments had mysteriously self-corrected the next time he used the camera. When he mentioned this to Blieu some days later, the other nodded and told him they had been fixed. When pressed for details, Blieu said he had to machine a couple of new parts, but that was no particular trouble. "We've got a good shop here, sir," was how he put it.

"Alex?" Rudd looked at his Executive Officer.

"Same old same old," Alex reported. "We're having some problems with the Paymaster, but it's nothing we can't work out. Some auditor picked up some irregularities, but we shifted things around a bit and it looks all right now." He gave a dry chuckle. "Not that we're getting rich skimming it off the top out here, but it's getting harder to hide our operation. Other than that, everything's up to snuff. We're even a little ahead on our training schedule. Our guys picked up the new drill pretty fast." He grinned and added, "For Marines, that is." Blieu ignored the good natured jibe.

Rudd nodded and said nothing, looking into the middle distance. The others waited patiently for a long while. Finally Blieu broke the silence. "So how's the Senator, Eric?" he asked.

"The Senator is very worried about the way things are going," the Commander sighed. "There are a lot of people who don't want us anywhere near this war and that makes it hard for us to do what we need for when it comes. Nothing has been able to stop the Germans and the Japanese aren't doing too badly, either. The problem is, we don't know what they're up to until after it's done."

"I don't know. We didn't do so bad calling the Polish invasion," White answered. "They were only three days behind our prediction. Not that it made any difference, but it could have."

Rudd shrugged. "We aren't at war and now everyone in Washington claims he saw the whole thing coming. Long before it happened, of course. They conveniently forget that before it did, we had a hard time getting anyone with clout concerned." He looked at the others. "I don't know if I told you about it at the time, but one of our ranking admirals advised me to stop making waves."

"So we couldn't do squat," Blieu observed tartly. "Except warn the British, which we did, but they didn't want to hear it, either." He shook his head sadly. "I guess I'll never understand. No one seemed to care that we had an agent on the ground in Germany giving us solid information."

"Which accounted for our 'lucky guess'," White added, nodding. "Shit, we knew what was going to happen even before Adolph shacked up with Joseph Stalin."

"Well, the Senator woke up after that," Rudd replied, pulling them back to the present. It was a discussion they had more than once before and the memory rankled. Yet it was no use chewing bile. "He also woke up to the fact we were right on target, too. Now he's trying to make up for lost time and he wants us to check out what the Germans are up to in South America. Apparently he got wind of something from one of his sources in the State Department."

"South America?" Blieu asked. "I thought we were pretty tight with the governments down there, except for Brazil and maybe Argentina. Something going on there?"

"There's apparently a large German population in every country that counts," Rudd answered, "and the Germans are going after raw materials. Especially on the western coast."

"Lot of nitrates in Chile," White nodded. "I seem to remember a war over those. Peru and Bolivia got into it with Chile?"

"That's right," Rudd replied. "The War of the Pacific, which Chile won and which turned out good for us now. We're on more solid ground with the government there than in some other places. But there are lots of other mineral resources the Germans are after beside nitrates. They're after rare metals, oil, bauxite. You name it and they're trying to corner the market for their war effort."

"So where do we come in?" Blieu wanted to know. "This sounds more like business for Treasury or Commerce. Or even the State Department."

Rudd nodded. "That's who is handling the obvious connections," he said. "Thing is, what the Senator caught wind of was something else. There's not much hard information, but it sounds like the Germans may be building military installations somewhere along the west coast. Submarine bases and maybe hidden airfields to protect the bases."

"Damn," Blieu responded. "It makes sense from their point of view. From there they could strike at Canal shipping pretty easily when we get into the war. Depending on which way the governments down there go, they'd have a close supply of fuel, too."

"Exactly," Rudd nodded. Nor did he miss the unstated assumption in Blieu's statement. There was no question in their minds that the United States would eventually find itself in the war, and no real question which side it would take. The only question was when and how this would happen.

"Wait a minute," White objected. "Denis is right. We are tight with the governments down there. Why not get the information to them? Let them take care of it."

"That was my response but it's not that simple," Rudd explained. "The Senator tells me that the best we can hope for in practical terms down there is neutrality. There are large communities of German colonists in every South American country, and they are a pretty powerful group. A lot of them agree with what the Nazis are trying to do. They may or may not like Hitler, but they're good Germans and the last war left a bad taste in their mouths."

White nodded. "So they basically neutralize any allies we have there. Even if we give them the information, they may not act on it." He shrugged. "Just like the British."

"Precisely," Rudd told him. "Unless we force their hand. What the Senator wants us to do is to put together a team to do just that. The first part of the mission is to find out what they are doing and where, and the second is to send in a team to make enough noise the politicos can't ignore it." He grinned. "In other words, gentlemen, it's time to rumble."

"Hot damn!" Blieu declared. "It's about time we did something. When do we start?"

"Wait a minute," the taciturn White insisted. "What the Senator is talking about could get us shot as spies. By a friendly government. It could push them the other way, too, if it goes sour."

"He mentioned that," Rudd told them. "He thinks it is worth the risk, and I have to agree. I don't see we have much other choice. We just have to be damned sure not to get killed or caught."

"Or not identified as Americans if we are," Blieu remarked with an evil grin. "We could always carry German documents and wear German clothes. That might even help us slip up on the bastards."

"Denis you are one devious soul," White observed. "I worry about you."

"That's what all the ladies say," Blieu confessed.

28

"I wonder who we have on the ground down there?" White asked no one in particular. "It would really help if we had someone in place we could trust. I'll call BUPERS tomorrow and find out."

"Save yourself a nickel," Rudd told him. Opening his briefcase he took out several files. "I had the same question and so did the Senator. He had it run down for me before we even talked." He took out one of the files and opened it. "There are several good possibilities in other areas, but I think this guy is the best shot. He's the best located and he's locally connected." He handed the folder to White who opened it on the desk. Blieu looked over his shoulder as he read it.

"He's been on the ground almost four years," White agreed. "So he should be well established by now. And he should know the country if this is correct."

Rudd nodded. "He's a geologist working for an American company and he's covered the back country pretty well. At least around Lima and to the north. According to this, he moved his base south to Pisco a few months ago."

"Any idea why he did that?" White asked, suspicious.

Rudd nodded. "I wondered about that, too. On the other hand, it makes sense. Apparently no one else is looking at that area. Not much there but sea lions and coastal desert, but it could have good minerals. Like Arabia."

White nodded. "It could be a good area for the Germans, too, if it's that isolated. Depending on what they're up to."

"Exactly," Rudd nodded. "From what I was able to find out in Washington, it would make a perfect place for a hidden sub base."

Blieu was staring intently at the hazy identification photo in the file. "Hey, I know this guy," he exclaimed. "He and I went to communications school together." He nodded. "We also hung around the same bars at night."

"What's he like?" Rudd wanted to know.

"I don't really know," Blieu said thoughtfully. "We didn't hang around together. He seems to be a quiet type. Minds his own business, but I don't think there's much he misses. He asked good questions in school." He started to say something more but shrugged. "That's all I know."

"Come on," White demanded, suspicious at the other's reticence. "What is it?"

"Nothing," Blieu shook his head. "Just a personal thing."

"Alex is right, Denis," Rudd insisted. "If there's anything off center about this guy we need to know about it right away."

"No, it's nothing like that," Blieu shook his head, then grimaced. "He was the reason for one of the few times I missed," he admitted.

"Missed what?" Rudd wanted to know, but White suddenly broke out laughing.

"You got to be kidding!" White gasped, staring at Blieu. "You?" Rudd had never seen Denis Blieu so taken aback.

"Missed out," Blieu muttered, answering Rudd's question. He glared at White.

"Missed out on what?" Rudd demanded. "What in the hell are you two talking about?"

"Curse you, Red Baron," Alex laughed, pointing two index fingers at Blieu and shaking them like machine guns firing. "Our own Denis Blieu, shot down in flames by a green American."

"Tell me it ain't so!" Rudd laughed, finally catching on and looking at Blieu for confirmation.

"I'm afraid so," Blieu admitted, giving White a poison look. Then he shrugged and grinned. "I gave it my best shot but the young lady had her heart set on Radford. The sad thing is, he could have had her on one of the tables and he acted like he didn't even know it! When he left, it was with a crowd."

"So you rescued her from her loneliness," White suggested, sardonic.

"I have my standards," Denis replied stiffly. Then he grinned. "But that wasn't one of them. The poor dear was so crushed I had to do something." White made a gagging noise and Blieu laughed.

"Wait a minute," Rudd insisted. "This is important." The other two were instantly serious. "Was he unaware of it, or was he with someone else? Or maybe too drunk?"

Blieu thought a moment. "No, he wasn't drunk. He only had a beer or two at the most, and he nursed those. If I had to guess, I'd say he was aware of what was going on but just not interested."

"He's not queer is he?" White asked. Rudd nodded, seconding his executive's concern.

"No," Blieu answered. "No hint of that. None at all. The lady was a little...forward, I think, and that must have put him off. She was pretty but rather empty headed, too. So I think he may have been deliberately obtuse to her overtures."

"And you weren't interested in her mind," White snorted and Rudd smiled.

"Just her soul," Blieu shot back, grinning. Even Rudd laughed.

"All right," the Commander said. "Then you need to be the one to initiate contact, Denis. Do you have any problem with that?"

"No," Blieu told him. "It was no big deal. Nothing personal. It was a long time ago and there's been a lot of water under the bridge."

"You mean a lot of souls between the sheets," White snorted, correcting him. "And you did get the girl, after all."

"There is that," Blieu laughed. "It was only a temporary setback."

"How long will it take you to get down there?" Rudd asked, pulling them back to the problem at hand. "We need to move on this as fast as we can."

"Without making any ripples, ten days," Blieu answered. "Maybe less if we can get a civilian plane. A two-seater would do nicely. I'll fly myself down and bring your man back if you want."

"No," said Rudd. "You make contact with him and make the call. If you think he will work out, then send us a wire. While you're gone, we will put together what we need and join you in Lima. Even if Radford is a no-go. we're still going in. We'll work out a cable code to use before you leave."

"Right," Blieu answered. "Am I traveling in coffee or cocoa this time?"

"Neither," White answered. "This time, my friend, you're going bananas."

3. Other People's Mail

"Well, we will miss you, my friend," the old priest said. The three of them were sitting in the courtyard of the rectory, though the hour was still early. Since Radford was leaving, supper had been early and the two men sat in what was their accustomed places while Rosario quietly sat to one side making one of her baskets as she listened to their talk. She looked up at the padre's words and smiled agreement.

Seeing movement out of the corner of his eye Radford turned his head to give her a smile and Rosario blushed. Juan Calderon smiled, too, but kept it to himself. *If these two aren't lovers by now*, he thought, *they will be soon.* Once again he silently gave thanks for the mercy which had brought this strange young man into their lives. To this he added a prayer to bring him safely home, to himself as well as Rosario.

"I'll miss you, Juan," Paul answered simply. "You, too, Rosario." She nodded but didn't look up from her work. "You know, this place has really become home to me. Not Pisco, although I like it here, but you and Rosario. You've made me very welcome."

Juan Calderon made no answer, but simply nodded, and Rosario smiled shyly. To change the mood Radford laughed and patted his full belly. "On the other hand, I have to say walking the mountains will be good for me. I must have gained ten pounds since I met you all. Not that I regret a bite."

This time the padre chuckled and Rosario looked up, smiling. After a moment, the old man's face grew serious once again. "What concerns me, Pablo, is the area where you are headed. This part of the country is new to you, isn't it?"

Radford nodded. "Yes, but that's why I'm going there. There's not much use scouting around where I trip over every other geologist in the country. From what I can tell, very few have bothered with the area I'll be looking at."

"Did you not wonder why that is?" Calderon asked.

"That was on my list to ask you tonight," Radford nodded. "I didn't want to be obvious in asking around about it, but I haven't heard much mention of it around town. I overheard a couple of

Portuguese talking about some trouble the militia ran into near there, but I only caught part of the conversation."

The padre nodded. "You did well not to ask if you're going there," he said. "Locally that's known as a place to avoid. Several people have gone into the area and have not come back."

"That's something I didn't know," Radford replied. He thought a moment. "Are you advising me not to go up there?"

"Not at all," Juan Calderon assured him. "That is incredibly beautiful country up there. Just be very careful with the people you find."

"It sounds like you've been there," Radford invited.

"Oh, yes, although it's been several years since my last visit. I got lost and wandered through there on my way south many years ago. I was able to be of some small service to them and we became friends." Radford waited patiently, but the old man was through talking history. "They are good people," he continued, "but they won't tolerate much foolishness. Given the history of the Europeans here, I can't say I blame them. I suspect some of those who didn't come back thought they could ride roughshod over the stupid *indios* and I suspect the rest simply perished from their own mistakes. The country where you go is not very forgiving." He looked up. "Who's your guide?"

"I thought I'd take Quito. I used him before and he did a pretty good job."

The padre snorted. "I imagine he did in country every one knows as well as they know the market square. He's good enough, I suppose, but keep in mind that he works for the highest bidder. Have you told him where you plan to go?"

"Yes," Radford answered. "We're supposed to leave tomorrow as soon as he gets back from up the coast. What are you saying, Juan?"

"I'm telling you he works for the Germans," the old man replied. "I happen to know that for a fact, but don't ask me how. Not that they use him for a guide. Even they know better than that. No, I suspect he's far more useful to them selling information about where he takes others."

"Son of a bitch!" Radford exclaimed. Rosario looked up at Paul's sharp tone and the old priest translated the unfamiliar English phrase. Rosario nodded and added something in a dialect Radford did not understand. Calderon caught his look and explained.

"I don't think the phrase would mean much literally translated," he told Radford. "What she is saying is that you're insulting the bitch calling Quito her son."

Radford chuckled and looked at Rosario with new interest, but she didn't look up. The basket she was weaving seemed to need all her attention. Then Radford's face turned serious. "I don't know what to do," he said. "I've already hired Quito and things are pretty well set. I hate to put off going at this point. I guess I could tell him I changed my mind."

"When does he get back?"

"He told me it would be noon at the latest, but I'd be surprised if he got here by mid-afternoon. I've had to wait as much as two days for him before."

Calderon nodded. "He has that reputation so it's simple. Leave the first thing in the morning, even before light. When you get back, you can tell Quito you didn't want to wait. Does he know exactly where you are going?"

"No, but neither do I," Radford told him. "That's the problem. If I knew where I was going I wouldn't need a guide. Who else am I going to get to guide me who knows the country? Especially at this hour?"

"Ye of little faith!" the old priest said in English as he grinned. He turned and spoke rapidly to Rosario in the same dialect she had used before. To Radford it sounded like a variation on Quecha, but he couldn't be sure. Rosario listened intently, then nodded and put aside her basket and hurried out of the room. A moment later Radford heard the street door to the rectory close behind her.

"So you have someone in mind," Paul observed dryly. "Anyone I know?"

Juan Calderon nodded. "Yes. His name is Pico. He comes from the area you want to look at."

"Pico?" Radford asked, frowning. "You're not talking about the one-eyed swamper who works over at Romero's, are you?"

"Ah, you've met him," the padre answered, nodding.

The younger man looked at the padre like the old man was crazy. "Juan, if it's the same man I'm thinking about, he's half blind and crippled, too. He stays drunk most of the time."

"Have you ever seen him drink?" Calderon challenged gently.

34

"Well, no, but...."

"He was born with one leg shorter than the other," the old man told him. "Did you notice the bad scars on his face?" Radford nodded. "Pico lost his eye killing a jaguar with his *machete*. The thing was attacking the man next to him and Pico killed it with a single stroke." He shrugged. "Not before the cat clawed him. That's how he lost his eye."

"It sounds like you were there," Radford observed, intrigued despite his personal concern.

"Yes," Juan Calderon told him. "I'll tell you about it some time. We were on our way to Santa Ana where I was to marry Pico's niece and baptize her child, which I did." He opened his cassock, revealing his chest, which was covered with old scars. "I was the other man."

"Well, all right," Radford admitted. "I understand your loyalty to Pico but he's still half blind."

"You still don't understand," the padre told him. "Pico sees more with one eye in a week than most people do all year. No one pays him any attention because he works in a *cantina* and seems drunk, but he hears a lot of things there and he understands what he hears." He shrugged.

Radford nodded doubtfully and the priest continued. "You see, no one thinks much of Pico, just like they don't think much of Rosario. Few look beyond the obvious. So if you hire him, people will think you're just another foolish *norteamericano.*"

"Why do I want people to think I'm a fool?" Paul Radford asked. "I'm paid not to be."

Calderon nodded. "Yes. And you are no fool, either, which your employers know. But if a fool looks in the area no one's found anything, no one cares. A smart man looking there draws attention."

Radford looked at the old man with new apprehension. "There's a lot more to you than meets the eye, too, Juan Calderon," he observed.

"Who, me?" the old man glowered. "Me, I'm just a crazy old priest with a bad disposition and a retarded housekeeper." He laughed.

"Right," the other responded. "And I'm the King of Siam." He thought a moment. "All right, it makes sense to me. I'll take your man, Pico. The animals are ready so we can leave at first light." He gave the old man a strange look but said nothing.

"Something is bothering you, my friend," the padre told him. "What is it? Does it bother you I know so much about these things?"

Radford laughed. "I can't hide much from you, can I?"

The old man opened his eyes wide and wiggled his fingers like a Mesmerist. "Padre Juan sees all and knows all," he replied in a ghostly voice. Radford laughed more. "I did ride with Villa," the old man said, serious again. "I was one of his spies, and I became very good at gathering information for him. Mostly I did exactly what Pico is doing now, pretending to be a drunk."

"Ah," Radford nodded, but Calderon could see reservations in his face.

"You want to know why I'm still doing this," the other said, more as a statement of fact than as a question. "Well, in your place, I'd want to know what I do with this information. Right?"

The young man grimaced and nodded. The padre smiled. "No one else knows about this," he told Radford. "Only me and Pico and Rosario." He shrugged. "At first, it was just that the old habits die hard and life in a small town like this can be deadening to the mind. So Pico and I talked about things he heard since we had nothing better to do. Then, when the Germans came, I wanted to know what they were up to. For my own protection. There is no question they are after more than minerals and I wanted to know what it was." He shrugged. "I still haven't found out, but I do know something is up. There are many more Germans in Lima than one would think necessary for such an isolated place, and this place gets too many strange visitors."

Radford sighed, almost in relief. "So you gather the information for yourself," he said, but there was a question left unspoken in his statement.

Calderon nodded. "Until now I've had no one to pass along what Pico has told me and what I have learned on my own," he said. "I'm telling you so you can pass along what you think is necessary to your government. All I ask is that you keep your source to yourself."

Paul Radford chuckled. "From what I've seen of our embassy people, they wouldn't believe me if I told them the Andes are tall mountains," he said. "They seem to be very caught up in their own affairs and in love with their own preconceptions."

"More fools, them," Calderon nodded.

Just then they heard the door to the rectory open and soon Rosario came into the courtyard. She was followed by a nondescript man not much taller than herself. He was dressed in wear stained clothes, with a long shirt which had once been white hanging loose over baggy trousers. The shirt was gathered at his waist with a cloth belt, woven in a subtle rainbow of dark colors. A leather thong held what Radford guessed was a crucifix tucked away under his shirt and his feet were shod in native rope sandals, well worn but still very serviceable. In his hands was a tattered hat Radford had seen him wear in the *cantina*, now taken off in respect to the house.

Though the man walked with a slight limp, there was no evidence of drunkenness in his gait now, and a closer examination of his tunic would have revealed that while it was old and stained, it was clean. The man himself was lean and wiry and a wispy, sparse mustache and beard hung from his chin. Yet it was the man's eyes which caught Radford's attention. Dark as unblinking obsidian, he was sure they missed nothing. Nor did they reveal anything, and the young man suddenly realized he had never looked directly into the man's eyes before. Doing so now he felt a passing sense of compassion for any jaguar which would be so foolish as to attack this man or anyone in his care.

Then he remembered one of these eyes was glass and laughed inwardly at himself. The eye which was normally covered by a black patch was now uncovered and only the deep scars across the man's face revealed which eye this was. Yet he understood why Juan Calderon had said this man saw more with one eye than most do with two. The sense Pico was looking out of both was uncanny.

Seeing Radford, Pico stopped cold, fixing the younger man with his gaze. Calderon spoke up, telling Pico something in what sounded like the same language he spoke earlier to Rosario, and she translated for Radford. "He's telling Pico you are a good man, a smart one who is to be trusted," she said simply. With the old man's words, Pico nodded and the tension went out of his stance. Yet Radford saw that even relaxed, the man was like a tightly coiled spring which could explode into action in a flash. *How could I have missed something so obvious,* he wondered.

"I beg your pardon, my friend," Calderon said to Radford. "I am so used to talking to Pico in his native tongue I forgot my manners. Rosario didn't tell him about you, but just that I wanted him."

Radford nodded, beginning to appreciate just how tight-lipped his new friends were. The old man continued. "May I present my friend, Pico. This is Pablo," the padre told the smaller man. "At least, that's what Rosario and I call him."

This was news to Radford. "I like that," he said. "It is good to meet you." He extended his hand to Pico, who after a momentary hesitation, took it. Surprisingly, taking Pico's hand was like grasping a limp, thick fold of warm leather, and Radford remembered that shaking hands was not a custom among the Indians. He started to release the other man's hand, but Pico grinned and squeezed. It was like having his hand in a vise, though the smaller man was careful not to hurt him.

"I see what you mean," Radford told the priest. "There's a more to Pico than I ever suspected. He'll do very well if he cares to go."

Quickly Juan Calderon explained what Radford wanted, this time speaking Spanish sprinkled with a number of words he did not recognize. When he was done, Pico nodded and turned to Paul. "I will take you there," he said simply. "Where do you wish to meet?" His Spanish was as clear and unbroken as Calderon's.

Radford told him. "I'd like to leave at first light," he added. "I'll go by tonight and tell the man to have our burro ready."

"Let Pico do that," the padre suggested. "He can sew a few seeds of misdirection."

Pico smiled and nodded. It struck Radford that Pico and the old man were really enjoying this. "Good idea," he said. He reached in his shirt and handed the guide a list. "That's what I'm taking. Do you have any suggestions."

Pico looked at the list. "How long are we going to be gone?" he asked. "Six months?"

"I've been told I travel a bit heavy," Radford said, a little defensively. "That's why I'm taking the burro." Pico waited and he realized he'd not answered the man's question. "Two weeks, I think. Maybe three. That should be long enough."

Pico nodded and looked at the list. He named about a dozen items. "That's all we need," he told Radford. "The rest isn't necessary."

"Not even a rifle?" Paul asked. "And what about rain gear and a tent?"

Pico shrugged. "We're not going hunting for jaguar," he said. "Our *pistola*s will be enough and you don't need a tent or a raincoat. Don't you have a *poncho?*" Radford shook his head. "I'll bring you one in the morning," the guide told him. "Bring a warm shirt, too. It will be cold where we go."

"What about food?"

Pico grinned for the first time. "I supply the food," he said. "If you have some money I will get what we need tonight."

Radford handed him a sheaf of bills. Pico took less than half and handed the rest back to Paul. "I guess you need to tell the stable we won't need the burro," he added.

"No, we take the burro," Pico told him. "It will make a good gift. When we get back I will tell the stable it died. It will cost more that way but...." He shrugged.

"Gift?" Paul asked. "Who's the gift for?"

"Trust your guide, Pablo," Juan Calderon told him. "You will see." Reaching under his cassock he pulled out a silver medallion on a black silk cord. Seeing it, Pico nodded and smiled, and the old man handed it to Radford. "Here, wear this," he said. "The man who gave it to me is who the gift is for. Or for his son if he is not still alive." He shrugged. "He was very old when he gave me this and that's been many, many years ago."

Paul looked at the medallion. He could tell it was very old, but the deeply etched figure at its center was still clearly visible as was the elaborate design ringing the perimeter. It was a pictograph, the figure of a man, obviously a male, with both hands raised, as if in victory. In one hand was what looked like a spear or some other weapon, and in the other was a round object hanging from the man's hand by three strands. Suddenly Paul understood that what the man was holding was the head of an enemy and an involuntary shudder went up his spine.

Juan Calderon saw the flash of recognition in his eyes. "Yes," he said. "This is the medal of a great warrior, passed down from generation to generation." He shrugged. "The story behind it is lost in the centuries but the basic meaning is still quite clear, although I suspect there is much more to it than that. That could have been his head hanging from the hand of his enemy."

"A clear warning, too," Radford added. "Don't mess with this man."

"Yes," the old man said. "You may find it useful." He nodded to Pico and the guide reached into his shirt. Lifting the thong around his neck he showed Radford what was suspended there. Rather than a crucifix, it was another medallion exactly like the one Paul held in his hand.

"So you see how it is," Juan Calderon spoke and Radford nodded. The priest rose from his seat and addressed Pico. "Well, Pico, you have things to do and it's time for a walk for me." The smaller man rose to go with him and Radford got to his feet, but the padre grinned and stopped him. "I think perhaps a couple of love birds need so say goodbye, too."

"Padre!" Rosario scolded, and Radford flushed. Seeing his color, the old man cackled as he left the courtyard. Pico kept his eyes down but Radford knew he was smiling, too.

The letter arrived three days after Radford and Pico left for the interior. The regular clerk was off duty the day it came so it lay in Radford's mail slot at the hotel desk almost a week before the clerk saw it as he was leaving a message in the next slot next. Glancing around quickly to make sure no one was watching he took the letter and stepped into the back room. There he gave it a careful examination.

There was not much to be learned from the outside. The envelope was a common light blue air mail fold-over addressed in a strong, clear hand to Paul Radford at the hotel. The return address was a T.M. Radford from somewhere in Texas, and the stamp bore a postmark dated more than two weeks before in Ft. Worth. It looked like a thousand other personal letters the clerk had seen and he started to replace it in the box, then changed his mind. Tucking the letter into his jacket pocket he picked up the phone and placed a call to a local number.

That evening after work, the clerk stopped by his brother-in-law's cantina for a bottle of beer as he often did on the way home. The usual local people were there, but tonight two foreigners sat at the table nearest the front of the bar, paying little attention to the rest of the occupants. They smoked as they talked quietly and sipped their beer. On the table between then was a pack of American cigarettes, but as he passed, by the clerk heard a few words he thought were German. What caught the clerk's attention as he seated himself at the owner's table at the other end of the bar was the smaller of the two men. He recognized the other as a local business man, but the smaller man was someone the clerk had never seen before. He was dressed completely in black, which was unusual, but it was his eyes, his cold blue pitiless eyes, which were so striking. Without intending to, the clerk stared.

As if the man in black felt the clerk's gaze, the cold, hard eyes turned and locked with his. For a long moment, and without knowing quite how, the clerk found himself unable to move, even to breathe. He was frozen in his chair like a bug pinned under the harsh light beneath a powerful looking-glass and he found himself remembering ancient sins, things done and left undone, he'd not thought of for years. Nothing within him was hidden from this man. Nor was there any doubt in the clerk's mind that the man in black would not hesitate to use this knowledge against him. Then the man in black shifted his gaze and released him, and the clerk almost crossed himself in relief.

"Hey, brother, what's wrong?" a voice beside him asked and the clerk turned his head to see his brother-in-law taking the seat beside him. "You look like you've seen a ghost."

"Not a ghost," the clerk muttered. "The devil himself." As if hearing his name, the man in black glanced their way but this time his gaze moved quickly by them and returned to the other man sitting at his table. The man in black said something and the other man laughed quietly. To the clerk that was even more chilling than the man's gaze.

"*El negro?*" his brother-in-law asked. The black one? The clerk nodded and the other nodded. "I'd hate to have him mad at me," he agreed. "Who is he?"

"I don't know," the clerk answered. "And I don't want to know, either," he added, to himself, but his brother-in-law heard him and chuckled.

"I've got something for you," the clerk told him. "But wait a minute. I've been holding water since noon." He got up and made his way to the open-air urinal in a small walled court behind the bar.

The barkeep nodded and returned to the bar. The man in black's companion caught his eye and signaled for another round. Getting up he fished out some change and stacked it on the table to cover the round. Then he made his way toward the *pissoir*. The man in black said nothing but shook out a cigarette from the pack on the table and lit it, laying the worn brass lighter on top of the pack. As he set the fresh round of beer on the table the bar tender noticed the lighter was deeply etched with two jagged black lines shaped much like lightening bolts. Yet the bartender got only a glimpse. Noting his interest, the man in back picked up the lighter and returned it to his pocket, turning to stare at the bar tender.

"*Gracias, senor,*" the barkeep murmured, not raising his eyes as he scooped the stack of coins from the table. *My* cunado *is right,* he thought to himself, returning to the bar. *This man is evil.*

Thirty minutes later Rott was reading the letter. He and his companion were seated at a table in the other man's kitchen. Steam rose from the spout of a teapot still bubbling on the gas stove which they used to open the envelope after carefully examining it for tell-tale markers. There were none they could see, but that didn't mean the envelope was only what it appeared to be. The presence of tell-tales itself would have told anyone who knew of such things almost as much as the contents of the letter. Had there been such tell-tale markers, the letter would have never been delivered. It would have been forwarded to Berlin for careful study by their best cryptologists. This would not work in Europe, but here in South America, mail from the north often went astray.

The letter was a brief one, two pages, hand written, one on the inside of the envelope itself and the other on a half-page of onion skin paper which was enclosed. Yet before taking the half page out and unfolding the envelope, Rott carefully examined the whole thing again for tell-tales placed inside. A subtle trap, yes, but the presence of that would tell Rott much more than tell-tales outside.

Satisfied the letter was probably what it seemed, Rott quickly read over the clear, strong hand and then gave it to his companion. He sat patiently until the man was done, then asked, "So what do you think, Wilhelm? Quickly, first impression."

"My first impression is that it probably is a letter from his mother," Wilhelm answered. "That's confirmed by the language usage, too, but there remains the possibility it still contains code." Before entering foreign service, Wilhelm had been a student of linguistics at a major university and American idiom had been his specialty. "The language pattern is regional, specific to Texas and the Southwest." He pointed to a couple of phrases. "However, that is not to say someone from that area was not used to write the letter to convey exactly that impression." His bases covered should he be proven wrong, the former professor fell silent.

Rott nodded. "What makes you think it is actually from his mother?" he asked.

The professor thought a moment. "The obvious thing is the mention of his naval commission, but the whole tone sounds maternal. She even chides him for not writing more often, but she does so gently."

Rott read the passage in question again, then handed the letter back to the other. "Read it once more," he said, "but aloud this time. I want to listen to how it sounds."

"Dear Paul," the professor began and the first part of the letter was bright and cheerful, talking of people and events which would be noted and carefully checked out by Rott's superiors. It ended on the same note and was signed, "Love, Mom," but the onion skin page was different. While it was written in the same strong, clear hand, it was dated the day after the first part was written, and the tone changed.

"You know, the mail service from there is really terrible. Sometimes two of your letters arrive in the same day, and sometimes we get the ones you've written later first. I hate to whine, but it's been at least three weeks now since we heard from you and even though you're grown, I worry. I know you're out where you can't always send mail, but maybe you could write as you travel and then send us the whole thing when you can. Maybe like a journal. The journal of your South American adventure.

"Paul, I'm not telling this for you to feel guilty." At this point the linguist rolled his eyes and Rott actually grinned. "And I don't ask for myself so much as for your father. While he may not admit it, he really misses you and he is afraid for you. All this war business really gets him down. Did you know he still wakes in the middle of the night frightened with nightmares of France? I don't know what all he saw when he served there, but it was really bad and with all the war talk he's afraid the Navy will call you up to active service. I think if he had known war was coming again so soon he would have been much more vocal when you told us you wanted to try for a commission. So please write as often as you can. It will mean so much to him. And me, too.

"Your father and I are also concerned about your new friend. Not the priest. As you know, we are not the kind of Baptists who think all Catholics are going to hell and the old fellow sounds like a cultured man. Who we are concerned about is the girl. I know she must be very nice, son, but you have to remember who we are. There are many people in our community who are not as broad minded as we are, and we don't want you to make a mistake you might regret all your life. I would not say anything, but the way you write about her tells me this is not a casual acquaintance. All I ask is that you think things through carefully before you do anything foolish."

"Mothers!" Wilhelm murmured, shaking his head. "They all sound alike."

"So he has a commission," Rott frowned. "I wonder why our agents in America didn't find that out when we asked for his background?"

Rott was talking to himself, but his companion answered. "Either someone was not very careful when they checked or it has been kept secret," he said. Rott glanced at him sharply for stating the obvious but the linguist didn't catch the look. He, too, was thinking out loud. "Given the quality of the information we normally get from them," he said, looking at Rott absently and nodding, "I would have to assume the latter. That raises the question why it's being kept secret."

Rott sighed. Sometimes the linguist could be a pedantic, obtuse pain in the ass, but the man had a first rate mind. *Which*, he told himself, *is why I chose to endure these occasional lapses. Among other reasons.* So he decided the carrot was better just then than the stick. "Exactly, Wilhelm. Exactly my thought. Great minds all work alike, *nicht war?*"

"Of course," the linguist murmured. *Rott is such a pig,* he thought, covering his contempt with a distracted smile perfected while he was at the University to hide his thoughts from colleagues. *And such a fool. He's shrewd and cunning, and nobody to fool around with, but he's not really intelligent. Certainly not cultured or cultivated, though he knows his manners when he chooses to use them.* Even so, such men had their uses, like that mad corporal in Berlin, and the former professor took comfort in the thought that when this war was over, and the generals had killed each other off, the real leadership of the Reich would step forward and take charge.

Rott nodded and carefully refolded the letter. It would be carefully photographed and resealed for delivery the next day. As he did this he wondered how long he would have to suffer this too educated idiot. It was bad enough being an object of the man's contempt without putting him firmly in his place, but having to pretend not to notice grated on what passed for Rott's soul. Yet suffer him Rott must, for the man was well connected. By someone very high in the Reich, someone who thought well enough of the professor to put the word out. Rott wondered who this someone might be and promised himself that the next time he was in Berlin he would find out.

Quito is another matter, thought Rott an hour later. Though he had not met the man before, in his own way Quito was far more dangerous than Wilhelm, for all his political connections. What made Quito so dangerous in Rott's estimation was his almost complete lack of imagination. That and his reputation for being the worst hard-case around gave the man an arrogant confidence which carried him through situations where fear, born of imagination, might have defeated him. Like Rott, Quito could not imagine his own defeat going into a fight, for he had never lost a one.

The difference lay in the fact that looking back on things later, Rott learned from the mistakes he might have made. Quito, having won the immediate conflict, never gave the matter another thought, and Rott understood clearly this would be the cause of the man's first, and last, defeat. Even were he not killed, Quito's confidence would be shattered and he would never be the same. Whoever defeated him would own the man completely, and for a brief moment he considered taking him down right then. What stopped him was Wilhelm's presence. There was no sense taking the risk. No doubt the professor would be jealous of Rott for stealing his agent. *Another time, my friend,* Rott promised himself, glancing at the Indian and then back to the linguist.

Quito, seeing the ghost of the thought come to life and die in Rott's eyes, felt an uncharacteristic shudder run down his spine. There was something *muy malo,* very evil, about this man, as if he were not human at all, but a spirit-devil dwelling in human flesh. Without thinking he touched the amulet hung by a thong around his neck, the strange stone bought from the *brujo* from the mountains. It cost him dearly, six *animales* and some trade goods, but it was worth it. No spirit had troubled him since.

Gottcha! Rott thought, knowing at that moment he had won without lifting a hand and with the linguist none the wiser. The guide, seeing Rott's small, tight smile, knew exactly what it meant and cast down his eyes. For the first time since he was a tiny child, Quito knew fear, the same fear he'd seen so many times written in the eyes of his victims. It was not a comfortable feeling.

Obtuse as he was, Wilhelm saw something happen between the two men and wondered what it was. Somehow he was suddenly on the outside and to regain control of the situation he spoke to Quito harshly. "So you didn't go with him?" he asked, demanding information Quito had already given.

Don't push it, Quito thought as he responded to the linguist's tone. *Just because you have this devil present now.* "Yes," he said shortly. "Just as I told you. When I got back from taking your people up the coast, he was gone."

"Why were you delayed?" Rott asked quietly. His quiet tone was far more fearful than Wilhelm's snarl though there was no threat in his eyes.

"Some of his people held us up," Quito said simply, nodding toward the professor. "They insisted in taking an extra day, but it didn't accomplish anything. Then, when we got back to town, some of them got drunk and we had a hard time finding them." He shrugged. "Still, I was only a day and a half late. The American has waited for me for as much as three days."

Rott nodded and said nothing and Quito went on, angry now, remembering what the delay had cost him. The American paid better than the Germans, much better. "That *hijo de puta!*" he declared. "He cheated me! Then he took off with that one-eyed drunk for a guide. I hope they get lost."

"That's too much to wish for," Rott observed dryly. "He'll be back. Like a bent *pfennig.* Did he tell you exactly where he wanted to go? Or what he was looking for?"

"No," Quito shook his head. "He only said he wanted to look around up near Santa Ana in the mountains. I don't know why. Everyone knows there's nothing there." He grinned. "Yet, if a fool wants to be separated from his money for nothing, who am I to tell him different?"

Wilhelm laughed nervously, trying to hide the alarm he felt. "This isn't getting us anyplace," he said. "We'll bribe the other man when they get back."

Rott nodded, the soul of calm. *Why didn't you just shout it from the roof top, asshole,* he thought. *This man can read you like a book.* "Yes, I think you're right. Why don't I meet you later at your room? I have another job I want to talk over with Quito."

Though Rott's words were calm, Wilhelm understood them for a command. "Very well," he said, stiffly. "At the hour?" Rott nodded and the linguist made his way out the door.

When the professor was gone Rott fixed Quito with his stare. He knew Quito was aware he had just learned something he was not supposed to know, although Quito didn't know what that was, and Rott watched the panic rise in the man's eyes. Once he was sure Quito would agree to whatever he asked, the man in black said quietly. "Now, it's just you and me." The other looked like he was about to die of fright in his chair and Rott loosened the leash a bit. "Tell me about this young American, and don't leave anything out. Where did you take him and what was he looking for?"

Without a moment's hesitation, that strange raptor named Quito began to sing like a caged bird.

4. Ambush

"Goodness," groaned Juan Calderon. "I haven't eaten like that since you left." He chuckled and looked at Rosario, who blushed. Three weeks had passed since Rott's visit to Pisco and the two of them were sitting in the courtyard after supper talking to Paul Radford.

"I haven't, either," Paul Radford nodded. "I'm not bad at campfire cooking and Pico isn't, either, but neither of us come close to Rosario." He smiled and the young woman flushed even more deeply. "It's good to be back." He took out a handkerchief and wiped his forehead. Even though the sun was long down, the air in the courtyard seemed close. "After being in the mountains it's hard to get used to the coast again. The air seems so...thick."

The padre nodded. "It takes a few days for the blood to change. Going both ways. Whenever I go inland I feel a fish out of water. Even a short walk leaves me gasping. Then, coming back, it's like you say. Swimming through the air when you get to the coast. The mountain people really don't like to come down here at all."

Rosario nodded and said a few words in the strange dialect. Without waiting to be prompted, she turned to Paul and spoke in Spanish. "They get sick, too," she told him. "In their lungs."

"Which may have saved the first Spaniards," Calderon added, but clearly felt too torpid to pursue the subject. Instead he grinned. "You need to spend more time with Rosario so she can teach you her native language," he teased.

"It also seems hotter than when I left," Radford cut in smoothly and Rosario flashed him a look of gratitude not lost on the old padre. "Or it that my imagination?"

"No," Juan Calderon replied, too full to even pursue his gambit. His eyes were almost glazed, as if he were about to fall asleep sitting up. "It gets warmer here through December and really doesn't cool off much until May," he added absently.

At Radford's startled look he smiled and shook himself awake. "Remember, we're south of the equator here, so the seasons are reversed." He yawned. "Goodness, I feel like a lizard lying in the sun after he's eaten a big bug." Rosario made a face and he chuckled again. "So tell us about your trip," he said, rubbing his neck and turning to Paul. "How was it?"

"After I got used to the elevation it was marvelous," Radford answered. "Pico took it easy the first few days to give me time to adjust, but it was still difficult. The mountains seem to go straight up out of the sea, but the country is gorgeous. It's amazing how much the mountains affect the vegetation. On the coast it's so thick and then it thins out so quickly as you go inland. I've seen deserts with more plants than some of the places we crossed between here and the highlands. And all that changed when we got over the first divide." He nodded, remembering, and continued. "It's all such wild, beautiful country, but when we got to the highlands, it was incredible. I've never, ever seen anything quite like that," he added with awe. "Not even the northern Rockies. I can't wait to get back up there next week."

The old man nodded. "Yes, it makes the whole trip worth while doesn't it? Just to see the highlands." He sighed. "There's no describing it."

"I don't know what it is," Radford agreed. "It's very dry up there and it seemed like I could see for a hundred miles. Pico told me that was true," he said, looking to Calderon for confirmation. Not that he really doubted Pico's veracity. While exaggeration about one's native land may not be factual, as seen by those who count beans, it is none the less true in the eyes of the heart. As such, it is a statement of a deeper truth, a poetic truth which lies beyond empirical reality.

"Depending on where you are, you can," Calderon told him. "One can see at least that far in places. So very little rain gets that high there's nothing to cloud the air, especially on the western side." Then the old man turned quiet, reflective. "The first time I was there it was like looking through the gates into Heaven," he murmured and sighed. "I'd like to see it again before I die." There was a poignant edge of loss in his voice.

"Why don't you come with us next time?" Paul invited. "We're headed back next week. You, too, Rosario," he added, seeing her disappointment at his news.

The old man shook his head sadly. "My friend, these old legs get me around well enough here in town, but I would never make the first pass going up the mountains." He shook his head, cutting off the other's protest. "No, please believe me. I don't talk about it much but there are already days when I can barely get out of bed without help." Rosario looked up and nodded.

"Well, if you change your mind, we can take it a step at a time," Radford answered. "Or we can put you on a burro."

Juan Calderon chuckled. "Then I'd have to listen to you and Pico ask each other which one was the burro. No?"

Radford's laugh answered him. "I can't promise you wouldn't," he said. "The point is, you don't have to do it on your own strength, Juan. I'll get you there if you want to go. Just say the word."

The old priest looked at him a long time. "You know, my friend, I may just take you up on that. It's been at least five years since I've been up there and there are probably lots of babies to baptize." He laughed. "And many of their parents to marry, too."

"Don't they have their own marriage customs?" Radford was surprised.

"Oh, yes, but the Spanish taught them they needed the rites of the Church, too." He snorted. "As if God hadn't blessed their unions, anyway! But they like a good Church wedding and it's marvelous the way they do it. Several of them get together, several couples, and I marry them and we have a big party." The old man nodded, remembering. "I think you're right. I think maybe I need to go there again. Not this next trip. That is a little soon and I will be busy here. Maybe right after the first of the year. Epiphany is a good season for marriage." He turned to the younger man. "That's less than six weeks away, but the Christmas celebration will be over and I can be back long before Lent."

"Consider it done," Radford smiled. "I'll have Pico get us another burro."

The old man's excitement was written all over his frame. "Yes!" he said. "It will be good to get out of the heat for a couple of weeks."

"Rosario can come, too," Radford offered again, but the young woman shook her head.

"No," she said. "I stay here. You boys go play."

Paul started to argue but Juan Calderon caught his eye and shook his head. "Rosario's right," he said smoothly. "Men need to get away every once in a while where they can scratch and belch and..." he grinned, "make other noises."

50

"Padre!" Rosario scolded, giggling. Then she did something Radford had never seen. She fixed the old priest with a stern eye and said, "Besides, you make those noises, anyway. When Pablo's not around." Her gaze brooked no denial.

"You're giving away all my secrets," the old man cackled. Radford had never seen Calderon so animated, so lively. "But we're not being good hosts. Paul's dying to tell us about his trip and here we are talking about rude noises."

"Yes, and who brought it up?" Rosario answered, surprising even the padre. Turning to Paul she said, "So tell us, Pablo. Did you find what you were looking for?"

"Well, yes and no," he told them. "That's why Pico and I are going back so soon. The geology is very promising, but the engineering would be the problem. It's not like the coast where roads already exist or can easily be made. Getting heavy equipment up there would be the problem." He shrugged. "I'm no engineer, but there would have to be a lot of high grade mineral there to cover the cost of getting it out."

Juan Calderon nodded. "That's what the Spanish found mining gold and silver," he said. "There was plenty to be found, but the cost of getting it out was very high. At least in terms of the lives of men and animals." He shrugged. "Although, that was not of much concern to the Spaniards. They took prisoners from among the Indian missions and worked them to death. When some of the clergy objected to this, they were either ignored or sent back to Spain if they were too troublesome. Not that many of them did," he added bitterly. "They may not have said so, but many of them were from wealthy families and considered the natives not as men but as two legged animals."

Radford nodded. "I seem to remember reading somewhere that there was even some question whether or not the Indians have souls." He nodded. "It's not so different from the attitudes you find about Negroes back home. Or Jews."

"Exactly," Calderon agreed, a little surprised, but very pleased, how quickly the young man saw the connection. "I believe you call it 'us and them'."

"And them that ain't Us is Them," Radford said. "We even call our country the US. I guess you could call it the land of the 'capitalized us', if you'll pardon the pun," he added, translating the phrase for Rosario, who smiled. Then she startled him by answering in his native tongue.

"The *padre* taught me English, too, Pablo," she said, smiling at his surprise. While her accent was distinctly Hispanic, her words were clear.

Juan Calderon shrugged. "Rosario helps me with the classes," he explained. "The children like to learn, especially something foreign and exotic. They like to talk together without their elders knowing what they're saying. Rosario had to learn in self-defense."

Radford laughed. "My brother and I used to do the same thing with Spanish," he said. "It took us a while to learn my dad was more than fluent than we. We didn't know he spent three years in Mexico before he married."

The padre nodded. "I tell them not to use English at home, except to practice, but, of course, they do. And now some of their parents are learning, too. So many Europeans and *norteamericanos* have come through here in the last three years they find it useful for business." He laughed. "But we're getting off the track. You were telling us about your trip and I keep chasing rabbits."

Radford shrugged. "Well, there's not a lot more to tell. You were right about Pico, and he was right about what we needed. The burro carried most of what we took with us up the mountains, and there wasn't much left to carry back. It was very pleasant after I got used to the altitude."

"You left the burro for a present?" the old man asked. "After you crossed over?"

"Yes, but that was odd. We never met whoever we were taking it to. Pico told me they knew we were there, so we tied it to a bush and left." He frowned. "We didn't see anyone at all after we left the upper river settlements, and even the people we saw there didn't have much to say."

"You'll find them different the next time you go up," the padre assured him. "Once they get to know you it may be hard to shut them up." He chuckled. "Among themselves they can be real chatter boxes. That's how you'll know you've been accepted."

Radford nodded. "You know, I didn't see very many animals there, either, now I think about it. The villages we came to on the other side of the mountain didn't even have chickens, although I thought I heard something that sounded like a chicken. That surprises me, but I don't remember seeing any kind of domestic animal further inland."

"They may have been hiding them," Calderon answered. "The people on the other side are hunters, not farmers. The vegetables in their diet are wild plants they've learned to gather and a lot of their meat is fish."

"Then, what would they want with a burro?" Paul asked. Rosario giggled and he realized his mistake. "Oh."

"Exactly," Juan Calderon chuckled. "Burro is a great delicacy for them. You left them more meat than they see in a month."

"Which is why Pico picked the younger, fatter mare," Radford replied. "I wanted the bigger, stronger animal but Pico was buying for the table, not for the trail."

"He saved you some money doing so, I imagine," the padre added.

"Yeah!" Radford shook his head. "I couldn't believe how little he paid. Quito must have been really putting it to me."

"In more ways than one," the priest agreed. "I hear he's really upset you left without him."

"Then I guess he just has to be mad," Paul replied. "He wasn't here when he said he'd be and the last time I had to wait four days. So if he doesn't like it I guess he'll have to lump it. Especially the way he's been cheating me."

"He could have easily gotten you killed in the area where you were going." Radford looked up sharply and the older man nodded. "Oh, yes, he very well could have. Both of you. The people you didn't see don't tolerate people like Quito."

"I don't understand. How could they tell what kind of man he is unless they meet him?"

"Oh, they can tell," Calderon answered. "You were watched every step of the way and I imagine there was little about you they didn't notice. Including the fact you were not carrying a rifle."

"You know, I had that feeling," Paul told him. "Like I *was* being watched. Then I decided it was just being in a strange place. I wonder why Pico didn't say anything about it?"

"Pico knew that with you he didn't have to," the other replied simply. "That's one of the reasons he agreed to take you." At the question in the young man's eyes he chuckled again. "The other reason was Rosario's *imprimatur*. Pico knows she's a good judge of character."

"I thought he took me because you vouched for me," Radford told him, wondering if the old priest was pulling his leg.

"Oh, that, too." The old man discounted his own words with a casual wave. "But mostly because of Rosario. She doesn't hang around with the shady types I do."

Rosario's reply was so soft they could barely hear. "I just live with the worst of them all," she said, primly putting down her basket and rising. "Would you like some beer now?" Both men laughed.

"Please," said Paul with a grin that brought a smile in return as Rosario left the room. "She doesn't let you get away with much, does she?" he observed, looking at the older man.

"Nor will she with you," Calderon answered, nodding. For a moment they men sat in silence, listening to the night. Then the padre spoke. "So. What else did you find up there? Anything unusual?"

"As a matter of fact, yes," Radford told him. "At one of the villages we picked up rumors that something was going on where we were headed but no one seemed to know just what. Only that there'd been lots of Europeans passing through."

"Europeans, primarily meaning Germans, I imagine," Calderon replied, frowning.

"No one seemed to know," the other answered. "Or no one was saying. I couldn't tell which and I thought it best not to be too curious."

"Very wise," Calderon agreed, patting the breast of his cassock as if looking for something.

Radford took the hint. Reaching for his cigarette case he frowned, then pulled out a light blue envelope. "Oh," he said, handing the case to the old man. "I forgot. There was a letter from home when I got back. I meant to read it after I cleaned up but I forgot about it."

"I imagine you had other things on your mind," Calderon observed, dryly, glancing toward the door leading to the kitchen. He chuckled.

"Why, of course I did," Radford answered, taking up the game. "Your excellent company, for one thing, and the thought of Rosario's food."

"Don't tell her that!" Calderon cackled.

"Don't tell me what?" Rosario asked, coming into the room with a platter of beer.

"He was in such a great hurry to get here for your marvelous food he forgot to read a letter from home," the priest said solemnly. "Or maybe it was something else."

"The food was not at the top of my list," Radford admitted and Rosario blushed.

"It must have been my brilliant company then," the padre nodded, glancing at the young woman.

Rosario ignored him. "What was your news from home?" she asked. "Was it your mother?"

"I don't know," Paul admitted. "I really forgot about it until just now, but it was from her."

"Well, aren't you going to read it?" Rosario asked.

"Right now?" Radford asked and Rosario nodded. Juan Calderon chuckled and gave him a look which clearly said, "You see?" The young man carefully broke the seal and unfolded the air mail folder, scanned it quickly and said, "It's mostly about people you don't know," he told them, but Rosario would not be put off. She said nothing but her look told him she wanted to know it all. So he handed over the letter and asked her to read it aloud. Delighted, Rosario began to speak and quickly picked up the flow of his mother's hand. Then, when she came to the onion skin sheet, her tone changed, and to Paul it was as if he could hear his mother speaking through Rosario's mouth. When she came last paragraph which talked about herself, Rosario hesitated, then read it aloud. There were tears in the young woman's eyes when she finished. "Your mother doesn't like me," she said.

Radford was aghast. "Rosario, I'm sorry. If I had known what she had written I would never let you to read it. That's not like her, believe me."

Rosario shrugged. "It wouldn't make any difference in how she feels," she pointed out. "She is very clear she doesn't want you to marry beneath you."

"You are not beneath me," Radford argued. "Look, she doesn't know you, *dulce*. Once she gets to know you it will be all right. I promise. She will like you."

Calderon looked doubtful but said nothing. Rosario dried her eyes on her apron. "Perhaps so," she said. Then she folded the letter carefully and handed it back to Paul. "I better check the beans," she added, getting to her feet and heading for the kitchen.

"Rosario!" Radford called after her, and started to follow, but the old priest stopped him. The grip on Radford's arm was like iron.

"Let her go, man," the old man advised. "Respect her pride. Let her lick her wounds in private." When the younger man started to argue, Juan Calderon shook his head. "Please. Trust me. There is nothing you can do except make things worse. She knows how you feel. That's enough. Let her be."

Radford sighed and sat back down. He looked at the letter. "Juan, I had no idea."

"I know," Calderon assured him. "So does Rosario. What you did in asking her to read was very natural. May I?" he old man asked, reaching out a hand. "I would like to see when it was sent."

Radford obliged and the old priest looked at the cancellation carefully. "I can't make out what it says," he told them. "It's smudged." He started to hand the letter back to Paul, then something caught his eye. Carefully he studied the back of the letter where it had been folded over. "Strange," he said.

"What?" Radford asked.

"The sealing glue left a double line," the old man answered. "Look there below the tab you tore off when you opened it."

The other nodded. "Yes, I see it, too," he said. "What about it?"

"Oh, perhaps nothing," the padre shrugged. "Maybe your mother opened it again when she put in the second sheet."

"No, I don't think so," Paul answered. "She always adds a note a day or two after she writes a letter and she never seals them until then. Or if she does, she uses a fresh envelope." He looked at the older man. "What are you thinking?"

"I'm thinking maybe someone opened your letter before you got it," Calderon replied. "Either here or before it left Texas."

"I don't understand," Radford told him. "Why would they do that?"

"That, my friend, is the question. Why, indeed?"

Yet as he walked home to his hotel that night, Paul Radford's mind was not on the question of the opened envelope. It was on the hurt his mother had unintentionally inflicted on Rosario. *How could I have been so stupid?* he asked himself. *I should have known how Mother would react. Juan is right. Rosario will never be accepted back home. Which means we will never be able to live in the States.*

It was only much later that Paul Radford realized his mother's letter was the catalyst which set his resolve to marry Rosario, come what may. *She did it herself,* he thought, smiling at the memory of what his mother told him of her proper Bostonian family's reaction to her decision to marry a roughneck from Texas, despite the money he'd made in the oil patch. *She will come around,* he assured himself. Nor was there any thought in his mind his father would fail to honor his decision, too. *Maybe my brother and sisters,* he thought, *but not Dad.* It never occurred to him he might be completely wrong.

The attack came without warning five days out of Pisco. One moment Paul Radford was making his way carefully across a stream on an ancient path and thinking of what he wanted to ask Pico about, something he'd seen since their last stop. An instant later the bullet from the first shot smashed into his oak walking stick, shattering it to splinters before smashing into the middle of his chest and knocking him to the ground. He never heard the second and third shots which passed an inch from his ear and buried themselves in trees beside the path. Yet even as he fell, Radford was dimly aware of men shouting, as if from a great distance, and several other shots fired from what sounded like rifles.

As he lay there gasping for breath and fighting for conscious against the waves of darkness which kept drifting across his mind, the sounds died away and he could hear men talking in urgent voices from somewhere above.

"Where's the other one?" demanded a harsh voice he knew but could not place. "The guide. Where did he go?"

The guide, Radford thought. This was something he knew he should remember but could not. Then a name drifted across his mind, but flitted away before he could capture it.

57

"I don't know," another voice answered, defensive. "He was in front and I was shooting at him."

"So was I," said another voice. "That's who you told us to shoot."

"You damned idiots!" the familiar voice answered harshly. "I ought to shoot the two of you! I told you I would shoot the *gringo* and you were to kill the guide."

"How were we to know it was the *gringo* in front?" the second voice whined. "The guide is the one who always leads."

"Look at his face, stupid!" the harsh voice exploded. "He doesn't look like an *indio*, does he? He's obviously a *norteamericano* or a European."

"Yes, but look at his clothes," the third voice argued. "He's wearing a poncho and a hat just like ours. I made the same mistake."

Any rejoinder the angry voice might have made to this was cut off by the second voice. "Look! He's still alive. I just saw his eyelids move."

Somehow Radford was able to keep his eyes shut and he held his breath, hoping whoever it was would decide he was dead. This proved in vain, for a moment later his side exploded in pain as a heavy foot kicked him in the ribs and left him gasping. Opening his eyes and looking up, he saw a familiar face which he could not name. Yet it went with the voice he knew.

"So you're alive, gringo," Quito laughed harshly, jerking a pistol from his belt and pointing it between Radford's eyes. "You should never have tried to cheat me." He grinned and cocked the pistol, clearly intending to finish what he had begun.

"Jesus," Radford whispered, and Quito laughed cruelly, never expecting the savage kick Paul Radford delivered to the back of his knee, or the iron hand which shot out and grasped Quito's wrist, deflecting the pistol just as it went off.

The sound of the shot deafened Radford and he felt a searing pain through the side of his head. Yet he somehow hung onto Quito's wrist and squeezed with all his strength, twisting his hand sharply as he pushed it backwards. Quito screamed and released his grip on the pistol as bones in his wrist gave way with a sharp snap, but his scream was cut off sharply and he fell heavily between Radford and the other two men.

Without conscious thought, Radford released the guide and grabbed for the pistol. Rolling away from the fallen guide he came up in a crouch, the pistol cocked and held out before him in both hands, but there was no threat. Quito lay on his side, staring in sightless amazement at the long thin arrow shaft which protruded from his chest. Nor was there danger from the others. Both lay slumped where they had fallen and Radford could see what looked like a short, strangely marked splinter jutting out from the neck of one of them.

Suddenly another voice called from the bush. "Don't shoot, Pablo!" and Radford swung the pistol in the direction of the sound, lowering it toward the ground when he saw Pico's face appear from behind a small tree. Slumping back, Radford sat on the ground where he had fallen, aware of a dull pain in the middle of his chest.

"Does it hurt?" Pico asked, gently pulling Radford's hand away from his breast and looking at the bloody hole made by Quito's bullet. Radford nodded dumbly and Pico gently pressed him back against the earth, carefully opening his shirt. Then he nodded. "You have a couple of bad cuts but this saved your life. The bullet must have hit it sideways."

Pico held up the medallion Calderon had given Paul. There was blood around the edges and a deep dent in the center, but the markings were still unmistakable and Radford heard a quiet murmur of voices from behind the guide. Looking beyond Pico he saw three men dressed in next to nothing with strange patterns drawn in subtle colors against their faces and bodies. While he could not understand what they were saying, their dress and markings brought a flash of recognition. "The people," he tried to say. "These are the people we brought...." but he could not finish the thought.

"Yes," Pico told him. "These are the people we brought the burro for. I don't know how you knew, but that's who it is. They are the ones who gave the padre the medallion." He turned to the others and spoke briefly in the tongue Radford had heard Calderon use with Rosario. One of the men, the older of the three, nodded and said something back to Pico.

"He says your power is strong," Pico told Radford. "The spirits protect you."

"He apparently did his part, too," Radford replied, smiling and nodding toward the Indian. "Tell him I really appreciate his help."

He was having trouble hearing, touched the side of his head. "Did I get hit there, too?"

Pico nodded. "Mostly powder burns, but the bullet tore your ear, too." He reached in his pack and took out a first aid kit, but the older Indian touched his arm and said something. Pico backed away and the older man crouched before Radford, looking intently at his wound. Taking something from his pouch he murmured to Pico, who handed him a canteen of water, and the Indian dampened what he was holding and began to carefully clean Radford's wound, chanting softly as he did. As soon as the damp poultice touched Radford's skin the pain began to diminish, and by the time the man was finished a few minutes later, the whole area felt pleasantly numb.

When he was done, the older Indian nodded and stood, saying something to Pico and then to the other two Indians. Pico replied in the same tongue and as suddenly as they had appeared, the Indians were gone, as if the earth had swallowed them up. Pico and Radford were alone in the clearing, and the young *norteamericano* was left with an overwhelming sense of unreality. Only the presence of the three dead men bore witness to all which happened in less than twenty minutes since the first shot was fired.

Seeing Radford's confusion, Pico nodded. "Rest here a moment, Pablo," he said kindly. "I will get rid of the carrion." Quickly the guide searched the bodies of the three men, retrieving little but a few rounds of ammunition and a very few personal items. Only Quito had much more, some papers in an oil cloth packet and a large bundle of paper money, and Pico handed these to Radford.

The oil cloth packet held a carefully drawn topographical map of the wild area they were exploring. The legend was clear enough but there were some curious markings at different points near the coast and in the margins, as well as hand written notes. These were done in a strong European hand, but written in Spanish, and the packet contained what looked like a list of items. The list appeared to have been written in the same hand as the notations. Judging from the easy precision of the lettering and even strokes, it was apparent to Radford both the map and the list had been given to Quito by someone else. The one time Radford had seen Quito's writing was in a note to him in an almost indecipherable scrawl.

Glancing up, Radford saw Pico had gathered the fallen weapons into a pile and was dragging one of the bodies off the path. Radford started to get up to help but was overcome by an odd sense of weakness and Pico waved him back. "No, senor," the guide said. "You rest and I will take care of this garbage." True to his word, the guide easily drug the corpse off the path and came back for another. When the last was gone he began cleaning up the signs of the ambush, carefully removing any traces of Quito and his men and brushing dirt and leaves over the blood left on the path.

Helping Radford to his feet, Pico took him perhaps a hundred yards further down the trail and told him to wait there. When Radford asked where he was going, Pico said, "If anyone comes looking, it will look like we stopped here, not there."

"What about the weapons?" Radford wanted to know. "What will we do with them?"

Pico shrugged. "I'll find a place to throw them so they won't be found. We'll throw the shells somewhere else."

Radford hesitated. The rifles Quito's companions had carried were military issue Mausers, and well worn, but the rifle the guide had carried was a sporting model. The deep blue finish was marred by light rust in two or three places, and the stock was scratched and ill used. The leather carrying strap was filthy, as well, but the clean lines of the gun marked it as a Mauser carbine, and Radford wondered where Quito had gotten such a fine piece. He'd never seen the weapon on the expeditions he'd taken with the Quito as guide.

"We'll keep Quito's rifle and the pistol," Radford decided. "Maybe we can learn something from them when we get back." Pico nodded and disappeared, leaving Radford alone in the clearing. Once again the sense of unreality descended upon Paul Radford, this time with a sense of loss and longing for home. Then, for the very first time, ever, he wondered if he would ever see his mother and father again. Or if it were his portion to die in this strange and awesome land so very far from the dusty hills of his native Texas.

"You were very lucky, my friend," the old priest nodded. "Or perhaps it was not luck at all."

"What do you mean?" Paul Radford asked. Eleven days had passed since the near fatal attack in the highlands on the east side of the Andes. After the ambush Pico suggested they shorten their trip, but the young American was adamant about finishing their survey and seeing the Ica patterns on their return trip. "We've come this far," he said. "I don't think whoever set the trap would think of setting up two." Pico was not altogether convinced, being concerned about Radford's wound more than a second attack. Yet after a good night's sleep Radford seemed back to his normal health, except for soreness in his ear, and when he saw no sign of infection, Pico agreed.

Not that there was that much to see when they reached the area near Ica. From the ground the patterns looked like well worn paths, barely discernible in spots, and it was only from the air one could appreciate the precision with which they were laid out. As many others before and after, Paul Radford wondered who had laid them out and why.

Juan Calderon smiled. "Sometimes coincidence gets a little weighed down by the burden of hard evidence. At such times Ocam's razor points toward a simpler answer."

"You mean divine intervention?" Radford asked, shaking his head. "I prefer to think I was just plain lucky." He fished out the medallion. "You really think this protected me?"

The padre shrugged. "No, not that, but something else. Or someone else. Yet such an answer raises more questions than it resolves, I think. I am just very thankful it all happened the way it did." He looked at Radford closely. "Something else about this is bothering you," he said, not as a question but a statement of fact.

Radford nodded. "I know what you'll say. It probably wouldn't do much good, but I'm bothered by not reporting it. I'm still not sure that's such a good idea."

"Doing so could precipitate a great deal of evil," Calderon answered him. "You have nothing to support your contention but your own word and that of Pico."

"We have the weapons," Radford insisted. "And I have my broken staff and a dented medallion."

"Which a bribed magistrate could turn as evidence against you," Calderon retorted. "Think, Paul, how it looks from outside. You could have ambushed Quito and stolen his weapons. Your staff could have been shattered by yourself and the medallion dented in the same way. There is also the fact you did not report it right away, but, in fact, continued your journey as if nothing had happened." Calderon waved away Radford's objection. "A magistrate could say you should have reported it immediately or in Ica, which was only a day or two away from where you passed."

"Yeah, but the longer I don't report it, the worse it looks," Radford told him. "Shouldn't I at least report it to someone at the embassy just for the record?"

"Not officially," Calderon said. "They would then have to act." He sighed. "Believe me, my friend, I know what a burden it is to carry another's life on one's conscience, but, after all, you did not kill anyone yourself. Not the way you told it to me."

"No," Radford admitted. "Pico and the Indians took care of them. But I was involved."

"You were attacked," Calderon corrected him. "From what you tell me, it was the Indians who did the killing, even as you were being threatened by Quito. Do you really want to reward them by giving the government an excuse to send troops up there?"

"No!" Radford protested. "Why would they do that?"

"That's exactly what would happen, my friend," the old priest assured him. "If you tell them the truth, they will jail Pico and send troops after the people who saved you. You don't know how frightened people here are of the Indians who live in the *montana*. With reason."

"Why?" Radford asked. "They don't bother anyone."

"No, but these are the people who defeated the Inca," Calderon replied. "They stopped them at the forest and fought them to a stand still. Not even the Spanish were able to do more. Not in their own country. And the people in Lima are descended from Spaniards."

"So I just say nothing?" Radford asked.

"No, I don't think you could do that," Calderon agreed. He thought a moment. "No, the next time you are in Lima let the embassy know you were attacked by bandits and your guide drove them off."

"What if they want to know details?" Radford wanted to know.

"Tell them the truth," Calderon answered, nodding toward Radford's ear, which was healing well but which would always bear a scar. "Tell them you were shot and wounded and are unclear on details. Can you say much more of your own knowledge?"

"No, I guess not, but they'll want to know where it happened."

"Can you point it out on a map?" the old man challenged.

"Not really, but Pico can. And speaking of maps, what about the documents we recovered? We need to give those to the authorities. They may be important."

Calderon shrugged. "Well, the facts as you know them is that Pico recovered the map. Who knows? The bandits must have dropped them. One of them must have been wounded and dropped the rifle, too. As for Pico pointing out where you were attacked, he is an ignorant Indian who can't read."

"That's no exactly true," Radford replied. "Pico can read as well as I can, and you know it. You taught him."

"Yes," Juan Calderon nodded. "I did. Pico is very bright. I am sure maps bear no mystery for him, even though I have never asked. Nor will I ask and I will not be talking to the authorities. So I will not have to lie. Neither will you. What they will want to believe is that Pico is an ignorant Indian, so that is exactly what they will believe."

"So we just let them?" Radford asked, still troubled.

Calderon sighed. "One thing which comes with age is learning to choose well the ditches in which one is willing to die, Pablo. Disregarding the consequences to yourself, are you willing to make trouble over this for Pico?"

"Of course not!" Radford answered at once. "I just don't like lying by silence."

Calderon nodded, sighing. "Neither do I, my friend. Neither do I. Nor am I callous to your feelings or the need for truth. Yet I have had a long time to learn to live with many things I do not like, and I prefer lying by silence to legal injustice. The truth is that Quito was going to kill you and Pico and his friends did not have time to stop him any other way. There was a great deal of justice in his death."

Glancing over Radford's shoulder the old man saw Rosario standing in the doorway. He smiled and said to Radford, "Look! Our angel is waiting for us to come to the feast she has prepared for her wandering prodigal. We can talk of this again after supper."

"First things first," Radford agreed, getting to his feet and following the padre into the other room. Seeing the feast Rosario had fixed he added, "Well, if we're still able to talk."

5. Making Connections

"Well, Mr. Radford, it sounds like you were pretty lucky," the foreign officer said, clearing his throat politely and leaning back in his chair. They were seated in a small office toward the rear of the embassy building in Lima and from the window behind the desk, Radford could see the high doors of a carriage house, now evidently converted to shelter official vehicles. A large black touring car was parked in front of one of the large green doors, being washed by a man whose uniform tunic was folded and laid out carefully over a stone bench to one side. As Radford watched, the man turned, polishing another section if the long, elegant hood and sending a shock of recognition through the young man. The driver he was watching was a dead ringer for one of the men in the mountains with Quito.

Radford started to say something about it, but the foreign officer didn't notice and went on with what he was saying before Radford could open his mouth. "What I don't understand is why you are coming to us. Did the police give you trouble over this?" The man peered out at Radford across long, elegant fingers steepled under his nose. Except for his eyes, he looked for all the world like a medieval monk taking a moment from his work for prayer.

The eyes, however, were neither kind nor gentle, and Radford felt as if he were being watched by a sniper from a great distance. "No, I haven't told them about it yet," he answered quietly.

The official blinked but showed no other sign of surprise, but the eyes gained interest. "Oh, you haven't, have you?" he asked. "Oh, my. This is not good at all, you know. Why in the world not?" A carefully measured frown of professional concern settled on his face.

Radford shrugged. "Well, for one thing, I didn't know who to report it to," he answered evenly, wondering how in the world such a phony ended up in such a responsible position. "I'm not even sure where we were at the time. It was somewhere near the border and we could have been in Bolivia for all I know." It was not an outright lie. Radford could not pinpoint where the attack took place on a map and Pico was neither talking nor available. Within a day of their arrival back in Pisco the guide was gone again, mostly at the recommendation of Juan Calderon.

"Just to be safe," the old priest told Radford when they talked again after supper. "Just to be safe. As a *norteamericano* the police will treat you with respect, but with Pico?" He shrugged. "With Pico they might decide to use... aggressive means of interrogation. Better he be out of sight a while until you get this cleared up."

"You mean torture?" the young man asked. The padre nodded "But we were the ones who were attacked!" Radford protested. "Why would they torture Pico?"

"To make sure you were telling them the truth," Calderon replied. "After all, to them he is just a drunk who works in a cantina. A...shadow man, I think you call it?" Calderon asked searching for the right American expression.

"A shady character?" Radford suggested and the old priest nodded.

"Yes, a shady character. Someone they can beat with impunity. Just to do it. Most of the senior officers are good men, but some of them?" He shrugged. "Some of them are pretty mean and their men are no better. Especially Delagdo. He's the Captain in charge of the area where you were attacked."

"Do you think he was in on it?" Radford asked, concerned.

"It would not surprise me," the padre told him. "Although Quito may have been on his own. Delgado's almost certainly in the pocket of the Germans, but they don't always let the one hand know what the other is doing, as the good book says." He thought a moment. "Yes, on second thought, I do agree. I think you had better report this, but we need to think how to do so and what to say."

Out of the discussion which followed, the strategy of working through the embassy was born, and except for his knowledge of where they were when the attack took place, Calderon advised Radford to stay as close to the truth as possible, even revealing the fact that at least one of the bandits had been killed. Radford suggested keeping the identity of the attackers secret, too, but Calderon vetoed it. "No," he insisted. "Even if Delgado did not know about it, the Germans would make it known if they were the ones behind the attack. Then the police would wonder why you didn't tell them you knew your attacker. I think it better to keep things simple. Quito was angry at you for not using him for a guide any more and must have followed you hoping to rob you. By luck their first shots missed but Pico's didn't. If they press you for details tell them you were hit and can't remember very well. That is the truth."

"I doubt they'll press too hard," Pico added. "Since it's not clear where the attack took place, it could be Bolivia's problem, not theirs. No one cares if bandits get killed trying to rob people."

"So we make it easy for them to do nothing," Radford nodded. It was clear he did not like what the old priest and Pico were suggesting.

"Yes," Juan Calderon replied. "Then, even if the Germans push, we have made it hard for them to get much cooperation."

"So why does Pico need to keep low, then?" Radford wanted to know. "All he has to do is to play dumb, too. At least as far as putting a mark on a map goes. I doubt anyone knows he can even read."

"True, but the Germans might be able to persuade their police retainers to make sure your story is true and the easiest way to do that is to interrogate someone who doesn't count in their eyes. If they could, the Germans would get the police to interrogate you the same way, but you are connected."

Seeing Radford's look of outrage, once again the old priest shrugged. "I know, it's corrupt and unjust and I don't like it, either. Yet, that's the way things are. You work for a big company who is investing a great deal of time and money in this country. The police would not want to stir things up by going after someone like you. Not unless they could justify it by first getting a 'confession' from Pico. Then they could do pretty much what they want."

So that became the story Paul told and the embassy official nodded. "I see. Well, that does put a different light on things, doesn't it. What is it you wish from us?" While the man's was bland, it was rather too bland, and there was no mistaking the irony of his small tight smile. Nor the fact he really did not want to be bothered at all.

Radford suppressed an impulse to slap the insolence from the man's face, remind him that he was a public servant. "I hoped you might advise me how it would be best to proceed," he replied quietly. "Who I need to talk with." He shrugged and put the ball neatly back into the other's court. "Of, course, Mr. Rea, if you're suggesting I don't have to do anything, that doesn't sound quite right." He left the implications of the thought for the other to supply.

"Oh, no," the foreign officer quickly assured him. "That is not what I intended at all. I certainly would not advise you to break the law. Not at all. I suppose you should report it to both governments to cover all bases." He sat back with a self satisfied smile, the problem off his plate.

"I agree completely," Radford nodded. "I thought perhaps you might suggest the name of someone I need to talk with here, and perhaps you could notify the Bolivian government for me. As a matter of courtesy to them, as well as to me and my company. Whether it was on their side of the border or not, they need to know there may have been bandits operating in that area. Who knows who else Quito and his gang may have robbed up there?"

"That is just one question, Mr. Radford," the police captain told him not an hour later. "Another is why did Quito follow you all the way up there before setting his trap? It would seem more consistent with a bandit's character to do so closer to home. Why wait?"

Radford nodded and framed his answer carefully. Dealing with this policeman was a whole different ball of twine than dealing with that fool at the embassy. For one thing, this man listened, not only for what was said, but for what was left unsaid, and he was not at all happy that Pico was not available for questioning. "I don't know," the young geologist told him. "I don't even know why the man turned sour on me. I was always very fair with Quito, very generous, and until this last trip, I was more than patient with him. Then my patience ran out and I engaged another guide."

"The town drunk, it is said," the captain reminded him. "Why did you engage him?"

"He was about the only other guide available and I was told he knew the country I wished to explore. As it turned out, my information was right. He knew the country very well and I made sure he didn't have anything to drink while we were gone." He shrugged. "I didn't have much choice. All the other guides work for other companies."

"I see," the captain replied blandly. He paused for a moment, carefully examining the young man's face, then asked, "What are you not telling me, Mr. Radford?"

Radford smiled ruefully. "You don't miss much, do you, Captain?" he said. The other shrugged and waited patiently. "One of the reasons I switched guides is that I was suspicious of Quito already," Radford told him, adding another piece of truth to what he'd told Rea. He hoped it did not come back to haunt him. "I am sure you can appreciate there needs to be a certain degree of confidentiality in what I do. The company I work for sent me here to find new areas of mineral deposits and I have to be careful with the information. Quito was a little too curious about my notebooks and my findings. I even caught him going through my map bag one time when we were out before. He claimed he was looking for something he needed, but that was in another bag and he had one of my notebooks in his hand. Then I caught wind that he was selling information to my competitors. I didn't have proof it was information he got from me, but when he was late it seemed like a good excuse to break things off."

"So you hired the village drunk," the captain nodded. "That's what bothers me. You don't seem like a foolish man. Quite the contrary."

Radford shrugged and grinned wryly. "Thank you. I try not to be. I had the same reservations about Pico, but I was told he knew the country and as things turned out, he worked out very well out in the field. I can't complain, can I? The man saved my life."

"Ah, yes," the captain nodded. "There is that." Holding out a hand, he asked, "May I see the medallion you told me the bullet struck?"

"Of course," Radford said, slipping it off over his head and handing it to the officer. "I was incredibly lucky the bullet hit my staff first."

"Incredibly lucky, indeed," the captain murmured, examining the medallion closely. "Who sent you to Pico, Mr. Radford?"

"The village priest," the other replied. "The one in Pisco. We've become friendly and I thought he would know someone I could trust."

"Ah, yes, Father Juan," the captain nodded. "An interesting man. Much more to him than one might suspect, I think." He continued his examination of the medallion, noting not only the lead smear which marked the dent concaving the disk, but also the ancient markings of the artisan who made it. "Where did you get this?" he asked, looking up. "I'm no expert, but I think it may be pre-Columbian."

"I guess it might be," Radford agreed, "but I don't think so. The design is very old, but from the size and some of the other markings I thought it was made from a Mexican fifty pesos. I picked it up for a couple of bottles of wine," he added. "I thought I'd take it home for my mother."

Radford could see the police officer was not completely satisfied with the answers he'd given, but apparently the other thought there was little point in pursuing it further. "Well, I'm sure your mother will appreciate it even more now," the captain nodded, reluctantly handing the medallion back to Radford.

"To tell you the truth, I wasn't thinking about telling her," the young man replied, and for the first time the captain smiled. "She worries about me enough as it is."

"Yes," the policeman replied, laughing softly. "I know what you mean. There are many things I don't tell my mother about my job, either."

A soft knock took the captain to his office door where he conferred quietly with an aide for a moment. Turning to Radford he said, "I think that's about all I need today. We have your address in Pisco and I will be in touch if I have any further questions. Perhaps you would write up a statement within the next few days and get it to me?" Radford nodded and the captain offered him his hand. "While we were talking your embassy called. Michael Rea. The fellow who sent you to me. He would like for you to stop by on your way out of town if it is convenient."

"Or even if it's not. I suppose I better go see what he wants," Radford grumbled, and they both smiled. There was no question in Paul's mind that Captain Molina shared his opinion of the monkish foreign officer.

"Thanks for coming back by, Mr. Radford," Rea told him as they walked down a hallway toward the back of the embassy. "After you left someone was asking where he could find you. One of our people just in from Washington." The foreign officer spoke the name of the city in hushed tones, reminding Radford of something and bringing a smile to his face. To his ear Rea sounded like a funeral director selling a line of walnut caskets and it clear he was impressed by the fact someone from the District wanted to see the younger man. Then they came to a small conference room and Rea pointed toward a chair. "Have a seat and I'll let him know you're here. Please feel free to smoke if you like."

The room was small and comfortable. Like Rea's office not far down the hall, it had a window looking out toward the carriage house turned garage and Radford could see the large black touring car he'd seen before. This time, however, there was no sign of the driver who had been polishing the hood, but Radford made a mental note to ask Rea about him.

"Well, well," a drawl sounded from the doorway. "Long time no see, buddy." Radford turned to see a familiar figure in a gray suit smiling broadly and offering him a hand.

"Blieu!" the young man exclaimed, getting to his feet and shaking the other's hand. "Of all the people I would not have expected to see down here. Did you quit the Navy?"

"No," the other grinned. "I'm on TDY here, and they wanted me to wear civvies. I heard your name mentioned and wanted to see you. How you been?"

The two men visited a while, renewing their acquaintance. While Radford had never been close to Blieu, he found himself glad to see the man. There is something about living as a stranger in a foreign land which makes even the most casual acquaintance from home seem a cherished friend and Radford was surprised to discover just how hungry he was for even the smallest details from his native land.

Yet when Radford suggested they continue their visit at an excellent restaurant he discovered while living in Lima, Blieu was oddly reluctant to accept. "I'd like to take you up on that, Paul," he evaded, "but it's probably best that we are not seen together in public. That's why I had Rea phone the police department rather than picking you up there myself." Blieu reached into his suit jacket and took out a plain craft envelope. "This will explain why I wanted to see you."

Radford opened the envelope and read the letter inside quickly. Looking up, he frowned. "This is a set of orders calling me to active duty," he said. "But it doesn't tell me when and where to report. It just says to report to the first Navy ship or command officer I encounter."

"Which is me," Blieu told him. "That is also why we didn't simply mail it. We didn't want you reporting just anywhere."

"Is this for real?" Radford wanted to know. "I don't even have my uniform down here."

"You won't need it, Paul," Blieu told him. "You are part of the reason I'm down here. If you choose to accept the mission it will be as an officer, but not in uniform."

"You want me to be a spy?" the other asked.

"Not exactly," Blieu answered. "I want you to be part of a special operations team, and I can't tell you exactly what our mission is until you agree to be part of it."

"You want me to buy a pig in a poke, in other words," Radford replied.

"Yeah," Blieu admitted. "I guess that's what it is. However, I assure you, it is completely in line with the Navy's mission and your oath as an officer. It's not anything illegal."

"I see. But it could get me shot as a spy, right? And not necessarily by an unfriendly government."

Blieu nodded. "I can't imagine that happening, but it could. If you agree, you would be a military officer operating out of uniform in a foreign country. It would be a country friendly to the US, but still..." He shrugged. "I won't lie to you, Paul. It could happen."

"So I'd be operating without the diplomatic status you have," Radford finished and Blieu nodded. "Well, if you need me so much, why don't you just attach me to the embassy here?"

"That would draw too much attention to you," the other answered. "Official attention which might damage your usefulness to the mission."

Radford nodded and rose. "Well, I guess I'll have to pass, then." He held up the letter. "If this is a legal order and you still want me, I guess I'll have to dig up a uniform somewhere."

"Sit down, Paul," Blieu said. When the other did not comply, he added. "That's an order, sailor." Grinning to take the sting out of his words, Blieu waved Radford to a seat and took out a pack of the vile French cigarettes he smoked, offering it to Paul.

Radford gave the other a hard look, then sat and took one of the offered cigarettes. He waited patiently for the other to speak. "I'd hate to play poker with you," Blieu told him. "You know when you're holding the high cards." Still, Radford said nothing, and Blieu went on. "All right, then. Here's a general outline of the mission. You understand what I am about to tell you is Top Secret and you must not talk about it to anyone?" Radford nodded and Blieu outlined quickly what the Senator wanted them to do.

"That makes sense," Radford said. Thinking for a moment he came to a decision. "There are some things you need to know," he said and quickly sketched in details of some of the odd things which had happened over the last few months. Yet he did not mention his friendship with Juan Calderon or the fact it was Calderon who helped him see the pattern in these events.

When he was done, Blieu nodded. "I think you are right. Rea told me about the incident with the guide and I don't think he was operating on his own. If I had to hazard a guess, it would be that he was working for the Germans. Despite official language to the contrary, they are not our friends."

"I don't think they're anyone's friends," Radford responded. "Not even their own."

Blieu looked at the younger man with new interest. "Why do you say that?"

Radford shrugged. "I don't know. It's just an impression I got studying their history and culture in school. It's like their barons were their own worst enemies. Poisoning each other's wells doesn't make much sense. Not in the long run. The Nazis don't seem that different from what I read."

Blieu nodded. "You'd fit well on our team, Paul," he said simply. "I wish you'd give it some more thought. We could really use you."

"Where does my company fit into the picture?" Radford asked. "I imagine they would have to be kept in the dark, right?" Blieu nodded. "So that would put them at risk, too. I don't know, Denis. Seems like it would put a lot of people at risk without their knowing it. It doesn't seem quite right."

"Wait a minute, Paul," Blieu interjected. "We're not asking you to do anything illegal. All we want is for you to keep your eyes and ears open. To let us know what you hear and see. That's all.

Anything else will be taken care of by the rest of the team. Other specialists."

"Other specialists?" Radford asked. "Who is this team, Denis? Anyone I know?"

The other shook his head. "You can't have it both ways, Paul. If you are a player, then you need to know the others on the team. If you're not, you don't. But I can assure you they're top notch people."

Radford nodded. "Fair enough. I guess I'd just as soon not know anyway, but I'd need to have some way of identifying myself to the others." He thought for a long moment.

Blieu remained silent and Radford grinned. "Damn. Sounds like I've already signed on, doesn't it?" Blieu smiled his reply and Radford laughed, "I guess I'm on then."

"Welcome aboard, Lieutenant," Blieu said, throwing the other an informal salute. "It's good to have you with us."

Radford held up the envelope which held his orders. "However, if it's possible, Denis, I'd rather do it without being activated. Can you get these orders canceled?"

The other nodded but was puzzled. "I imagine we can, Paul, but why?"

Radford grinned. "It's really not all that complicated. If I'm going to be doing the same work either way, my company pays better than the Navy."

"Consider it done then," Blieu responded and rang a bell. "How about a sandwich? While you're here I'd like you to bring me up to snuff on where you've been and what you've seen since you arrived. Especially anything out of the ordinary."

"Out of the ordinary?" Radford asked. "You mean, like my mail being steamed open?"

"So you answered duty's call," said Juan Calderon. As had become their custom, they were once again seated in the courtyard of the rectory sipping beer as they waited for supper. "Well, I'm not surprised at that. I would have been surprised had you not. What is curious is that they let you talk with me about this."

Radford shrugged. "Well, your name didn't actually come up, except when I was talking to a police captain named Molina. He wanted to know who referred me to Pico and he seemed to know you."

"Yes, he does, indeed. From many years ago." The old priest smiled. "Our paths crossed and I doubt he would consider me a friend. Or even a reputable companion for you. Yet, I believe he's a good man. Very thorough and therefore very dangerous, but he also has a reputation for being incorruptible. I suspect he's kept on a tight leash by the powers that be in Lima."

"Well, they wanted me on a tight leash, too," Radford replied. He told Juan Calderon about the quasi-official orders he received from Blieu. "But I wasn't having any of that. If they want me to be in the navy, then it needs to be through channels."

"Yet you agreed to work for them," the padre pointed out.

"Yes, as a civilian consultant or attached to the embassy. Not that it makes so much difference in terms of what I do."

"No," the older man agreed. "But it puts you on a different footing. You can at any point refuse without disobeying an order." He laughed wryly. "Doing so may get you shot either way, but at least you have the theoretical right to refuse."

"Or disappear with it being desertion," Radford added. "Plus the fact I can hire my own guide. If Pico is still willing. After our last adventure he might not be and I wouldn't blame him."

"Surely you jest!" Juan Calderon exclaimed. "I've not seem Pico so animated in years. The week you were in Lima he talked about little else, and I have to admit I envied him. That was more excitement than either of us has seen since we crossed the mountains twenty years ago." The old man shook his head sadly. "I know, my friend. I know. I left that life when I took these vows almost as many years ago and I don't regret it. But sometimes, when I think of those days...." Juan Calderon broke off with a sigh, a far away look in his eyes. Then he sighed again and grinned wickedly. "These days I have to enjoy such things vicariously. God forgive me, but I love it!"

"Yeah," Radford agreed. "It wasn't the call of duty for me, either, you know. It was that same thing you are talking about. The call of distant trumpets and drums. The call to action."

"The call of one burro to another!" Rosario snorted, bringing them another round of beer and setting the tray on the table more firmly than necessary. "I don't know which of you is worse," she declared, indignantly, looking from the one to the other. "You're both little boys playing spy. It could get all of you killed!"

Suddenly tears filled Rosario's eyes and she fled toward the kitchen. A moment later Radford ran after her, leaving the old priest alone in the courtyard. "Ai, yi, yi, yi, yi!" Juan Calderon muttered, shaking his head and raising his hands to the heavens. Yet the heavens kept silence, and the old man was left alone with the memory of his many transgressions. Nor was it true that the ones he regretted most were those he had left uncommitted.

The guard at the embassy was the same one who challenged Rott before. This time, however, the young man stared stonily ahead when the driver crossed the courtyard and mounted the steps to the main entrance, his Mauser rifle held butt down against the pavement as he stood at parade rest. Unlike the rest of the guards, who tended to relax a bit on embassy duty when the brass were not around, this one kept his uniform immaculate and his high black boots shined to a mirror gleam, and today was no exception. The man looked like a model for a recruiting poster for the Aryan Reich, tall and blond with ice blue eyes set in a pale Nordic face. And if the trooper felt resentment for the earlier incident, none of this showed in his stern, young face.

On impulse, Rott stopped at the entrance and turned to the soldier. Taking a cigarette out of his tunic, Rott lighted it and stood for a moment looking at the man. Except for a brief flicker of his eyes in Rott's direction once when the driver paused, the trooper gave no sign he was even aware of the other's presence. Even when moved closer, so close the smoke from his cigarette wafted into the other's face, there was no break in the man's composure.

"You'd like to shoot me, wouldn't you, private?" he asked softly, as casually as if talking about the weather. "You'd like to stick that long barrel up my butt and pull the trigger."

The soldier came to attention when Rott spoke. "To serve the Fatherland, yes sir!" he answered, almost as quietly as Rott.

Rott chuckled. "You don't have to come to attention for me, youngster," he said. "And don't call me 'sir', either. Understand?"

"Certainly, s...." The trooper caught himself in time.

"I'm going to need a good man," Rott replied. "Someone like you who no one will mistake for a civilian. How would you like to work for me?"

The guard was obviously at a loss for words. After the briefest pause he answered. "I don't see it matters whether I like it or not, Mr. Rott. I expect it would depend on what we were doing."

Again Rott chuckled. "You'd love it if it were lining me up against the wall," he suggested.

"Only if you were an enemy of the Reich!" the younger man declared.

"Or if you could get away with it," Rott suggested. "Do you drive?" he asked.

"Yes, s... Mr. Rott," the young guard caught himself again. "I was a taxi driver in Berlin before the war," he volunteered, making a decision. Working for Rott might not be his choice of duty, but guard duty was boring and Rott seemed to be all right enough as long as one didn't cross him.

"Don't worry about the honorific, man," Rott growled. "And relax that Prussian ass of yours a bit. Call me Rott. That will do." The young man went back to parade rest. "I'll have a word with your sergeant," the driver told him. "What's your name?"

"Weiss," the other replied. "Johannes Weiss."

"Weiss?" Rott asked, looking at the other closely. "You're not Jewish, are you?"

"Good God, no!" Weiss denied, horror breaking his composure briefly.

"You'll do, Weiss," Rott chuckled. "You'll do. This afternoon you'll be working for me. I want to see just how well you drive." Stamping the cigarette out, Rott turned and entered the embassy quickly, not waiting for a reply, and Weiss was left to wonder what Rott wanted with him. Then he decided surely it could not be as bad as the front lines.

"Still tormenting the help, eh, Helmut?" Schwartz murmured when Rott arrived in the office on the second story of the embassy. "What am I to do with you?"

Rott shrugged. "Yet, what would you do without me, Manfred?" he asked, completing the ritual he was beginning to find tiresome. "Besides, I wasn't tormenting him. I was recruiting him."

77

"There's a difference?" Schwartz asked and they both smiled. "But Weiss? I would not have thought he would be suitable. At least not to you."

Rott shrugged. "He's a driver and I could use another later on, but that's not why I want him. He looks German and that's what I need. More to the point, he's a pigeon."

"A pigeon?" Schwartz asked. "You mean like a messenger?"

"No, though he would be useful for that. What I mean is he's like a pigeon. When it's below you it eats out of your hand. When it's above you, it craps on your head."

Manfred chuckled and Rott waited until he was done. *One of these days the he's going to surprise me and get right down to business*, he thought, but there was no hurrying his protector, though today Schwartz seemed a bit on edge. Rott wondered why he'd been called back to the city when he was so urgently needed at the Project, but Schwartz would tell him soon enough.

He didn't have long to wait. The other's face turned serious. "I'm afraid I have some bad news, Helmut," he told Rott. "Radford was seen in the city yesterday."

"So Quito failed," Rott growled. "Well, I'll sort it out with him as soon as we're done."

"You won't have to," Schwartz replied. "Quito failed in the worst way. Radford was seen at police headquarters and he talked to Molina. Our sources there tell us he reported Quito was killed when he attacked Radford somewhere on the *montana*."

Rott shrugged. "Well, I don't see that's any particular concern to us. We have other people who can do the job and make sure it gets done. I never trusted Quito, anyway, but why worry? There's no way he can be tied to us."

Schwartz looked quite unhappy. "Unfortunately, there may be. See, he may have been carrying one of our maps when he was killed."

"*What!*" Rott exclaimed. "Where did he get that? How?"

The other shrugged. "We gave it to him." Rott was speechless and Schwartz hurried on. "He called here for you but you were at the project. So I took the call. He wanted a map and that seemed reasonable enough at the time. I made sure the one I got him had almost nothing on it."

"Almost nothing on it?" Rott croaked. "Where did you get it?" When Schwartz told him, Rott rushed from the room to a cabinet in a room down the hall and quickly looked through the documents he found there. Finding what he wanted, he nodded.

"What is it?" Schwartz wanted to know.

"We're all right, I think," Rott answered. "The map you gave him wasn't completely done yet. We had only started filling in details."

"Done?" Schwartz asked. "Except for a few pen marks here and there it looked finished to me."

Rott shook his head. "Nothing visible, Manfred. Treat it with the right chemicals and it's a different matter. We had only started work on the one you gave Quito." He thought for a moment. "Well, even if they have it, I doubt they will know how to treat the paper, so we're probably all right." He looked up at the other. "Is that all?"

"All?" Schwartz asked stupidly. He was still trying to absorb the implications of everything Rott had just told him.

"Is that all Quito asked for?" Rott spelled out.

"All the documents," his superior told him. "He wanted more money, of course, but I told him there wasn't a chance of that. He was whining something about having trouble finding the right kind of rifle, but when I gave him one of ours he shut up."

"You what!" Rott demanded.

"I gave him one of those new sniper rifles," Schwartz replied. "The civilian models. A pistol, too. I don't understand why he was having so much trouble finding arms, but we needed to get the job done so I went ahead and gave them to him." Seeing the look on the other's face, he asked, "What's wrong?"

"What's wrong?" Rott hissed angrily between clenched teeth. "What's wrong? Why didn't you just give him a frigging sign to wear around his neck saying 'I work for the Germans'?"

"Oh, come on, man, it's not that bad," Schwartz protested. "Every army down here uses Mausers," but Rott wasn't listening. He was headed out the door. "Where are you going?" Schwartz called after him.

"To Pisco, Manfred," Rott flung back over his shoulder. "To Pisco to try to save your sorry neck, and mine, too!"

6. The Map

"Any idea of what they were after?" The policeman asked. They were standing at the doorway of Paul Radford's hotel room, four of them, Radford, the sergeant, the manager of the hotel and a hall porter nervously wringing his hands.

"No," Radford answered. "I just got here myself. Who called you?"

"The desk clerk," the officer answered. "The maid saw your door ajar and looked in. When she saw the mess she called the desk and the clerk called me." He peered further into the room. "Do you mind?" he asked, pointing into the room.

Radford started to assent, then changed his mind. "Just a moment," he said. "Let me look to see if anything is missing first." Cautiously me made his way into the mess which had been his well ordered hotel room. Covers had been torn from the bed and thrown into a corner with the mattress which was ripped open. Contents of his worn suitcase had been dumped onto the mattress and casually sifted. The leather lining had been torn out of the suitcase and flung onto the pile, and all the seams of the grip had been carefully cut open and separated.

The only other items in the room were the reference books Radford used in his work and the few papers he kept filed in craft envelopes. The envelopes had been emptied and their contents searched before being thrown to the floor, and the books had apparently been rifled and tossed into the corner with the bed clothes and the remains of the suitcase. Even the leather pencil case Radford's mother had given him for graduation years before had been emptied and torn apart, and the satin lining was left dangling from where it was ripped from his leather jacket.

Seeing the jacket, Radford felt a flash of anger. By now it was well worn and comfortable from years of use, but when it was new it cost him several month's savings from a part time job he held in graduate school. The lining could be replaced, but along the waist was a long slit left when a knife cut too far through the fabric of the liner and into the leather.

"They were apparently after something other than money," the policeman pointed out, interrupting Paul's thoughts. He had come a couple of steps into the room and was surveying the mess with a critical eye. Several bank notes and a number of coins could be seen scattered in the mess and an expensive pair of binoculars had been left untouched on a small side table. The case, however, was torn apart and its remains added to the pile in the corner.

Radford nodded. "I suspect they were after my notebooks," he answered. "I had three blank ones left which seem to be missing. They must not have looked at them before they took them."

The policeman nodded. "How about the ones which were not blank?" he asked. "Did they not take them, too?"

"No," Radford shook his head. "I had them with me." He held up his rucksack and nodded. "You're probably right. It was probably one of my competitors after my notes."

"Strange they would be so bold," the policeman murmured. "One does not expect a thief to strike so early in the day. Even a commercial thief."

"Maybe that's why," Radford suggested. "Maybe they are smart thieves who knew nobody would be expecting them."

"Perhaps so," the policeman nodded, but Radford could see he was far from convinced. Nor was there any doubt in Radford's mind that Captain Molina would hear about the intrusion before the day was out. This officer reminded him of the captain, short, quiet and neat as a pin, with bland, intelligent eyes that missed nothing, and Radford was certain a word had been passed along to whomever was in charge here in Pisco to keep an eye on him.

Radford sighed and decided to grasp the nettle firmly. "I don't think we've met," he said to the officer. "Or that I've seen you around town before." He offered his hand. "I'm Paul Radford. I work as a geologist for one of the oil companies."

The policeman gave his hand a perfunctory shake. "Sergeant Gomez," he replied. "I was just transferred to Pisco. From Lima," he added before Radford could ask. "One expects a certain amount of pilfering in hotels, but this was a very thorough search. Whoever it was must want what they were looking for very badly."

"Looks that way, doesn't it?" Radford replied, nodding. "I met a Captain Molina from Lima quite recently," he added blandly. "An interesting fellow. I'm sure you must know him, Sergeant. A very tall fellow, as I remember," he said.

A momentary look of confusion crossed Gomez' face. "I work for a Captain Molina, but he is not all that tall. He's about my height."

"Oh," said Radford dully. "Well, I must have him confused with someone else. I met a number of people the same day and names are not that easy for me to remember. Maybe there was someone else with him."

"I can't think of anyone on the force that tall," Gomez replied, looking at Radford suspiciously.

"No matter," Radford answered shrugging, regretting his gambit. "What I remember was the man was very smart and very efficient. He was very helpful."

"Now that sounds like Captain Molina," the sergeant replied. "Always very efficient."

"I would imagine so," Radford said. "Well, if there's nothing else, I guess I better start cleaning up this mess." He looked at the reference books thrown on the floor. "People who treat books like this should be horse whipped. I'd like to get my hands on whoever did it," he muttered. Moving carefully he picked up the strewn volumes and gently stacked them on the side table.

The sergeant looked at him strangely. "So would I, Mr. Radford. So would I. You will, of course, tell me if there is anything else missing?" he asked. Radford nodded and a moment later the policeman was gone, leaving the young man to the company of the hotel manager and the hall porter who was still wringing his hands. Yet as he left, the sergeant made a mental note to have a quiet word in private with the porter later on. The man was nervous as a cat in heat, and Gomez was certain he knew far more than he was saying.

"Well, it's obvious they were after the map," Juan Calderon told Paul Radford not an hour later. "Did they get it?"

"No," Radford answered, "they didn't. I had it with my notebooks in my rucksack. I thought of giving it to Blieu when we talked, but I forgot." He reached into his pack brought out the map. "Maybe I should give it to him now, but I don't see why whoever it was would make such a big deal over it," he said opening the map onto the table which served as the padre's desk. "There's nothing on it but the usual map stuff. Except for these marks around the edge, but they don't make much sense."

The old priest pointed at the odd markings in the margins. "Not entirely," he replied. "If whoever it was took the risk of stealing it, there must be more here than meets the eye." He pointed to the legend which was printed in German. "The date shows it was drawn six years ago but it could have been printed anytime since. I imagine anyone could get one of these but there's not much doubt in my mind Quito got it directly from the Germans."

"No," Radford disagreed. "I've seen most of the maps available and this one is much finer work. I think it's a government map, but that doesn't make any sense at all. Why would they give it to Quito if it was so valuable?"

"Unless Quito was a messenger as well as an assassin," Calderon suggested. "If he was taking the map to someone else....." He broke off. "No, that doesn't make any sense, either. Who would he be taking it to in the middle of nowhere? Unless, of course, someone else was there, but if they were, then why would they need the map?"

"You've lost me," Radford told him.

"I've lost myself, too," Juan Calderon admitted. "I don't know what I am trying to say. The whole thing is very strange."

"As strange as the attack on me," Radford nodded. "I think I better let Blieu know about this. Maybe he will have some idea of what it's about."

"That's probably a good idea," the padre agreed. "He may be aware of something we are not." He looked at Radford intently. "Does he know you're talking to me?"

"No," the young man told him. "He told me not to mention it anyone." He shrugged. "Of course, even if he did, my confessor doesn't count."

"Your confessor, eh?" Juan Caldron raised an eyebrow. "Did I miss something or was I asleep in the booth? Since when did I become your confessor?"

"Well, you know," Radford answered, a bit embarrassed. "In a manner of speaking. Not that I was intending to tell Blieu about you, anyway. Why? Do you think I should?"

The old man sat for a long moment. "I don't know, Pablo," he said. "Were it just me, I wouldn't care. But telling him will involve Rosario, too." He waved away Radford's obvious objection. "Yes, man, I know. She is already involved, but they don't know that."

"I don't want to do anything to put her at risk," Radford replied decisively. "So I won't tell them about you and me except that we're friends. Captain Molina knows that already, but not how close we are." He was silent, clearly troubled.

"What is it, my friend," Juan Calderon asked gently. "Are you afraid of putting me at risk, too? If you are, then set your mind at ease. I've been there before, many times." He laughed. "I'm sure if I live so long, I will be again. At least, I hope so."

"No," Radford answered. "That's not what bothers me. I mean, yes, your safety does concern me. I don't see how it couldn't. But who I'm concerned about is Rosario. She's been awfully moody ever since we got back, like she was yesterday. She gets snappish and sometimes breaks into tears. That's not like her, is it?" He gave the padre a troubled look.

"Ah, that," the good padre nodded, but said nothing more.

"Do you know what's bothering her?" Radford asked. "Has she said anything to you? Anything you can tell me?"

"No," the old man said gravely. No, she hasn't said a word. Not that she would. Yet I suspect I know what it is. I suspect it's her child."

"Her child?" Radford asked. "What child? I didn't know she had a child."

"Ah, but she does, you see," Calderon replied, smiling gently and patting Radford on the arm. "A child she will have before the next year ends."

"Before the next year ends? You mean....?" Radford gaped. He could not quite get his mind around the thought. "You mean....?" he stammered again.

"Yes, my friend, I'm afraid I do," Calderon nodded. "I don't know for sure, but that is exactly what I do mean. I wouldn't be at all surprised to learn she's expecting your child." He shrugged and looked at the other directly. "Why? Is there any reason not to?"

"I thought I was being so careful," Radford told him. "I mean...."

"I'm sure you were," the old man chuckled. "Perhaps both of you were, although I would not think so with Rosario. Perhaps she and Someone else had other things in mind."

"You mean the baby might not be mine?" Radford asked, shocked.

"Oh, no, my friend," Juan Calderon laughed. "I'm quite sure you're the father, as sure as I am sure the sun will rise tomorrow. No, it's just that when a woman and God get together and decide there needs to be a child, a man doesn't have much choice."

Though Schwartz was far from pleased, there was little he could say. Not at the moment. The blame for the fiasco clearly lay in his hands, and while this did not particularly worry him just then, it could get sticky later on. Not that he was worried for his personal safety. He could sacrifice Rott as a last resort, if need be. Schwartz had the political connections to pull that off and the facts were that Quito was working directly as Rott's agent when it happened.

Even so, while shifting the blame to Rott might keep Schwartz from being shot, it could well mean his being recalled, and the last place he wanted to be these days was in Berlin. Even out here, halfway around the world, strange rumors of what was happening in Germany were going around, and those who found favor with the Reich today might well be considered traitors tomorrow. The lesson of the infamous "night of the long knives" seven years before was not lost on Schwartz. He had been in Berlin then, a rising member of the Foreign Service, and it was the Gestapo massacre which prompted him to ask for this assignment literally at the end of the earth. Nor could anyone have anticipated such an unlikely place would ever become such a hot spot of German interests.

"So you didn't find it," Schwartz remarked, looking at Rott askance. "I assume you were your usual thorough self, so that must mean he doesn't have it."

"Yes, or that he didn't have it in his room," Rott corrected. "Nor is it in the hotel safe. I made sure of that before we tumbled his room."

"Where else could he have it?" Schwartz asked. "Unless he had it with him."

"Or unless he hid it somewhere else or gave it to someone for safekeeping," Rott reminded him rather sharply. "It could be just about anywhere."

"Including in the mountains," Schwartz returned with equal asperity. "You may be overestimating our young Mr. Radford, Jergen. Not everyone is as thorough as you."

Rott ignored the flattery. "What are you driving at?" he asked.

"We know Quito was shot," the other answered. "Radford reported that. However, the police tell me nothing was turned in. No weapons, no papers, nothing. Radford told the police they simply left the body in mountains, but that he's not sure just where they were. He says they didn't bring the body out because he was wounded, but the police don't like the fact it took him so long to get back."

"What about the guide?" Rott asked. "You know, that one-eyed fellow he hired to guide him. What did he tell them?"

"Nothing," Schwartz replied. "He seems to have disappeared, according to the police. Which seems a bit suspicious to me." Rott nodded agreement and Schwartz added. "So maybe you should find the guide and ask him yourself, Jergen. And if he never shows up again...." He shrugged. "I'm sure he could tell you where they were."

Rott nodded. "Perhaps so, but I understand he's a drunk and who knows when he may show up? That may be why he disappeared so quickly, especially if Radford kept him on the wagon. He's probably on a binge. I think I better try to find out for myself."

"You mean heading into the mountains?" Schwartz asked. "Aren't you needed...elsewhere?" He caught himself in time, but flushed.

Rott gave him a baleful look. "Careful, Manfred," he murmured. "Loose lips lose lives. But, no, not for now. I have my other duties pretty well in order and I'll be back in ten days, or maybe less. Two weeks at the most. We simply have to recover that map."

"It's that important?" Schwartz asked, wondering what he had not been told. "I had no idea."

"The loss would be a major catastrophe for the Reich," he was answered simply. "Even the least hint of the information which it contains could be disastrous. So, yes, Manfred, it's that important.

Not even your political connections could cover us for the loss if it's traced to us."

For the first time in a long while, Schwartz began to be afraid. "Then get it, Jergen," he hissed. "I don't care who you have to kill. Just get it! Or we'll hang together."

"I think we'd be lucky to get off that easily, my friend," Rott told him. "So keep your ears open here. I'll leave before dark."

Denis Blieu was happy. Things were coming together well. Though it was not his custom to keep company with ladies of the night, he had discovered a number of lovely courtesans doing business in Lima. Normally it was not necessary for him to seek out brothels, or even independent operators, but this was business. Official government business. Thinking of the lovely lass whose company he shared for several pleasant and productive hours, he smiled to himself and sighed happily. *The things we're forced to do for the sake of the Republic,* he thought. Then he chuckled aloud. *I wonder how Alex will cover it with the auditors when I turn it in as a expense item.* For a moment he savored the scene in his mind, imagining his friend's response.

The thought of Alex reminded him he needed to get off a cable to the group, and soon. A large stack of notes awaited his attention at the embassy, notes he needed to condense into a concise report and encode for transmission to Rudd. Normally Blieu was conscientious about his paperwork. Yet ever since arriving in Lima he found himself unconsciously slowing down. Part of this was deliberate strategy, a self-imposed discipline of slowing down and keeping pace with the local rhythm of life so he wouldn't stand out. Because of his height he was too obvious as it was, so Blieu worked hard at cultivating the image of a junior embassy official assigned to the end of nowhere, and one happily going native. This was another reason for seeking out the fleshpots of Lima, and Blieu was certain by now his presence had been noted and his activities monitored. Hopefully, this would result in his presence being discounted and classified as harmless, and he was very careful to do nothing which was not consistent with the image he was so carefully cultivating.

Yet only part of this was deliberate. Here in the backwaters of the world the war in Europe was far away, out of sight and out of mind most of the time, and life went on at a pace Blieu imagined it had followed for centuries. So it was easy to slow down, easy to fall into the custom of the siesta followed by the afternoon's work and a late dinner, and it was easy getting into a casual attitude toward getting things done within a given time. Sometimes it took conscious effort to remember his mission, and this bothered him a great deal, for it happened more often than he liked to admit.

Blieu glanced at his watch, surprised to see it was well after ten o'clock. For a moment he debated shucking the drudgery of compiling and encoding his report until the morrow, instead stopping into one of the local cantinas for a nightcap and whatever gossip he could glean. There was no question that this was a direct part of his mission, however pleasant. Yet, he knew there was probably little he would hear which would not be reported in greater detail by his network of courtesans. So Blieu turned his steps toward the embassy, promising his scruples he would work for at least an hour before allowing himself the necessity of sleep.

Blieu's route took him through a number of deserted and poorly lighted streets of the city. Not that this was normally cause for concern. The streets of Lima were far safer than the streets of either San Diego or New York, and Blieu was trained to take care of himself. Yet tonight a sixth sense warned Blieu he was being followed, and whoever was doing it was very good. Not a sound reached his ears from the quiet streets, nor was he able to catch sight of a anything on the few occasions he could look back without giving away his awareness of being followed. Yet he knew for sure he was not alone in the empty streets, and not being able to spot his shadow heightened his sense of disquiet.

Suddenly a soft voice whispered out of a dark alley he was approaching. "Senor!" it called out urgently in Spanish. "Senor! Over here. To your left." *Shit,* Blieu thought, *a front shadow. No wonder I couldn't make him.* He stopped and looked in the direction of the voice. A darker shadow left the deep shadow of a doorway and moved toward him.

"That's far enough!" Blieu commanded in Spanish, reaching into his jacket and pulling out the snub nosed revolver he always carried on assignment, crouching as he did and aiming at the shadow.

Yet the shadow made no threatening gestures. "Please, senor, don't shoot. I have a message for you. From someone we both know."

"What's the message?" Blieu demanded, not relaxing for a moment.

The shadow extended an arm carefully and laid something which looked white on the ground between them. "That's part of the message," the voice said and backed up three or four steps.

Blieu did not move. "What is it?" he asked, nodding toward the light colored object on the street. Then he realized the other man could not see his nod. "What did you put down there?"

"A document, senor," the shadow's voice responded. "Please, when you look at it I think you will understand. Please. I intend no harm." The shadow began backing away up the street.

"Stop!" Blieu demanded, easing to one side so a solid wall was at his back. Quickly he glanced back up the street where he had just come, then back to the shadow. The man had not moved from where her halted and no one else was on the street. "Who sent you?" Blieu asked in a loud whisper.

"Please, senor." the shadow replied. "He told me not to say his name out loud, or yours. Only to say *The Sunshine Bar.*" He spoke the name in English. "He said you would know what that meant. If not, he told me to say 'Emma Jane'."

Blieu chuckled. "I expect I know what he was talking about. All right, pick up the document and bring it to me." He lowered his pistol and stood up, but did not return the weapon to his jacket. The man from the shadows figure stooped and picked up the white object and handed it to Blieu. In the dim light from the end of the street the officer could see he was short and walked with a limp. Yet what caught his eye was the black patch which covered one of the man's eyes. "So who are you?" Blieu asked, taking the document in his left hand. His eyes never left the man in front of him.

"They call me Pico, sir," the man whispered in clear English. "I work for the man who sent this."

"So what is it, Pico?" Blieu asked, finally holstering his revolver and glancing at what he'd been given. "What did you bring me?"

"Please, sir," Pico responded, again in English. "The walls may have ears. Take it with you and look at it carefully. I found it in the mountains and the man I work for will be here in a few days. Let him answer the questions. I think he already told you how I found it. He thought it best if I bring it rather than him and he said you would understand why."

"Maybe I do," Blieu answered looking down at the packet in his hands. It was tan, not white, and he could see it was some kind of oil cloth wrapped around something else. "All right, why don't you tell him...." Blieu broke off as he looked up again. He was alone in the street. There was no sign of Pico in either direction he looked and the dark alley was empty, too. Nor had he heard any sound of the guide's departure. *Damn*, Blieu thought, *I'm glad he's on our side.*

Glancing down at the packet Blieu suddenly felt weary. It was a familiar feeling to him, a letting down which followed sudden action. Combined with the effects of a large meal and a long day, it made him sleepy and he came to a decision. Tonight he would rest and tackle the packet and the chore of encoding his report tomorrow.

Thirty minutes later any thought of sleep was gone. Opening the packet and taking out the map, a thrill of excitement drove away any drowsiness left after the encounter with Pico. If this was what he thought it might be, there was no time for delay. Commander Rudd and the Senator needed to know about it right away. Changing to comfortable clothes and putting on a pot of coffee, Blieu washed his hands carefully and began a careful examination of the map Pico brought.

"Well, you really hit the jackpot, Paul," Blieu told Radford a week later. Once again they were sitting in the small office in the back of the embassy, and the afternoon was warm. Smoke from their cigarettes drifted lazily toward the open window looking out toward the carriage house, but this time the big touring car was gone. "I don't know why they let Quito have it, but that map was a helluva prize for us." He nodded. "Unless it's a hoax. That's always a possibility, you know, but I don't think so. I think this is the real McCoy."

Radford was silent a moment. "What makes you think it might be a hoax?" he asked, frowning. "I looked at it pretty carefully and it looked like a German map. The paper was good and the printing was very clear, like German work. Of course, I guess Quito could have gotten it almost anywhere."

Blieu nodded his head. "Yes, that's the point. He could have, but I don't think so. Nor do I really think it's an attempt to mislead us, but that's always an outside chance. That would explain why Quito had it in the first place."

"I don't follow," Radford replied.

"Suppose they wanted us to find the map," Blieu told him. "They wanted us to have information they put on it to keep us chasing our tails. So they gave it to Quito to get it to us."

"Yeah," Radford countered, "but they couldn't be sure we would kill Quito. As a matter of fact, we almost didn't. They couldn't count on him screwing up like that."

"You're right," Blieu explained patiently, "but they could have given it to Quito to sell to us. Or they could have made sure he got his hands on it. Maybe they let him steal it thinking he would sell it to us, or someone else so it would eventually get into our hands. Maybe killing you was Quito's idea and he just happened to have the map on him when he attacked you."

"Sounds kind of shaky to me," Radford told him. "Too many chances it could go wrong."

"I agree," Blieu nodded. "That's why I think it is exactly what it seems to be, but there is always the outside chance it's not, and we've got to remember that."

"So what was on it that got you going?" Radford asked. "I didn't see anything out of the ordinary, other than the fact it's very good quality work. Unless it's those strange markings in the margins."

"Those strange markings were what got me started." Blieu pulled a couple of large photographs, the size of full chest x-rays, from a large craft envelope on the small table. Paul Radford recognized the first of these as a very clear photographic copy of the map he sent Blieu, so clear the faint marks of the map's folds could be seen as vague shadows. Blieu placed the photo flat on the table and took out a ruler. "Let's play connect the dots," he said, aligning two of the strange markings on the margin along the edge of the ruler. "These two marks are the same, and if you align them, they give you a base line." With a pencil he made a faint tracing along the axis between the identical marks, leaving a red line across the photo at an odd angle. "These other marks are all exactly alike, but much different from those two. Align them in every way they can be drawn, and I think you'll see the significance." Quickly Blieu drew in lines with another pencil, producing a series of faint black lines which intersected the red score a number of points.

"Map coordinates!" Radford exclaimed getting excited. "They put them there to mark their map coordinates." He clasped a hand to his forehead. "I should of known!" he exclaimed. "I do that all the time myself."

"You do?" Blieu asked. It was his turn to be puzzled.

"Yeah, it's standard company practice. There's too much chance what we find will be stolen, like it could have been when my room was tossed. So I do a lot of encoding with my maps. It's a private key no one but me and the people in my company know, and it works. I use the same encoding in my daily log when I'm out in the field." He took a leather notebook out of his pocket and handed it to Blieu. "Take a look at this and I think you'll see what I mean. I would not be surprised if it was not standard practice with other companies, too."

Blieu thumbed through the book to the last entry. "From the date, I take it the last thing here is the trip when you were attacked. Right?" Radford nodded and Blieu continued his examination of the cryptic notes. "So, for example, 'AG.001@7.65/14.92' is something you can decode yourself, as can someone at your home office in the States if something happens to you."

"Yes," Radford answered. "That one is a shorthand that tells me I found a very small trace of gold at a specific site."

"Ah," Blieu nodded. "AG is for gold, and .001 tells how much. But if I could figure that out, what would keep a competitor from doing so if he got your notes?"

"The map key," Radford answered. "He might know we found a lot of gold from an AG1.5, but he wouldn't know where to look for it. On the other hand, someone else from my company could go right to the spot. Give or take fifty yards."

Blieu pounced. "But I imagine no one in your company would be able to figure out what you meant by 'QG+2@7.78/17.89', would they?" Radford said nothing and Blieu pushed harder. "Yet if I had the key to the map, I suspect that would put me within fifty yards of where Quito attacked you, right?"

Radford shrugged. "Even if you were right, you don't have the key. That's the point."

Damn, he's good, Blieu thought. *He should have been working for us all along.* "Want to bet I couldn't get it out of your company?" he challenged.

"You're assuming two things," Radford said calmly, refusing the bait. "One is that you could figure out who to ask and how to ask them. Even using the patriotic appeal, they would be reluctant to give the government the key to all their interests down here."

"That's one thing," Blieu reminded him. "You said there were two."

"You're assuming the code in the book for that entry is the same as the others," Radford told him with a small, knowing smile. "Assuming for a moment you are right about that notation, and I am not saying you are, ask yourself this. Why would I use the same code I use for my company business? Why wouldn't I use a different code, or even alter the one I use for company business? Particularly if it was only for the one event? That would make sense, wouldn't it? Someone else, like the police, could figure that out, too, just like you did."

Blieu looked at the entry again. It was smudged and he laughed. "Ah, it's been changed, hasn't it? All right, you win. But assuming there was something interesting to see there, you could take me to this spot, couldn't you?"

"Of course," Radford told him. "That's why I marked it. As I might tell the police, there are some interesting plants and rock formations in that area, among other things. Quartz and granite." Blieu rolled his eyes and the younger man shook his head. "Hey, Denis, I'm not trying to be difficult with you. You're right about that entry. I did enter it in company code at first but I thought I better change it over after my room was tossed."

The news took Blieu by surprise. "Your room was tossed? When did that happen?"

"Right after I got back from talking to you the last time." Radford quickly told him about it. "I started to write to let you know about it but I changed my mind. I decided to tell you in person. That's why I decided to send Pico on with the map. I thought you needed that right away."

"So that was Pico, then," Blieu observed and Radford nodded. "I see why you hired him." Blieu paused, was silent a moment. "Well, it's obvious they're pretty desperate to get the map back. Or, at least, that's want they want us to think."

"Double-think?" Radford asked.

Blieu laughed. "Sometimes more like triple or quadruple think," he said. "Sometimes we get so clever we step in our own traps. What I can't understand is why they were so obvious about it. It doesn't take that much more time to search without leaving much trace. They didn't even bother to make it look like a robbery. It's like they wanted you to know they were there."

"Do you think they're trying to scare me off?" Radford asked.

"What would be the advantage of that?" Blieu answered. "No, it doesn't make any sense at all. As Gomez said, casual thieves would have at least taken the glasses and the money." He looked at Radford. "I can't understand why you were leaving money lying out, either."

"I don't," the other assured him. "That was a gratuity for the maid. Less than a dollar."

A noise from the window drew Radford's attention and he saw the large, black touring car pulling up. When it stopped a man got out, glancing back over his shoulder down the drive as he closed the door and Radford recognized him. It was the driver he had seen before. "Denis," he said, getting to his feet and pointing out the window. "Look, quickly! Who is that?"

The driver was disappearing into the garage as Blieu turned around. "I couldn't tell for sure," he said, but I think that's Antonio, one of the embassy drivers. Why?"

Quickly Radford told him of the resemblance to one of the men with Quito in the mountains. "If I didn't know the guy was dead, I would swear that was him," he added.

Blieu sat a long moment thinking. "Damn," he said, finally. "It may be a coincidence, but I don't believe in those. If he's connected to Quito and saw you come here the last time, that might explain why they broke into your room. It might also explain some other strange things around here." He thought for another moment. "Look I happen to know Antonio's been gone all morning driving the ambassador's wife to market. I don't think he spotted you, but I think we better assume the worst. Just to be safe, let's try to get you out of here without him seeing you. The less Schwartz and his crowd know, the better."

"Schwartz?" Radford asked. "Who's Schwartz? A German?"

Blieu nodded, getting to his feet and ushering Radford into the hall. "Roughly my counterpart in their embassy, but I don't consider the comparison flattering. For all his charm, he's pretty vicious and some of the people who work for him are worse. Particularly one named Rott. He's on the embassy rolls as one of their drivers but our information is that he does Schwartz's dirty work."

As they walked down the hall Blieu was lost in thought. "I think you better stay out of sight for a while, Paul," he said, speaking quietly as he turned Radford aside into an alcove down the hall from the main entrance. "These characters are pretty salty and they play rough. Do you have anything to do that will take you away from Pisco for two or three weeks? Preferably away from settlements, too."

"Not really," Radford replied. "But Pico and I could check out those coordinates on the map."

"Good thinking," Blieu said. "If you can hang around town until tomorrow I'll work up a map of the hot spots you need to check." He grinned. "And I can plant some red herrings too, just in case."

"That's really not necessary," Paul told him. He touched his temple.

"Photographic memory?" Blieu asked.

"When it comes to maps, yes," Radford answered. "That's one of the reasons my company sent me down here. It helps in my job."

"I imagine it does," Blieu answered, opening a side door off the alcove. They entered a pleasant courtyard surrounded by hedges and shrubbery. "The gate across the court will lead you directly into a side street. Just be sure you hear it catch when you go out. When you get back from checking out the hot spots, find a hideout and send Pico to set up a meeting." He offered his hand. "Good hunting."

7. Strange Windings

Sergeant Gomez sat patiently in the outer room, watching the smoke from his *cigarillo* rise lazily to the high ceiling of the colonial building and thinking about the report he was there to make. The captain would not like the unresolved ambiguities of the case, he knew, but there was little Gomez could do about it except report what he knew and see what the *jeffe* wanted him to do. Nor was there much the captain could do except grouse about it, and the sergeant knew his captain would not blame him for the lack of information. While he could get more information with irregular methods, his superior looked down on such things. As he said more than once, there was no assurance any information obtained under physical duress was accurate. It was much more likely the poor wretch would tell his tormentors whatever he thought they wanted to hear, whether it was true or not, and the captain took the long view. Very few cases Molina was assigned went unresolved and while his methods were more subtle and less direct, they were effective and quite efficient.

Efficient. That was the word the *norteamericano* used to describe the captain and it was true. Sergeant Gomez and the captain had been together many years and had even started out in the police force about the same time. It was Molina's efficiency which brought rapid promotion, despite the political climate in Lima, and when he was promoted to Lieutenant, Gomez was surprised when Molina asked for him to be reassigned to his staff as sergeant. Gomez was a simple patrolman at the time and he was delighted with the opportunity to do something besides direct traffic and protect tourists from their indiscretions.

"You don't take bribes," was what Molina told him several years later when Gomez inquired why Molina had asked specifically for him. "That's most important. You also use your eyes and your ears and you understand what you see and hear."

"Well, *jeffe*," Gomez chuckled, "I don't know. Maybe I was just too dumb to know when I was offered a bribe. God knows I could have used the money."

"Maybe pigs sing, too," Molina snorted. What he knew, that few others did, is that Gomez supported a large extended family on his poor policeman's pay. Even though the sergeant had never married, he took care of the old people, and even a niece and nephew orphaned by disease. Easy as it might have been to accept a small gratuity here and there, or even to demand them, as far as Molina' could discern, Gomez had never done so. Nor was it a matter of religious scruples, for neither of them were religious men. Rather, it was a matter of personal integrity and the intuitive understanding that one who accepts a bribe has sold himself into a life of uncertain slavery by taking the first step down a steep and icy slope.

Now Gomez waited patiently, thinking of his report as he watched the smoke rise and wondering what was keeping the normally punctual captain. Yet he did not have long to wait. A few moments later Molina arrived, almost twenty minutes late by the clock. While this was not considered tardy by local standards, Molina had never adopted the attitude of *manana*, which was another reason for his rapid rise through the ranks of the police.

"Good morning, Juan," Molina greeted him warmly and Gomez followed him into the inner office. "What do you have for me today?"

Quickly Gomez outlined his investigation of the break-in at Radford's hotel in Pisco and his conversation with the young geologist. Molina listened intently and when the sergeant was done, asked, "What about the porter? What did he have to say?"

"He was very frightened, *jeffe*, and I had to really press him to get him to tell me anything. What he claimed is that a young European approached him and gave him money to bring him some fresh fruit and a paper from the market." Molina raised an eyebrow and Gomez nodded. "Which is a lie, of course, but I could not budge him from that. When he got back, of course, the European was gone and the room was a shambles. Not that he discovered it right away. He left that for the maid."

"And the fruit?" Molina asked quietly. "What became of that?"

"He had no idea," Gomez chuckled. "Somehow in all the excitement it disappeared, too, like the mysterious European."

"So the European was not a guest in the hotel, after all," Molina concluded.

"Nor would anyone else verify having seen him except for the desk clerk. He described him as good looking, blue eyes and blond hair, and said he was young and well dressed. He thought the man might have been a German or maybe an American, but he couldn't be sure. Nor could he remember seeing the man at the hotel before, but he also said there had been a number of people passing through and he could not be sure of that, either."

"How was he paid?" Molina asked. "The hall porter. Foreign currency?"

Gomez shook his head. "No, he claimed not. Nor was there any money left over from buying the fruit and somehow the newspaper had disappeared, too." He chuckled again. "When I asked if there was not even loose change he claimed to have had to pay extra out of his own pocket for the order and tried to convince me he was angry at the European for leaving him in debt."

Molina laughed. "Our porter seems to be a most gifted story teller," he said. "Did you confront him with his lies?"

"No," Gomez replied, shaking his head. "I didn't know how hard you wanted me to press or how much interest you wanted to show, so I pretended to accept his story. I don't think he really knows much that he didn't tell me and he might be useful to us later on. Do you want me to question him again?"

"Not necessary," Molina replied. "Did you ask him how the man walked?"

"Yes," Gomez answered. "I asked him if he noticed anything unusual like scars or glasses or the way the man walked, and he said not. As did the desk clerk. From their descriptions, I am pretty sure it wasn't Rott, or even Schwartz."

"Which doesn't mean Rott is not involved," Molina observed. "This sounds like his work."

"Why would he be so obvious? So crude?" Gomez wondered. "That's what bothers me about this. Why not take the money and field glasses to make it look like a theft?"

"Maybe he wanted Radford to understand very clearly it was not a thief," Molina suggested. "Or that he is being watched, but why warn him? Unless he is trying to scare Radford off, but if Rott was behind the attack in the mountains, that doesn't make much sense, either. Why be so blatant?" He shook his head. "We don't have enough information to make an intelligent guess."

Gomez smiled. "Which means you want me to do some more looking around."

"Exactly," Molina agreed, smiling back. "What I want you to do is talk to Radford again and see what else you can find out from him. Then ask around town some more and see what you find out from that. Ask around about that old priest, too, Juan Calderon. Talk to him, too."

"He's involved?" Gomez asked. Molina nodded. "You know, I met him a few years back," he told his boss. "When I was assigned in the *montana*. He used to come through once or twice a year to visit the wild people on the other side."

Molina looked up sharply. "I didn't realize you knew him," he said. "Did he have a guide?"

"Oh, yes," Gomez answered. "Although I doubt he really needed one by then. The guide was a strange fellow with only one eye, but he seemed quite competent."

"Ah," said Molina. Another piece of the Radford puzzle fell into place. "I don't suppose his name was Pico, was it?"

Gomez looked at his captain in surprise. "Yes, it was. Why? You know him?"

"No, but I've heard about him," the *jeffe* nodded. "He passes himself off as a drunk and works in a cantina in Pisco. So keep an eye out for him, too, but don't question him directly. Just keep your eyes open and tell me what you find out."

When Alex White brought the news, the commander was still at hard at work at his desk. Though the hour was getting late, the sky was bright with the light of a brilliant sunset and streamed in the dusty window as Rudd squinted over his papers in the gathering dusk and White snapped on the light as he entered the office. "No need to go blind," he remarked. "We have this marvelous thing called electricity these days. It doesn't cost much and I think the taxpayers can stand it."

Eric Rudd chuckled. "I've been wondering what that thing on the wall was for." Seeing the look of excitement on White's face he asked, "So what have you got?"

"I just talked to the guy from Washington. He came in on the flight with the new equipment and he'll be here in a minute. He's in the head but from what he was telling me, the map Radford came up with was a real gem."

Looking back down the hall, White spoke to someone and a moment later another officer came into the room, wearing the uniform of a first lieutenant of the Army. "I'm Paul," he said. "Jacques Paul. I take it you're Eric Rudd, sir," he added, saluting and handing the commander an identification card. Rudd gave a half hearted salute back. "Army Intelligence," the lieutenant added. "The Senator sends his salutations. He's asked me to brief you on the material you sent and to return it to you so you can get back to your man in South America."

"Get it back to him?" Rudd asked, waving Jacques Paul to a chair. "What in the world for?"

"That map is hot," the Lieutenant told him. "We put it through various tests and found out the real information on it is on the back. Under black light the lab wizards found part of a set of blue-prints to what we believe is a military installation. We think it is possibly part of a submarine base or maybe it is something else. What it appears to be is a storage bunker for high explosives, and one too expensive for a commercial operation. We think it might be storage for torpedoes or bombs, or perhaps both."

"All right," Rudd told him. "Assuming it is for real, we scored big. But why give it back?"

"We considered that, too," the lieutenant told him, ignoring his question. "This could be very, very clever disinformation, but we think not. One reason is that the courier was shot attacking our people, and while we still don't understand that completely, the consensus is that the map is for real. The hoax is far too elaborate for far too little gain otherwise."

"So we don't want them to know we have the information on the back," Rudd nodded. "That's why you want us to get it back."

"Exactly," Jacques Paul replied. "Without giving the Germans any indication we know what is on it." He pulled on a pair of white cotton gloves and took a craft envelope out of the leather briefcase he was carrying. Cautiously he opened the envelope and extracted the map, but it looked nothing like it did when it arrived from Blieu. The whole surface was stained and wrinkled from what appeared to be hard use and a small ragged hole about a third of an inch in diameter extended through one corner area. What caught Rudd's attention, however, were rust colored stains covering the area around the hole.

"Real blood," Jacques Paul confirmed. "And a real bullet hole. Microscopic examination will show cotton strands from Peruvian fabric, traces of lead from a bullet, and human sweat crystals."

"Damn, you're thorough," Rudd said with open admiration. "I wonder who thought all this up?"

"Actually, I did," Paul told him. There was no trace of conceit or false humility in his answer.

White nodded. "I gather the idea is when they get it back it will be hard for them to tell it's been through a lab." Jacques Paul nodded. "That's the easy part," Alex continued. "How in the world are we supposed to get it back to them? We can't just hand it to them and say, 'Hey, is this yours? We found it on a dead body we think belongs to you.'"

The lieutenant laughed and shrugged. "That's your part of the operation, gentlemen. I suppose you could have someone sell it to them. That's what I'd do in your place. That's a motive the people you're dealing with credit and it would cut out the possibility of anyone else having it."

"No, that's too risky," Rudd told him. "Too complicated and too many things can go wrong." He grinned. "Hell, we might find one of our own people in another agency buying it back. No, I think we better let them steal it back. Alex?" White nodded.

"See," Jacques Paul said. "You're much better at that kind of thing than us support types. I would suggest that no one be allowed to handle it directly except for your man in South America. We would not want an inappropriate set of fingerprints to appear on it."

"Fingerprints off paper?" White asked. "I didn't know that was possible."

"We don't know how to do it at this point," the lieutenant admitted. "But it is theoretically possible and who knows what the Germans have come up with? They have some incredibly clever people when it comes to technical things."

"They make the best cameras in the world," Rudd agreed. "That's what the best photographers use around here. Expensive as hell, but nobody can touch their optics." He nodded. "All right. We'll keep it clean. What else can you tell us, lieutenant? What are we looking for down there?"

Jacques Paul took another sheet from his briefcase. "There are a number of things to be on the watch for," he replied. "The problem is, they are all common to large-scale construction and may be perfectly legitimate commercial projects. We've come up with several things to watch to be able to tell the difference, and here are just a few things your man down there needs to look for." The page was three quarters filled with single spaced type, and by the time Jacques Paul was finished with his briefing, the moon was riding high over the horizon in a deep blue desert sky.

For a long time after Paul quit speaking Rudd was silent. Then he looked at Jacques Paul and asked, "I take it the Senator briefed you on what we're after?"

The lieutenant nodded. "Yes, on a need to know basis." He shrugged. "I couldn't very well tell him what to look for unless I knew what he was looking for and where. May I?" Rudd nodded and Paul reached in his briefcase and pulled out a large area map of southern Peru, northern Chile and Bolivia. "I have given it some thought," he said. "What we are talking about is an engineer's nightmare or his idea of paradise, depending on how he looks at it. The challenge is incredible, and keeping it secret is even more difficult." He pointed at several areas of the map and circled them lightly with a pencil. "If I were in charge, these are the areas I would look at first. Mostly because they are relatively unpopulated. That or the people there have little or no contact with the outside world." He went on to explain his analysis of each of the areas he had circled. "Of course, this is based on the information I have now," he said. "All I have is second-hand and I might have to rethink the whole thing once I was on site."

Again Rudd looked at White. This time he raised an eyebrow and White smiled and nodded. "Tell me, lieutenant, what do you like to be called?"

"I prefer Jacques, sir," the other answered. "Although Jock is fine, too."

"Well, Jacques," the commander asked. "How welded to that desk in Washington are you?"

"I'm not sure exactly what you are asking," Paul replied.

White grinned. "He's asking if you would like to join our group. It looks like we might have a real rumble going in South America."

"Damn, sir," Jacques Paul grinned. "I thought you'd never ask. That's why I asked the Senator to send me down here. Where do I bunk?"

"What do you see?" The words were on Paul Radford's lips but he said nothing. For the last five minutes he had been squatting by the path, watching Pico look at tracks in a damp stretch of soil running across a low place along their way. Instead, Radford looked more intently at the tracks, trying to discern what it was his guide saw there.

Suddenly Pico settled back on his haunches and nodded. "Three men," he told Radford. "Two of them are Europeans, maybe Americans. The other is wearing rope sandals. Maybe a guide." He nodded to himself. "All carrying packs. And in a hurry."

"How long ago did they pass?" Radford wanted to know.

"Yesterday morning," Pico responded. "Maybe the afternoon before." He looked around at the misty clouds gathered in the peaks above them. "It's hard to tell up here, but it didn't rain."

Radford absorbed the news quietly. "I wonder why they didn't pass us on the path? We haven't been moving that fast."

Pico shrugged. "They came down the path we joined this morning I think. There were signs of people ahead of us back there but no clear tracks." Suddenly he became very alert and reached for the pistol in his belt. Following his gaze up the path, Radford retrieved his own weapon. Signaling Radford to stay put, Pico disappeared into the brush by the path without a sound.

Again Radford waited, this time for fifteen minutes which seemed like an hour before he heard a bird call which told him all was clear. A moment later Pico appeared not twenty yards up the path and beckoned the young man to join him. When Radford arrived where he was squatting by a rock beside the road, Pico pointed. "That's what I smelled. I thought it was old, but I couldn't be sure." Radford craned his neck and saw Pico was pointing at cigarette butt. As he watched, Pico picked up the butt and sniffed it. "American made," the guide observed, pointing toward the small icon of a camel on the butt of the cigarette.

"Same brand I smoke," Radford said, then felt foolish. He was certain Pico had noted this, as well as many other personal habits of his, in their weeks together in the mountains. "So it's Americans, you think, then. Right?"

Pico shook his head. "Only someone with money to buy ready made. American cigarettes are very popular, especially among Europeans." Then, in answer to Radford's unspoken question, he said, "I think these men are Germans." He pointed to yet another track in soft ground near the rock where the smoker sat. "See the nail marks? Those are German."

"I wear German boots myself," Radford told him. "Why do you think they are Germans?"

"I've seen the tracks of one of the men before," Pico told him. "The man walks with a limp and is a very evil person. He is a German and I hear much evil said of him." He shrugged. "He's a German devil if it is the man I hear of."

"You've never seen him yourself?" Radford asked, but Pico shook his head. "You don't think they're looking for us, do you?" Radford exclaimed, suddenly alarmed.

Pico shrugged. "Who knows? But I don't think so. They are in too much of a hurry." Again he pointed at the cigarette butt, which was only about a third consumed. Then he pointed across the path. "They stopped because the limping man had to piss."

Radford nodded, suddenly aware of the faint smell of urine mixed with the much stronger smell of half-burned cigarette. At the same time, he was struck by how much a creature of the lonely reaches of mountain and rain forest Pico really was, how alive he became here in the wildness, relying on smell as well as sight and hearing, and how alien what passed for civilization must be to his companion. Once again Paul Radford thanked Whomever Is There for sending him the gift of the man Pico. *Out here*, he thought, *I'm literally a babe in the woods compared to Pico. And it doesn't matter a bit how well I know the wild country back home.* It was a humbling thought.

Suddenly Radford realized that Pico was grinning at him. "I did it again?" he asked, knowing he had just missed something the guide told him.

Pico nodded and chuckled. "I said we need to watch for traps, but I don't think they are after us. They are in too much of a hurry, I think."

"Unless that's what they want us to think," Radford replied and Pico grinned and nodded. "So how do we avoid a trap?" Paul asked, feeling foolish for stating the obvious.

"We go a little more slowly and smell our way," Pico told him. "The smoker makes it easy." He chuckled again. "It will come, Pablo. It will come. Stay out of town long enough and it will come. You will be the one guiding Pico."

"Fat chance of that," Radford replied. He looked at the sun. "Maybe we need to camp around here for the night. Give them more time to get ahead of us." He shrugged. "Or more impatient waiting for us to walk into their trap."

Then Pico laughed, a quiet musical sound. "See?" he pointed out. "It's happening already."

"I don't think there's much reason looking around here any more," Radford told his guide three weeks later. "What do you think?" As far as he could tell, they were standing at the exact center of the fifth site they had checked, a high ridge between two distinctive peaks. A steep slope rose from the deep valley below and from this vantage Radford could see the path they had followed switchbacking its way through the low vegetation. They were far above the tree line here, and the path came to an abrupt halt in a low, worn depression in the ridge. Opposite the entrance to the depression was a short rock cairn, and beyond the cairn the ridge dropped off in a vertical face hundreds, if not a thousand, of feet to the rocks below. *Three steps beyond the cairn,* Radford thought with an involuntary shiver. *Three steps and thirty awful seconds.....* He left the thought unfinished.

"No one here," Pico agreed. "No tracks on the path. No water anywhere near. Looks like no one's been here since the Incas." He looked around, clearly uneasy. "You want to stay here tonight? We have two more hours of light left."

Radford debated. The ascent from the main path had taken them the better part of the afternoon and he had seen nowhere on the way up they could camp. Not that water was a problem. They carried plenty for the night and even the lack of fuel for a fire was not a problem. They had at least three days' dried provisions, and surely there was some sort of game available even in this desolate country. The problem was flat ground. *Roll over in your sleep up here and wake up in the creek at the bottom of the gorge,* he thought. *If you wake up at all. Or even worse, roll the other way and wake up in free fall.*

All but one of the other sites etched in his mind from the pencil lines Blieu had drawn on the map in the embassy had come up negative. Since they left the main trails there had been no further sign of the Germans, and not much sign of anyone else, either. There was still the one other site left for them to check, but Radford had no doubt it would come up empty, too. It was in an area which was physically inaccessible and far too close to settlement, making it vulnerable to discovery. When they discussed this as they planned their journey, Pico had agreed, and Radford would have written the site off completely except for the counsel of Juan Calderon. "The Germans can be very subtle," he pointed out. "They might use the device of the purloined letter and cover their actions with the appearance of a mining camp."

"Any overflight would spot it," Radford protested. "There aren't any significant mineral deposits up there." Then he grinned, catching his own mistake. "At least none anyone knows anything about. That's why people like me are prowling all over the country."

"Ah, yes, and any overflight in that area would tell them someone was looking, too," the old priest answered. "Looking for something besides mineral samples." He shrugged. "From the air any mining operation looks like a construction site. No, there is no urgency, Paul, not that kind, and the best way to keep them from knowing you are looking is to search on the ground."

Now Radford came to a decision. As tired as he was it was doubtful he would move in his sleep and the low depression would give them some protection from the wind. "Yeah," he said. "We've been pushing pretty hard. We can turn in early and get a start at first light tomorrow." Then he grinned. "You can teach me how to play that flute I picked up in Santa Maria."

Pico looked at Radford, then looked around. "No," he said, shaking his head. "No flute, Pablo. Not here. This is not a good place. Too many ears to hear it."

Radford looked around in surprise, trying to see whatever Pico was looking at. "People?" he asked. "We haven't seen anyone in days."

"Not people," Pico replied gravely. He said a word in his native tongue Radford had never heard before. "Like evil spirits. Very bad."

"You mean demons?" While Radford's western mind rejected what the other was saying, he had learned to trust the guide in all things over the days and weeks they had been together on the trail. "Like this place is haunted?"

"Worse than demons," Pico told him, uttering once again the word Radford did not know and making a strange gesture with his left hand the young man had never seen but recognized as a warding sign. Then Pico crossed himself with his other hand. "Very bad," he continued. "Very evil."

Suddenly the significance of the depression with its low rock cairn dawned with a flash of insight which hit him like a ton of brick. "You mean...." he asked, and Pico nodded. Then a very strange thing happened. In an instant of clarity it was as if a veil were lifted across hundreds of years and he found himself standing at the cairn, surrounded by two dozen people standing in a semicircle, and watching with dread certainty as a priest in Inca clothing, with eyes as hard as the obsidian ceremonial knife he was holding, came toward him while four strong men held him down. Then he could see himself, still alive and conscious though his heart was cut out and laid on the altar, falling through the vast emptiness beyond the cairn.

Seeing the comprehension in Radford's eyes, Pico nodded and repeated. "Very bad. Better to not stay here at all."

Still in shock, Radford nodded. "I see what you mean. We'll camp below." He looked around again, but the high ridge appeared normal, as if nothing had happened there since it was pushed up between the high peaks when the mountains were created. There were no signs of priests or acolytes or blood spilled on the mountain stone. Only the stone cairn and worn depression remained to bear mute testimony to human presence. Radford started to say something about this to Pico but discovered he was taking to himself. The guide was over the lip of the depression and twenty yards away, headed down the path they had followed climbing the ridge and walking at such a rapid pace it took Paul several minutes to catch up.

When Radford talked to Juan Calderon about this a week later, the two of them were alone in the rectory courtyard in Pisco. Rosario had gone to market to buy food for a special meal and Pico was out gathering whatever gossip he could glean. "I'll go with Rosario," he told the others, finishing his beer and getting to his feet as Rosario was about to leave. "I'll see what they are saying around the market. Then I'll go to the cantinas to listen to the talk there." He grinned at Rosario. "After a month of Pablo's cooking and mine, I certainly won't be late for supper."

Now as Radford told the old priest about what had happened on the high ridge, Calderon nodded his head. "No, you weren't crazy, Pablo," he assured the young man. "Not even temporarily. I have no doubt what you saw and felt was something that happened. Maybe five hundred years ago, and maybe more."

"How can you be so sure?" the younger man asked, shaking his head. "I've never experienced anything like it. I mean, those weren't people I know, and certainly not people I'm related to. I thought at first it was just an overactive imagination, but I 've never seen anything like that. It was like it was taking place right before my eyes."

"Precisely," the padre answered. "That's my point. You are a very down to earth fellow." He grinned. "Not to make a pun about your work. The point is, you don't dabble in strange things. You are also a very spiritual young man, but you don't fool around with the occult." He shrugged. "I don't wish to minimize the experience, but the one you had is not too uncommon."

"I'll take your word for that," Radford answered. "What I can't figure is what brought it on. I was just standing there, not thinking anything in particular except what had Pico so spooked, and then there it was. Then, as quickly as it came, it was gone." He laughed, embarrassed. "Of course! I see what you mean. We were a long way above the tree line."

"I am afraid you've lost me," Calderon said cautiously.

Radford smiled. "Don't you see? It's so obvious. We were above the tree line and we had just climbed up a steep slope. We must have been close to eleven or twelve thousand feet. What must have set it off was hypoxemia. Lack of oxygen. One of the symptoms is hallucinations."

A ghost of a smile crossed Juan Calderon's face. "I don't think so, my friend. While it might be a comfort to think the source of such theophanies in high places is physical, I don't believe it for a minute. You have been in the mountains for weeks and your body has had plenty of time to acclimate. Nor were you that high up." He shook his head sadly. "No, you saw what you saw, and I have no doubt it was an event which happened long ago. For some reason, the evil done under the sun seems to cling to certain places. I don't know why this is, but I could show you other places where you might experience the same thing, and worse."

"I think I'll pass, thank you," Radford said dryly, bringing a chuckle from his companion. "Once is quite enough, believe me." He frowned. "Still, it's hard to give credence to it. You know?"

The padre nodded. "Yes, I know. Yet, if you think about it, there is not that much difference from what you saw and what I celebrate in the Mass. Human life given so that others might live."

"Or so an angry god might be appeased," Radford replied bitterly. His normally gentle features were bleak, hard as stone.

"Ah," the old priest nodded. "You know, I have never asked, but I wondered why you never came to Mass. Too much pain there?" His eyes were grave with compassion.

Any reply Radford might have made was interrupted by a soft knock at the door. Looking over his shoulder, he saw Pico standing at the entrance to the courtyard, and behind him someone stood in the shadow of the hall. "Pablo," the guide said. "There is someone to see you." Turning to the priest, he added. "I apologize for bringing him here, padre, but he said is was very urgent."

"Then bring him in," Juan Calderon said, a mask of neutrality coming down over his face. "By all means, bring him in."

A moment later Denis Blieu entered the courtyard. "A thousand pardons, father, but I needed to see Paul here very urgently and Pico told me he was here." He offered his hand to the priest, who stood and returned the handshake.

"Have a seat, please," the padre told him. "You can talk here privately if you wish. Pico and I will leave you alone. Would you care for a beer?"

"Thank you," Blieu replied, taking a seat. "That would be very good."

"No," Paul Radford interjected. "I'll get the beer. I want Juan and Pico in on this." At Blieu's look of concern, he added. "They know more about things than I do, Denis. The padre is who put me onto the fact Quito was betraying me."

The priest and the guide stopped and waited, looking from Radford to the lieutenant. Then Blieu nodded his assent and Pico spoke up. "Sit down, padre, and you, too, Pablo," he ordered. "I'm the hired help around here. I'll get the beer."

Juan Calderon laughed and took his seat. "See what I have to put up with around here?" he asked Blieu. "First this young fellow steals my housekeeper's heart and now my help is giving me orders."

"You're telling me there *is* a just God?" Blieu quipped, and they all laughed.

8. Strike Two

Manfred Schwartz had never seen his companion so tired or harried, not even in their long days on the European front. The man across the low table in his office was ragged from fatigue, as ragged in spirit as his military field jacket and trousers, worn thin from constant use and streaked with grime from days and weeks of constant wear. Whenever Rott paused to light a cigarette his hand danced with a tremor as he cupped the flame of his lighter, and deep gray shadows stained the severe lines in his haggard face.

The hand tremor troubled Schwartz, though it was not surprising. Rott was running on nervous energy. He had not slept for the last ninety-six hours and the food had run out five days before. Too driven to stop even to hunt the sparse game which could be found and taken, the normally spare Rott was gaunt and appeared to be teetering on an abyss of collapse. Despite this, the man's eyes burned with fierce determination. For Rott, collapse, and even death, was simply not an option.

"We failed," he said as he slumped into one of the leather chairs in Schwartz's office. "I didn't have much hope when we left that we'd find them, but we had to try. There was no trace of Quito or his men anywhere. And no one we talked to would admit seeing them."

"*Sheiss!*" Schwartz swore. "How could they disappear without a trace? How could they not be seen? Did you look everywhere?"

The determination in Rott's eyes exploded into rage. "Of course we did, you prick head!" he snarled, his voice a savage rasp. "What do you think we were doing up there for the last three weeks? Playing jerk-off?"

"No, of course not," Schwartz assured him, ignoring the insult. "That's not what I meant. Of course, you looked everywhere and interrogated everyone. I am sure you were very thorough, as you always are. What I was asking was if there was anywhere you did not look. Places so obvious you didn't think to look there."

"Well, we didn't look under your bed," Rott growled, relenting. "Although we did look under the First Secretary's. You know his tastes." He gave Schwartz what was intended as a grin but appeared as a ghoulish grimace. "We were saving that for later this afternoon.

111

After tea at the British embassy." He chuckled at the thought. "No, we looked in all the obvious places and even in all the not so obvious ones, but there was nothing there. Not even any birds."

"Birds?" Schwartz asked.

"Carrion eaters. One of the more obvious places to look," Rott answered, rubbing the other's nose in his ignorance. "No condors and not even any shit-birds. Nothing." He shook his head. "Not even any old tracks, except for animals. That's what puzzled me. There aren't many people up there, but there are some, and we should have seen traces of someone."

"Well, perhaps even that tells us something," Schwartz offered, choosing his words carefully. "Perhaps it tells us someone was careful to hide their tracks."

Rott nodded. "Yes, I thought of that, too. But it's impossible to hide everything. From what little we found you would think we were the first men up there since the Incas," he said, unknowingly echoing Pico's assessment.

Schwartz stood and walked to the window, looking out on the courtyard. "So how did Johannes do, Jergen?" he asked absently, looking down at the guards at the embassy door as he lit a cigarette.

"Better than I expected," Rott admitted, hiding his irritation at Schwartz's question. There was no hurrying the man and it did little good to waste time being impatient. Instead, Rott stubbed his cigarette out and allowed his head to settle back against the cushion of the chair, intending to rest his eyes for a moment. He was instantly asleep and never heard Schwartz's next question.

When Rott awoke, he was still sitting in the soft leather wing chair. His arms and legs were felt cramped, as if someone had bound them in a plaster cast while he was sleeping, and his mouth tasted vile. Blinking the sleep out of his eyes he looked around and saw Schwartz working at his desk. Yet the light coming in the windows told him hours had passed and the clock ticking on a side table confirmed this. What was morning light when he sat down was now mid afternoon shadow, and only intense pressure from his bladder had awakened him. Throwing off the lap rug someone had draped over him and swinging his legs off the ottoman, he hobbled to the wash room off one side of Schwartz's office. There Rott took care of his business and splashed fresh water on his face to wash the sleep from his eyes.

"Why did you let me sleep so long?" he asked, returning to the office and lighting a cigarette.

"As if I had any choice," his companion answered, pointing to a fresh urn of coffee. "It would have been easier to wake the dead. Drink your coffee and we'll talk."

Rott was curious about the change in attitude he sensed in the other but nodded and walked to the window. Sipping his coffee he looked out the window and saw Johannes walking across the stone pavement, freshly bathed and dressed in clean clothes, looking none the worse for wear from the trek. A frown crossed Rott's face. Something was not right. "How long was I out?" he demanded.

Schwartz glanced at his watch. "Approximately twenty-seven hours," he said. "I had the doctor take a look at you, but he said let you sleep." He looked at Rott curiously. "You don't remember waking up and talking to me, I suppose?"

Rott shook his head, clearly disturbed. Schwartz chuckled and shook his head. "Well, no matter. Your strategy paid off, anyway." He picked up an envelope on his desk and handed it to Rott.

Opening the large envelope, Rott took out the map given to Quito. Carefully unfolding it, he took it to a large table near a window and laid it out flat. Looking at the markings in the margins and at a small typographical error in the legend, he nodded. "I can't tell for sure just yet, but it looks like our map. How did you get it?"

Schwartz looked at him oddly. "About a half hour after you passed out you awoke briefly and told me we needed to send someone to Pisco to check Radford again. Then you passed out again. Since you were out and Johannes wasn't in much better shape, I decided to go myself. I got lucky." He smiled and brought something out from behind his desk. Rott could see it was a canvas rucksack, and not of European design. "I saw Radford in the street and he didn't have this with him, so I checked out his hotel room, and there it was."

"How did you get into his room?" Rott asked. His voice was disturbingly quiet.

"A small bribe," Schwartz responded. "The same man Johannes bribed before. He was scared but I threatened to go to the police if he didn't let me in." He shrugged. "And there it was."

"It sounds almost too easy," the other said, frowning. "What else was in it?"

"Very little, actually. Some pencils, a couple of other area maps, and an unused notebook." He reached into his desk and handed Rott a pair of Zeiss field glasses. "This time I made sure to make it look like a petty theft," he said smugly.

Rott shook his head. "I don't know, Manfred. It sounds too good to believe. I wish you had waited until you had talked to me."

"I did talk to you!" Schwartz snapped. "You may not remember it, but I did, and going to look was your suggestion!" Then he shrugged. "Come, come, my old friend. Sometimes we get lucky."

"Mostly we make our own luck in my experience," Rott reminded him. "But still, it could be as you say. The map looks real enough, but we will have to have our laboratory check out the stains."

"Not only could be, but is," Schwartz assured him. "As I am sure the lab tests will show." He hesitated. "You know, I've been thinking, Jergen," he continued tentatively.

"I promise not to tell," Rott answered dryly, but not even sarcasm could dampen Schwartz's good mood. Ignoring the jibe, the former professor continued.

"I think we may be taking this fellow Radford too seriously," he said. "What if he is no more than he appears to be? A geologist working for an American oil company. If he is, we're wasting a lot of time chasing our tails."

"And if he is not, we ignore him at our peril," Rott asserted. "This is much too important to take any chances, Manfred. Besides, have you forgotten about Quito?"

"Not at all," Schwartz assured him. "But what if Radford were telling the truth? What if he really did not know where he was when the attack took place? What if the information he gave the police was wrong and the bodies turn up somewhere else?"

Rott sighed. "I thought of that, believe me. That is why we were out so long, looking in many other places. We even searched as far north as Quetzal, but there was no sign of Radford or Quito, either." He looked at the map again. "You could be right, of course, but I think we still need to keep an eye on him."

"Of course we do," Schwartz agreed, "and I have just the man for the job. I found him when I was in Pisco this morning. I need your sense of him, too, but I think he's our man. He's a cousin of our hotel porter, and he runs a bar in Pisco."

"Are you wanting my job, Manfred?" Rott asked quietly. There was no mistaking the tone of his voice. "Are you pushing me out?"

"No, of course not," the other declared. "You were incapacitated and I was just trying to help things along. That's all."

"Good," Rott told him. "Because if I go down, we go down together, *old friend*. Understand?"

"Truly, my friend, I was just trying to help," Schwartz protested. "You were dead to the world."

"Well, I'm alive and kicking now," Rott told him. "And perfectly able to run my end of things. So be sure whatever you do helps." Satisfied with Schwartz's response, Rott said, "All right, then. No use duplicating effort. Who is this fellow and how did you come across him? Maybe we can use him."

"I don't understand it," Denis Blieu said. He was seated at the dining room of the rectory and a large relief map was spread out before him. While this was a larger map than the one taken from Quito, and drawn in full relief, the strange markings found in the margins of the original had been duplicated exactly to scale. The other difference was that the original lines drawn by pencil at the embassy were gone, replaced with circles in each of the areas intersected. "Those marks are there for a purpose," he went on. "I don't know what it is, but I'm certain of it."

"We came to the same conclusion in Washington," Jacques Paul agreed. "At the time it seemed your analysis was the best. There should have been something at one of the intersections."

"Assuming we are reading the marks right," Radford told them, and Juan Calderon nodded. "We may have been too quick to go with the obvious answer."

"You checked out all the sights thoroughly?" Jacques Paul asked. He had flown in the day before and come down to Pisco with Blieu to talk to Radford.

"All except this one," Radford answered. "Both Pico and I agreed it was fruitless to bother with that one. It's far too close to settlement and engineering just building a road in would be a nightmare." He shrugged. "We were going to check it out on our way in, but it was a week out of our way. So we decided to come on in and check it out later. From here we can do it in three days up and back." He looked at Pico, who nodded his agreement. "We can check it out tomorrow if you want, but I don't think we'll find anything. "

Blieu shook his head. "No, I suspect you're right. I doubt anyone much goes up there, but the chance of discovery is just too great that close to settlement. I checked out the current mining operations registry in Lima and there was no activity up there. At least, none reported. The official I talked to had heard of mineral surveys in the area, but not much else."

"Maybe we are not reading the marks right," Radford said. "How close are these to the original marks on the map?"

"They are just as accurate as we could make them," Jacques Paul answered him. "I have blown up photos of the original marks if you'd like to look at them."

Radford nodded and Jacques Paul handed him a large craft envelope. Taking out the eight by ten glossies, Radford studied them for a moment and then laughed. "I thought so," he said.

"What do you see?" Blieu asked.

"Look at these," Radford told him, pointing to the marks on the topographical map. "Without a glass these all look pretty much the same. As a matter of fact, the pairs we used to draw the lines look exactly alike, but they really aren't. Not when you enlarge them. That's the reason we chose them, and we chose pairs because the closest distance between two points is a straight line."

"All right, professor," Blieu laughed. "I'm with you so far. I don't see where you're headed, but I'm right there with you."

"The thing is, we're not talking about lines," Radford him. "We're talking about the points where lines cross. We're talking about intersections, and we don't necessarily need six of those. All we need are one or two. Right?"

"Yes?" said Jacques Paul, frowning.

"What if the intersections were drawn with two sets of three lines rather than one set of six?" Radford asked, taking a long straight edge and lining it up between two points after checking the photo enlargements. He drew a line, then checked the enlargement again, and located a third point. Drawing a line from that to each of the ends of the first line he drew, he formed a triangle. Then he joined the

116

other three lines and formed another. When he was done, the lines formed a lopsided star with six points. Then Radford drew a circle around each point two lines crossed. "There," he said. "Six more spots. Maybe we've been looking in the wrong six places!"

"Damn!" said Blieu. "What gave you that idea?"

Radford grinned. "I do the same thing all the time. The other is too obvious. Anyone with half a noodle can figure that out."

"Ouch!" said Blieu, and Juan Calderon smiled.

"I didn't mean you, Denis," Radford assured him. "I meant it was just too obvious. To really hide something means going beyond the obvious, and if this map is that important, I think we have to assume the Germans would be more careful than that. I would if I made a major mineral find. I wouldn't want it to be easy to figure out if someone stole my map."

"That's odd," Jacques Paul said, pointing at the area they had been discussing earlier. "See how close that intersection comes to the first one?"

"Actually it's an exact match," Radford told him, drawing in pencil lines the way Blieu had the first time in the embassy. "Or damned close. Maybe we better check out that place, after all."

"I'd check this one first," Blieu told him, pointing to another area where the intersections were close, but not identical. "That looks like a lot more promising spot. It's a long way from anywhere and the terrain is not as challenging."

"It's not that far from the coast, either," Jacques Paul added. "I think Denis is right."

"I disagree, gentlemen," said Juan Calderon. "I think you should check the area Pablo passed up first. I don't think it's by chance the two intersections coincide."

"I wonder what this one is here?" Radford asked. "This one just off the coast. It looks like there isn't anything there. Not even any islands."

"Probably a red herring," Blieu told him. "Or just coincidence. That's probably just where two lines happened to cross."

"I beg your pardon?" Jacques Paul asked Calderon.

"I was just remembering an old Portuguese saying," the priest told him. "Coincidence is like a virgin birth, and happens about as often."

117

"We've got to go with the probabilities first," Blieu argued. "We could spend months chasing our tails trying to cover every possibility."

"You are probably right," the old man admitted. "It's probably just an old man's notion. What do you call it, Pablo? A hoonks?"

"A hunch," Radford laughed. "I like that. Hoonx. But your hoonxes are better than most people come up with using hard information." He looked at Blieu. "Why don't we check out the double marks first. At least the one. It will only take a couple of days and then we can scratch it off for good."

Blieu was not moved. "I don't think so. After all, look at that one spot totally out to sea. No, we will look in the other sites first." His tone booked no further discussion.

Radford looked at Calderon and Pico, then shrugged. "Well, you're the man in charge," he said. "I'll wire my company that I have some new leads. Pico and I will take off as soon as we can get things together." He looked at the map. "With any luck, we can cover them all in three weeks. Maybe less." He glanced at Pico, who nodded.

"Less, if possible," Blieu told him, looking at Jacques Paul. "I can't say much more than this, but time is really getting short. Things are heating up in Europe and the Pacific."

"You are saying we may be at war soon?" Radford asked.

"Any day now," Jacques Paul told him. "The way things are now, all it will take will be a spark in the wrong place."

"Like Peru?" Juan Calderon asked dryly.

"Possibly, but more likely it will be an Japanese attack on us in the Philippines." He shrugged. "Or maybe even Pearl Harbor."

"I thought that was well protected," Radford answered. "Isn't the whole Pacific Fleet based out of there? It would be insane to attack Pearl Harbor."

Blieu and Jacques Paul exchanged another look. "That is official doctrine at this time," the latter said. "There are others of us who disagree, though not publicly. An attack at the right moment could seal the whole harbor and make the entire fleet vulnerable." He shrugged. "Most people in the District still think like civilians in peace time. They want to believe we can avoid going to war. The rest of us are trying to avoid a disaster."

"Can you tell us more?" Juan Calderon asked. Jacques Paul looked at Blieu, who nodded, and then began to speak. When he was done there was silence for a long time, and when the talk began, it went on through supper and into the evening. Even Rosario broke with her own discipline and put off her evening chores, listening closely as the men talked, quiet as a mouse in the corner. While she said little, her mind was full of questions, questions about what the future held for herself and her man, and mostly, for the new life she now felt growing within her.

Later, when the others had gone, Paul ignored Rosario's protests and helped her clean up the kitchen. This was something he often did, and normally she was glad of his company. Yet tonight she was very quiet, and when they were done she left the room without a word and began preparing for bed. Following her into the room they often shared, Radford stopped her just inside the door and turned her toward him. He was surprised to find her cheeks were wet.

"*Mi corazon*," he asked gently. "What's wrong? Has all this talk of war upset you?"

"Why should it?" she replied noncommittally. "There's always talk of war. That's the thing you and the padre talk about most these days."

"But always before it's been far, far away. Now it's come here. Is that it?" he asked. Rosario nodded and he went on, trying to reassure her. "Don't worry, my love," he said, holding her close. "Don't worry. I won't let it come near you or our child."

"It already has, Pablo," Rosario sobbed. "Those evil men almost killed you!"

"Almost, but not quite," he answered. "My angels were looking out for me."

"I'm not a child, Pablo," Rosario looked at him directly. "Please don't try to tell me not to worry. The war is here and it will take you away from me."

"No, it won't," he answered quickly. "I won't let it. You're my wife and you're carrying my child."

"We are not married," she pointed out. "It doesn't matter to me, but I am not your wife."

"Well we will be tomorrow!" Radford declared. "I'll get Juan Calderon to marry us in the morning and if he won't do it, I'll get the mayor to!"

To his surprise, Rosario broke into tears. "You don't understand," she sobbed. "You are such a smart man but you don't understand!"

"I understand I love you with all my heart and I understand I want to spend the rest of my life with you," Paul insisted. "So I want you to be my wife. What more is there to understand?"

This made Rosario weep all the harder. "What is it?" Radford demanded gently, looking down at her head buried in his chest. "Are you already married to someone else?"

At this Rosario snorted, then began to laugh. "No," she answered, looking up and wiping away her tears. "If I were it would be simple! I would leave him and marry you!"

"Then what is it?" he persisted, kissing her softly on the brow.

"The padre told you," Rosario answered. "One night when you first started coming to visit. I didn't want to believe him, either, but he was right. I don't belong in your world."

"You were listening?" Radford asked, aghast. He couldn't have been more stunned if she had admitted to axe murder, and his repugnance showed in his face.

"Of course," she said simply. "I thought you knew that. I always do unless I'm out."

"That's not right!" he objected, trying to remember anything he had ever said to Juan Calderon he didn't want Rosario know, or hadn't told her himself.

"Why not?" Rosario demanded. "After all, you were talking about me."

"That's not what I mean," Radford answered. "It's just not right to listen to other people's private conversations."

"Wouldn't you listen in on the Germans if you could?" she asked, indignant.

"Well, of course, I would, but that's different," he declared.

"How is it different?" she snorted. "Why can you listen to your enemies and not your friends!"

Radford opened his mouth to say something in reply, but there was no response he could think of to answer Rosario's question. "I don't know," he said. "It just is."

"Then maybe I shouldn't do it anymore," Rosario answered, turning away so Radford couldn't see her smile.

"Just because you shouldn't doesn't mean you won't, does it?" he asked, laughing at himself and tickling her ribs. "Does it, woman?"

"You know me too well," Rosario said, giggling as she turned to tickle him back.

"Or maybe not well enough," he replied softly, trapping her hands and pulling her to himself. He looked down into her eyes, giving her a kiss that gave rise to a low moan in her throat as she responded. "Not well enough at all," he murmured huskily as he began to kiss her neck.

Even so, their conversation stuck in his mind and he brought it up again the next day as he was walking Rosario back from the market. "Tell me something, *corazon*," he said, handing her some fresh flowers he had just bought from a vendor. "What did you mean last night when you said you don't belong in my world?"

Rosario's smile faded, replaced in her eyes by a deep sadness and Radford regretted asking the question. "I'm sorry," he said, waving it away. "I didn't mean to ruin the day. Please, never mind."

"No," she said. "Ignoring it won't make it go away, Pablo. It's still there whether the sun shines or it rains." She shrugged. "It always will be."

"Then please help me understand," he asked her.

"Look at me," she said. "I belong here, in this country and among these people. Could you see me with people like those two men and the padre at your home? You and I are not from the same class of people. I wouldn't know how to act around them. Especially if the women are like the men." She held out an arm. "Look at me, Pablo! My skin is brown. Yours is pink. You are European. I am a *mestizo*, a person of mixed blood. Do you think your mother would accept some *indio* for a daughter-in-law? Do you think she would accept my child as her kin?"

"I guess she would just damned well have to," Radford said defiantly. Yet in his heart he knew his beloved was right. He knew exactly what his mother would say, and just how hurtful her words would be, to Rosario, if not to his face. "Besides, what would be wrong with me staying down here?"

121

"Nothing, if that is what you really want," Rosario answered carefully. "But I don't think it is. I don't think you want to spend the rest of your life in Pisco."

"We wouldn't have to live here," Radford answered. "We could live in Lima or anywhere we wanted to. I can always get a job as a mining engineer, and if I can't, with my contacts I can go into business for myself. Making a living is not a problem. We might even get rich!"

"You don't understand," Rosario told him. "It would be worse in Lima than in America, I think. People there are very prejudiced about *mestizos*." She shook her head sadly. "Even if we were rich."

"Look, Rosario, I'm willing to risk it," he told her urgently. "All that other just doesn't matter to me. I'm willing to give it up if I have to. Don't you understand that?"

"Yes, I know you want to mean what you say, Pablo," she replied. "Yet I know that other world will always have a place in your heart. It will always be able to call you back."

"No, it won't," he argued. "Just watch me. I'll prove it to you."

"It already has, my love," she answered, her eyes to the ground. "Every time those men show up it happens all over again. They come for you and then you go and I lose you to them." She looked at him with tears in her eyes. "What if they tell you to come home? What then? Can you honestly tell me you would not go? I do not care so much what happens to me. I would always wait, but what of the child? The padre is an old man now. I know he will always protect us, but when he dies. Who will raise our child if you are gone?"

Paul Radford was struck by the simple truth of Rosario's observation. There was no denying she was right. When it came to his sworn duty to the Republic, he would always go, just as he always had, no matter what the personal cost. Nor was it a simple matter of patriotism. It was embedded within family tradition, in everything he had ever been taught, and there was no denying it. It was simply who he was. "I'll come back," he told her, hoping desperately he would be able to honor his words. "I will always come back to you, no matter what! And to our child!"

"Even if they kill you, Pablo?" she asked. "Even when they kill you?" Shaking her head sadly, Rosario looked at him with a sadness too deep for words, or even tears, then turned away and started home.

For a moment Paul Radford stood watching her, too shocked to move, then he hurried after her.

I wonder what that was about? the watcher in the shadows thought. Then he shrugged. His job was not to think. Rott had made that very clear, and his first meeting with the man outside the embassy door was still painfully etched in his psyche. His job was to watch and to report whatever he observed. Rott could decide what it meant. Jotting enough details to remind himself what he had seen, Johannes tucked the leather notebook away in his bush jacket and started down the street in the direction Rosario and Paul Radford had taken.

"What it means is that he is vulnerable where the woman is concerned," Rott declared. He and Schwartz were sitting in the latter's office. "Not to belabor the obvious, but any time we wish to get at our lucky Mr. Radford, we have an easy target in the woman." Looking at the young man sitting at attention in the other leather chair he said, "Tell us again, Johannes. Close your eyes and think very carefully about what you saw, every detail. Then tell us again, leaving out nothing."

The young soldier closed his eyes and imagined himself back at the market plaza in Pisco. As he spoke, it was in first person as Rott had taught him, and as if the scene were playing itself out before his eyes. The whole thing took him the better part of twenty minutes, and when Schwartz shifted in his chair impatiently, Rott held up one hand and shot him a warning look.

"Excellent, Johannes," Rott acknowledged when the other was done, giving him what was meant to be a warm smile. "You have a real flair for this kind of thing."

"Thank you, sir!" Johannes stammered. This unexpected praise from Rott was as frightening as the cold fury he remembered only too well. "I'm glad to be of use."

Rott actually chuckled, scaring the young man even more. "A very correct answer, Johannes, but I meant what I said. You have a very good ear for things and you know how to use your eyes. Not that this should give you a swelled head, of course. I will expect even more from you in the future, but for now we are pleased. That will be all."

"Thank you, sir," the other responded, leaping to his feet at almost snapping a salute before he realized he was in civilian clothing. Instead he snapped an arm straight out. "Heil Hitler!"

"Sieg heil," Rott answered casually, waving him out the door. When the young man was gone, Rott looked at Schwartz and asked. "What do you think?"

"I think your man, Radford, is a spy," the other answered. He looked at Rott directly. "I also think you would do well to be less casual where the Chancellor is concerned. Especially in front of our younger men. Word might get back."

Rott snorted. "I make sure I am too valuable to them to dispose of lightly," he answered. "Still, you are quite right. It doesn't do to make unnecessary enemies. However, there is not much to worry about from Johannes, I think. Did you see how he almost pissed in his pants when I paid him a compliment? I own him, body and soul. The Chancellor may be Odin, himself, but as far as Johannes is concerned, I am Thor." He chuckled. "And my hammer is a lot closer to his head."

Schwartz nodded. "I hope so. What do you think of his description of the Europeans he saw talking to Pico? Do you think they are Americans?"

Rott nodded. "Almost certainly. One man he described reminded me of the new military attaché to the embassy." He waved his hand. "That new fellow with the French name. I have no idea who the other one is. Probably someone from Washington."

"Blieu?" Schwartz asked and Rott nodded. "You're right," Schwartz added. "The description does fit him, although I didn't think of it until you pointed it out."

Rott nodded. "That's why you keep me around, Manfred. I see things others don't." He thought a moment. "It may be that the guide is in the American's pay and Radford is not, but I think we have to assume he is. Until we know different. Which means we have a vector of attack through the woman."

"You believe he's that attached to her?" Schwartz asked. "Are you sure she is not just a local ... convenience? I understand she's as ugly as a mud hut."

"Even so, the way Johannes described their encounter does not sound like a casual affair," the other responded. "And if it is anything but that....." He shrugged.

"So, where do we go from here?" Schwartz asked. "How do we use this information."

"I need to think about that a bit," Rott answered. "We also need a lot more information. So I think I'll have Johannes poke around a bit about this new American who came with Blieu. Maybe we can figure out what they are up to."

Rott sat lost in thought, a frown of concentration on his face. Then after a moment he looked up at his superior. "I assume that when I do come up with something I have a free hand." Schwartz nodded and Rott grinned, and it was Schwartz's turn to suppress a shudder at Rott's humor. Not for the first time he was grateful he and his subordinate were on the same side. No matter how lucky he might be, with Rott on his case, Paul Radford's fate was sealed.

9. Foul Play

Sergeant Gomez was not fooled by his warm reception, not for a moment. While the old priest's manners were impeccable, and the hospitality of the rectory, flawless, Gomez knew there was something going on beyond what he was being told. All his years spent as a policeman, first in the remote districts and then in the capital, had acquainted Gomez with every kind of liar and every form of lie and honed his nose for falsehood. So most often he could tell when he was being told the truth, or at least when he was being told what those talking believed to be the truth. There is a difference and Gomez knew well that the greatest lies are told by those who believe they are speaking the absolute truth.

So it was very clear in his mind that there was something not quite right with what Gomez was hearing. Not that he would dream of accusing Calderon or Rosario of lying through their teeth. No, it was something far more subtle, and his sense of things was that there was something, and perhaps a great deal, he was not being told.

Nor was there any doubt in his mind that the old priest was aware Gomez knew this, and was also aware Gomez knew he knew it, too. He doubted Calderon would tell an outright lie unless he had no other choice, and if the padre did, it would be utterly convincing. No, what was going on behind the padre's polite smile was serious effort to avoid direct falsehood.

Gomez sighed, a sigh he often uttered when he considered the many mouths he had to feed on his small policeman's pay. There was no response to this from the old priest but the young housekeeper looked up with obvious concern. "So you don't know where I might find our elusive Mr. Radford," Gomez asked, shamelessly taking what advantage he was offered and looking directly at Rosario as he spoke.

Even so, he might as well have never bothered. Rosario was as skilled at hiding her thoughts as the old priest. Yet, when she spoke of Radford there was something in her voice which told Gomez their relationship was more than casual. Whether they were lovers or not, it was obvious the housekeeper's feelings for the young geologist ran deep.

"I'm afraid not, Sergeant," Juan Calderon answered for both of them. "It's been over a week since I last saw him. He had supper with us and said something about being up in the mountains again, but exactly where he was going or for how long...." He finished the sentence with a shrug. "Truly, I wish I could help you more, but I can't." He looked at Rosario, who nodded agreement.

The sergeant nodded, too, and sat in silence for several long moments, frowning and staring vaguely into the middle distance among them. It was a technique he found useful over the years with nervous folk with something to confess. Silence seemed to encourage them to run on until they said something he could use to pry forth more information. Yet Rosario and the old priest simply sat very patiently with the silence, watching him impassively. They seemed perfectly comfortable and Gomez wondered how long they would allow the silence to continue. He guessed it was longer than he cared to sit in this straight backed chair, so he shifted direction.

"I imagine he told you about the attack in the mountains not long ago, didn't he?" Gomez probed, looking for something to keep the conversation going.

"Oh, yes," the padre replied. "He told us all about that. He was very lucky to come out alive."

"Lucky, padre?" Gomez chided gently. "I didn't think people in your profession believed in luck."

Juan Calderon grinned. "Only in a manner of speaking, my friend. Some would say his guardian angel was working very hard that day." He shrugged. "Even so, it could have gone either way. So, yes, he was very fortunate it happened the way it did. At least from a human point of view. I am very glad I gave him that medallion."

"Oh, you were the one he got it from," Gomez pounced. "That's odd. He told my captain he got it for a couple of bottles of wine."

Juan Calderon cursed himself for a fool, but allowed none of this to show on his face. Instead, he grinned. "Well, in a manner of speaking, he did, Sergeant. A couple of bottles of good wine and several hours of good conversation with a boring old fool. It was a good bargain from where I sit."

"I might call you many things, padre," Gomez assured him, watching Juan Calderon like a hawk. "Yet I don't think either boring nor foolish would be one of them. What did you talk about, if you don't mind my asking?"

The padre chuckled. "Well, thank you, sergeant. I may have you put that in writing to give to my bishop. Actually, it would probably be easier to tell you what we didn't talk about. Our Mr. Radford is interested in many things. Yet, if I had to say, I would think we talked most about the country and the people here. I think it must have been our talk about the native people which reminded me of the medallion. He liked it and so I gave it to him."

"A man of many parts," Gomez replied. "What I don't understand, padre, is why you gave it to him in the first place. The captain said it looked quite old and very valuable."

"Bread upon the waters," the old priest answered smoothly. "The medal was doing no one any good in my desk drawer, and if it could gain the good will of a generous benefactor of the Church...." He shrugged. "Then, why not? I doubt I could have even gotten the fifty pesos it was made of."

"Ah," Gomez answered, nodding. It was plausible, even though he was certain he was being sold a bill of goods. From his assessment, Juan Calderon was far too proud a man to stoop to graft, or at least its second cousin, but it was a reasonable explanation. This was the way things were often done and few would think to question it.

Rosario spoke to the priest in her native tongue, asking if he wanted to invite the sergeant to stay for the meal she was preparing. While Gomez understood everything she said clearly, he decided to feign ignorance. This was a game three could play, so he gave the padre a bland look, raising his eyebrows in question.

"Forgive our poor manners," Juan Calderon said in Spanish. "Rosario was asking if you would like to eat with us."

Gomez gave Rosario his brightest smile. It was amazing how this transformed his face. "Well, thank you," he said. "I appreciate the offer and my nose tells me I would be a fool to say no. Yet I would not think of imposing."

"It would be no imposition at all," the priest assured him. "It is not often we have distinguished visitors like yourself and we would be honored."

Gomez laughed. "I am afraid I am more extinguished than distinguished at the moment," he said. "I got up early and it has been a long time since breakfast. I would be most grateful."

"Excellent," Juan Calderon replied and Rosario got up and hurried into the kitchen. "Tell me, my friend," he asked, turning their conversation into a safer vein, "what is going on in Lima these days?"

Gomez laughed. "That depends on whether you want gossip or news, padre."

"There is a difference?" the old man cackled and Gomez found himself telling this strange and likable old rogue about the latest escapades of his most outrageous uncle in Lima. When Rosario called them to dine, the conversation paused for grace and then continued in this vein until Rosario was giggling like a school girl and Juan Calderon was laughing so hard he couldn't eat.

Even so, it was not lost on the padre that they were dining with a potential adversary. Though he knew the sergeant's reputation for integrity, he also knew that very integrity could be dangerous to them. What Paul Radford was doing for his country, and for the free world was honest and moral. Yet there were many ways of looking at it and there was no denying what Radford was doing was spying for his own country. This was not contrary to the best interests of Peru, but sovereign nations prefer to decide for themselves what is in their best interest. There were those in power in Lima who would not like Radford's acting against the interests of Germany. Some of those same people were Gomez's superiors in the police department.

Nor was it lost on Calderon how well the sergeant was drawing Rosario out of her reserve. Even Paul Radford had never made her laugh like that, and the padre wondered how the young man might feel if he were there. Yet he knew he would say nothing of it to his young friend. Though he loved Pablo like a son, the welfare of Rosario and the child must come fist, and padre Juan understood very clearly the young man would agree. He might not like it, but he would agree. Right or wrong, it never hurt to have a police officer on your side, and this was something Rosario knew as well as he did.

"Goodness," Gomez said an hour later, groaning as he pushed his chair back from the table. "You better keep how well Rosario cooks a secret, padre. If word gets out to Lima you'll have people beating down your door to hire her away from you."

Juan Calderon nodded. "I hope our secret is safe with you sergeant."

Gomez glanced at Calderon sharply, but there was no irony or sarcasm in the padre's face or voice. "Only if you share it with me," Gomez laughed, robbing his own words of their irony. "I never take bribes, but I never ate Rosario's food before, either. For that I might be tempted."

Rosario looked down and found a spot on her apron which needed her attention, but it was clear she was blushing with pleasure. "You think I am joking," Gomez told her, "but I assure you I am not. You would make a man a fine wife."

The part of Rosario's face they could see turned beet red, and she got up quickly and left the room. "The flan!" she said. "I forgot the flan."

Gomez looked after her, clearly distressed. "What did I say, padre?" he asked Calderon. "I didn't mean to offend her."

"She's spoken for," the padre told him gently. "And she is very shy about it."

"Ah," said Gomez. "I see." Yet it was clear to the padre he did not. "Who is the lucky man, if I may ask? Anyone I know?"

There was no avoiding the truth. A direct lie would be quickly found out if the sergeant asked around town, and Calderon was sure he would. "The young man you wish to talk to," he answered. "The American, Paul Radford."

"Oh," Gomez answered, clearly surprised. In his experience Americans and Europeans went for the slender beauties of the capital, not for plain girls from the countryside like Rosario. He wondered if this were what he sensed going on under the surface. *Probably not,* he thought. *At least, not completely. There is something else bothering the old man, too.* "But they aren't married yet?" Gomez blurted out, not thinking how the question might sound.

"Not yet," Calderon told him, missing nothing. It was clear to him Gomez was interested in Rosario, and not just as a cook. He shrugged. "I try to mind my own affairs," he said, knowing full well just how outrageous a lie he was uttering. "Well, at least, as much as I can," he added, throwing a sop to his conscience. "Some things are hard to miss."

Gomez laughed, telling himself the last remark was not about himself, yet disbelieving it even as the thought crossed his mind. Juan Calderon knew full well how he felt about the padre's housekeeper. "He's not from here," Gomez pointed out. "Is be being honorable?"

"As honorable as a man can be with a woman in love," Juan Calderon replied. "Look, sergeant," he added. "The man is my good friend and Rosario is as dear to me as a daughter. I don't mean to give offense, but I am reluctant to speak of this much more. Especially to a policeman when it has no bearing on what he needs to know. Surely you understand?"

Gomez nodded. "Of course, padre! My apologies. I wasn't speaking as a policeman," he added, the confession surprising him even as the words left his mouth. "I was speaking as a man. A thousand apologies." He looked toward the kitchen and murmured something even the sharp ears of Juan Calderon could not catch.

"I beg your pardon?" the padre asked. Nor was he surprised at the answer he got.

Gomez shook his head sadly. "I was just thinking how sad it was that I did not find Rosario first. Your friend is a lucky man, indeed."

At the moment the lucky man was in a foul mood. Swearing softly, he slapped the side of his neck, missing the tiny predator looking for a meal there. Yet even as he did, another attack was launched at the other side of his head. "Shit!" he roared, flailing his arms wildly and accomplishing little but adding to the sweat running down his back. "Let's get out of here before these little bastards eat us alive!"

Pico did not have to be told twice. He set off at a gentle lope and within minutes the high marsh was far behind. When they came to the top of a ridge he stopped and laughed. "The wind will keep any of them who followed us," he said. "You looked like a.... what do you call it?" he asked, flailing his arms in a wide circle. "It pumps water."

"A windmill," Radford grinned sheepishly. Here in the cool breeze coming up the slope his sense of humor returned quickly.

"Weend-meel," Pico answered, testing the word and nodding. "They use them to make electric power, too. No?"

"Yeah, but they aren't very efficient," Radford answered. "They use them in rural areas back home where power hasn't come in yet, but the things are expensive. It's cheaper to use a generator run off a fuel oil engine." Pico nodded thoughtfully and Radford asked, "Why? Have you seen one?"

"Yes," the other said. "It was down the coast, not far from Pisco. Maybe fifty miles and up in the mountains. I saw six of them, like a row of trees, in a valley where the wind always blows. "But they were very big and different."

"What do you mean?" Radford asked, wondering why six windmills would be found in the middle of nowhere. One would be odd enough, but six?

"They were big, like this," Pico told him, circling his arms as if wrapping them around a tree. "And they turned in a circle like this," he added, drawing a circle in the air parallel to the ground. "They were fifteen, maybe twenty meters tall, and most of it was the part that tuned. On the side were big things, like scoops, to catch the air." He made a large "S" with his arms held out, one to the front and one to the back, and turned around where he stood.

Radford nodded and thought for a moment. "That would work," he said. "We used to do that with cans back home. We nailed them to a fence post and called them twirl-a-jigs." He frowned. "I never heard of anyone doing that with something so large, but I don't see why it wouldn't work. As a matter of fact, it might work better. You wouldn't have to have a tower." He looked at Pico intently. "How big were these things? How big around?"

Pico spread his arms wide. "Two meters, maybe more. But they turned very slowly."

"Something that big would," Radford replied. "Like the windmills in Holland. But they could also generate a hell of a lot of power." He rummaged in his pack and took out his map. "Can you remember where this was?" he asked.

"Here," Pico pointed. "South of Ica and not too far from the sea."

"Damn!" Radford exclaimed, excited. "That's not far from that site we didn't check out! That's where we need to go next, Pico."

However, the guide shook his head. "There was nothing else there, Pablo."

"There's got to be if someone took all that trouble to build the things. When did you see them?"

"Maybe three years ago and I thought the same thing as you. I was told they were built there by some people who wanted to build a town there, too. But they never did." He frowned. "That sounded strange to me, but they were right. There was nothing there but these things turning in the wind."

"You looked yourself?" Radford asked.

"Yes, but not that carefully," Pico replied. "There were signs where someone had been digging and there were still stakes in the ground, but nothing else."

"Stakes in the ground. You mean like marking off streets?"

Pico nodded. "Just like that. Like where the streets would go. And one of the windmills pumped water up to a reservoir a few hundred meters up the slope. There was nothing else there."

Paul Radford grinned. "Unless you wanted to hide something. Then you would do it to make someone think no one was there. Like put stakes in the ground. Tell me, did the windmills look like they had been neglected?"

"No," Pico nodded. "They were in good shape, like someone was taking care of them. That didn't make much sense when I thought of it later but I thought maybe the windmills were the last things built."

"Could be," Radford answered, "but I still think we need to check it out right away. Even if it does mean we have to double back later." He pointed at the map again. "We're right here and it is out of the way, but I think we should do it."

Pico shrugged. "That's what Juan Calderon thought. But it's four days from here. We'll lose a week if we are wrong."

"And we'll gain a week if we're right," Radford replied. "I think we need to take the chance. If things are getting as touchy as Bleu says, the sooner we find the German operation, the better."

"It was Germans who built the windmills," Pico told him. At Radford's startled look he added, "At least that is what I was told, but I don't know for sure."

"Why didn't you tell me about this?" Radford asked. "We might have saved some time."

Pico shrugged. "I didn't think about it," he said simply, then grinned. "Until I saw you beating at the insects. Then I thought

133

about it right away." He chuckled, waving his arms. "I wish I had a *cine* to show you. And Juan Calderon."

"Why not all of Lima?" Radford muttered. "Let everyone have a good laugh." Then he relented. "I guess it must have been pretty funny, after all."

"Chit!" Pico mimicked, dancing around flailing his arms. "Chit! Chit! Chit!"

"All right," Radford told him, laughing. "I get the picture. How about let's head out for Ica now?" There was no question in his mind he was going to hear about this again when they got home to Pisco, and probably before then, too.

The attack on the rectory came two days after Sergeant Gomez's visit. Though it was not customary to lock the church itself except in times of riot or insurrection, Juan Calderon was always careful to lock the door which led from the nave into a hallway connecting with their living quarters. Nor did he forget to check the gateway which led from the rectory courtyard into the street, or the one on the opposite side of the compound which was used by delivery men in years past. Years of living on the run among the *guerrillas* ingrained such precautions deep within his soul, and even when he was ill, he always asked Rosario to check the doors if he could not.

It was also the padre's custom to keep a small watch dog, despite the stir this caused among some of the gentle folk of his congregation who questioned the presence of such a beast on holy ground. Yet few ever saw the padre's dog, though it could be heard from time to time, and the beast was carefully kept out of sight whenever the bishop came to visit. The man was a fastidious soul, one who had trouble believing the ox and the ass were really present at the manger, and Juan Calderon did not wish to offend his nominal boss deliberately. Or the powerful patrons who held the Church captive with their pitiful gratuities, irregularly given and seldom with grace.

Even so, there was no dog in the rectory to warn Juan Calderon that night. Many months before the padre's dog had died of old age, and the old man had not yet resigned himself to the discipline of teaching a new pup its house manners. Had he done so, the attackers would probably have never gotten so far, a fact he reminded himself of bitterly in the days which followed.

Yet the padre was being unduly hard on himself, for the attack was not an act of random violence or casual thievery. It was carefully planned and executed, and the absence of a dog only made it easier for the attackers. For on that particular day, one of the attackers, chosen for his small stature, hid himself in the sacristy closet after the last mass. Hours later he emerged from among the vestments, half suffocated and in pain from hours of cramping legs and a distended bladder, almost raising the alarm when he stumbled into the tall Paschal candle stand and knocking it over. Only an act of desperate dexterity kept the stand from crashing to the stone floor, and lying under the heavy brass, having cushioned its fall with his body, the small attacker discovered his bladder had emptied itself in the excitement. "*Sheiss!*" he exclaimed softly, appreciating neither the irony of the event nor the inaccuracy of his assessment.

Easing himself from under the candle stand and setting it upright, the small man scurried to the hall door and gently lifted the heavy wooden bar from its cradle. When he opened the door to the nave of the church he was joined at once by three other men, all dressed in rough, dark clothing. Two of these men were toughs from town, hired for the night's work, who would be paid off in much harder currency than they expected, in lead rather than gold. The third was the commander of the raiding party and clearly European though he was dressed as the others.

"What kept you so long?" the commander hissed. "We've been waiting for over two hours." Then his nose wrinkled, visible even in the low light of the hall. "What did you do?" he hissed. "Piss your pants?" Waving away any response, he signaled the others to follow him down the hallway to the rectory.

Another solid door stood closed at the end of the hallway, and for a moment the commander thought his careful planning was wasted. Yet the heavy door was not locked and swung open silently on its hinges. Quiet as wraiths, the four men fanned out into the open sitting room of the rectory.

At a signal from the commander, the small man moved toward the courtyard door while the other two men took up positions in the short hallway leading to the room where the housekeeper slept. The leader took up station where he could cover the doorway to the priest's quarters and still see the others guarding Rosario's room. There he waited until the small man joined him, signaling that the courtyard gate was now unlatched.

The commander nodded his understanding and approached the door to the padre's room, carefully reaching out to grasp the door knob. Intending to open the door wide before the attack began, he turned the knob gently. Yet the mechanism was rusty and left unoiled, another cautious habit of the padre, also born of experience, and it gave a soft rasp as it was turned.

Soft as it was, the warning almost spelled disaster for the raiding party. While the commander stopped turning the knob instantly, and stood breathless listening for the slightest sound of waking from Juan Calderon's room, it was wasted caution. Within the silence from the other side of the door came the unmistakable sound of a single action Colt pistol being cocked.

The commander made a quick decision. "*Jetz!*" he shouted, as he ducked behind the thick wall beside the door. Now! The small man ducked to the other side of the door and on the other side of the sitting room the two men waiting outside the housekeeper's quarters rushed into Rosario's room.

Moving quickly, the leader bumped the door to the padre's room with the side of his hand, quickly jerking his arm back to safety. Instantly six shots rang out, splintering the padre's bedroom door and filling the rectory with the roar of the pistol and the high whine of ricochets screaming off the plaster walls.

The thunder of the big Colt was punctuated by a scream of fright sounding from the housekeeper's room, a scream broken off as quickly as it was uttered. After the sixth shot the small man threw open the door to the padre's room, bringing his revolver to bear on the old priest standing naked near his bed and holding a huge pistol which was still smoking. Too late the small man saw the second pistol, a Colt automatic which Juan Calderon held in his left hand, and his body literally flew back out the doorway as three more shots took out his heart and ripped through his neck, showering the leader crouched by the doorway with blood.

As the commander scurried for cover along the wall, the two men assigned to get Rosario broke out of her room, one of them carrying her punching and kicking over his shoulder as the other tried to keep the others between himself and the padre's open door. Even so, the old priest's automatic roared twice more, the first shot breaking the second man's ankle and bringing him down, and the second smashed its way into the man's chest, abruptly ending his scream of pain. Then another scream arose, this time a cry of rage from the padre's room as the old man flung himself into the sitting room, leveling the automatic for another shot.

This time the commander fired back, and he saw the old man go down, blood streaming from a gaping wound in his head. "*Schnell! Schnell!*," the commander said, shouting to the man holding Rosario behind the shelter of a heavy chair and waving his pistol toward the courtyard door, forgetting the man did not speak German. Yet it was clear what the commander wanted, and the ruffian carried Rosario out the door over his shoulder like a sack of potatoes. Grabbing the small man by his belt, the commander carried him like a heavy suit case to the car waiting in the alley outside the courtyard wall, heaving him into the boot and leaving the fourth man for the police.

Let them figure than one out! the commander of the raiding party thought as the car sped away, wondering when the bodies would be found. As planned, the thick walls of the rectory had worked well in their favor, confining the sound of the shots, and only two pairs of eyes observed their sudden departure. One was a mangy dog they had seen in the headlights of the car, searching the alley for any scrap of food. The other was a watcher in the night who slipped out of the deep shadows across the street and cautiously entered the courtyard of the rectory.

News of the attack came to the American embassy in Lima in the person of Captain Molina. Since protocol prevented him from going directly to the embassy, he simply waited until his people told him Denis Blieu was off the grounds and waited for him to appear in his normal haunts. Approaching him in the cafe where he was having an early lunch with Jacques Paul, Molina saluted sharply and said, "Good morning, Lieutenant. May I have a word with you?"

Getting to his feet, Blieu returned the salute and extended a hand. "Good morning, Captain. Is this something official?"

"Actually, it is, but I hoped to have a private word with you," Molina responded, looking at Jacques Paul. "That is, if it is convenient," he added.

"This is my personal assistant," Blieu replied smoothly, introducing Jacques Paul. "Since it is not personal, why don't you join us for lunch?" He looked around at the empty restaurant. "Unless you wish to talk some place more private?"

Molina glanced around and nodded. They were seated at the very back of the restaurant and there was very little chance of them being seen there except by the serving staff, three of whom were in Molina's personal network of informers. Taking a chair he said, "Forgive me for getting right to the point, but the situation is rather urgent. I am looking for one of your people, a Mr. Paul Radford."

"I know who you are talking about but he's actually not one of our people," Blieu replied. "He is a private citizen who works for an American oil company."

"I understand that," Molina replied. "I also understand your government does not hesitate to call on such people to provide information." He held up a hand stopping Blieu's automatic protest. "Not as a spy, necessarily, but simply as a ... source. Please, hear me out first." Quickly Molina outlined what had taken place two nights before in Pisco. "So you understand why I need to find Mr. Radford," he added. "I think his life is in grave danger if we don't reach him before he returns to Pisco."

Blieu was silent a long moment. Looking at Jacques Paul, he raised an eyebrow in question and the other shrugged. "All right," Blieu agreed. "I'll tell you what I can. We did ask Radford to work for us as a source of general information. Our concern is what every government's concern is, and that is what our potential enemies might be up to."

"Peru is not your enemy, sir," Molina replied, somewhat stiffly.

"No, it is not," Blieu assured him. "Our governments are very close and we are very careful not to do anything to put that in jeopardy. However, certain Continental governments are not exactly our friends and it is those whose activities we monitor." He paused a moment, then went on. "As you know, Captain, there are certain parts of your government who are quite friendly to some of our potential enemies, and that is why it is sometimes best to be less than direct, even with our friends."

Molina considered this for a moment, then nodded. "Very well, Lieutenant. I understand your position and I realize I cannot compel you to speak frankly. Yet if I am to protect your citizens, I do need your cooperation. I need to know what provoked this attack. Two people are dead and the housekeeper is in grave danger. I don't care about the *desperado*, and my government is not concerned about the woman." He shrugged. "I disagree, but that's the way it is. The point is that the archbishop does care about his priest and he's raising the devil. So I have a certain ... freedom of action."

"We can probably help find Radford," Blieu assured him. "I think he may have discussed where he was going with Lieutenant Paul. Why don't I send him with you?" He looked at Jacques Paul. "Can you put things on the back burner for a few days?" he asked.

"That won't be necessary, Lieutenant," Molina protested. "If you could just give me some idea of where to look that would be most helpful."

"I would consider it a personal favor, Captain," Blieu answered smoothly. He decided to stretch the truth a bit. "You see, Radford's family has a certain degree of influence back home and anything we do to help....." He left the though unfinished.

Molina didn't like it, but the Americans were bargaining from a position of strength. "Very well," he answered. "However, he must agree to accept my command while he is in the field."

"Of course, Captain," Jacques Paul answered. "We're military people and we understand that's how it has to be. How soon do you want to leave?"

"We better finish lunch first," Molina answered. "I don't know when we will get to eat next. Or where. The next stop after this is Pisco."

"Then it's a good thing Denis is picking up the ticket," Jacques Paul answered. picking up the menu and looking at it carefully. "Tell me, Captain, are you from Lima? Your accent sounds like you come from further north."

10. Strange Visions

Paul Radford was weary, so weary he could barely put one foot in front of the other. Sweat ran down his face, drenching his shirt, soaking through the field jacket he put on not an hour earlier against the cold wind of the high elevation. *What's the matter with me?* he thought, shaking his head to clear his vision. *It's too early to be this tired. We've only been on the trail a half hour and this slope isn't that steep."* He stopped for a moment, fished in a pocket for a handkerchief, rolled it into a band to keep sweat out of his eyes. *It must be something I ate.* Then an all too familiar voice spoke from within him. *There is no time to be sick, Paul. People are depending on you. You've got to go on.*

Right! Radford answered the voice. *I've got to go on.* Focusing his whole attention on the path before him, he unbuttoned his jacket and started up the trail again. *You can do it Paul,* he told himself. *Just walk this thing off. That's right,* the voice responded. *Mind over matter. One step at a time.* Yet at that moment a violent chill came over him, shaking him so badly he could barely keep his feet. Buttoning his jacket again and hugging his arms to himself closely, he tried to move forward, but the ground beneath his feet began to melt away before his vision, as if he were looking into a stream of shimmering water. "Pico!" he heard his voice cry out, as if from far away. "Pico!" Then Paul Radford felt himself falling as the darkness overcame him.

The tall figure in white shook his head, sadly, it seemed, and held up a restraining hand. *Not yet, my friend,* the thought came to him, unbidden. Nor was it 'never' but 'not yet', and the reassurance this gave him was surprising. *Why is that?* he wondered. He knew he'd always understood how things were, at least to some extent. Yet even as the thought crossed his mind, he understood there was part of him which always wondered, and this was the part of him which craved knowing for sure.

Ah, but you don't know for sure, another voice spoke from the darkness to his left. This was also a voice he knew well, a voice which at times brought him to the depths of despair. Yet even as he began to respond, the figure in white raised a warning finger and the Adversary fell silent. *Now is not your time,* the gesture seemed to say.

For a moment he thought the figure in white was speaking to the Adversary. Then he understood the words were for himself, and there was sadness in the knowing. For looking beyond the figure he could see the land of his dreams and it was spring there, high spring. The sun was warm, the breeze was soft and loving, and in the distance he could hear a lazy hum of bees working the magnificent array of bright wildflowers of every color he could imagine. He had never seen the meadow grass greener and far in the distance, beyond a deep river flowing through this broad, fertile valley, there were deep blue snow capped peaks, heights of the most incredibly beautiful mountains he would ever see.

Home! Came another thought. *This is Home!* Yet at the same moment he realized he could not enter there and the sadness which came over him with this thought was almost more than he could bear. *O, Zion!,* he whispered, echoing the lines of a psalm which had always haunted him. *O, Zion! How can we sing thy happy songs in this alien and bitter land?*

Once again the figure in white raised a hand, this time reaching out to touch him lightly on the shoulder. With the touch he found himself filled with joy, with such radiant joy nothing else mattered. No pain he could ever suffer, no loss he had ever experienced, no sense of self betrayal or anguish over his own shortcomings could matter. There was only I and Thou and the profound joy which went with this.

Soon, my friend, another thought came. *Soon enough. There is still work to be done, work which only you can do.* With this thought the figure in white began to fade quietly into the shimmering light which surrounded them. *Yet, remember. I am with you always.....*

Suddenly the Voice gave away to another sound, another voice coming from behind him. This voice was not so familiar, and it was calling his name. Turning his head he found himself looking down a long tunnel, a tunnel of light flowing through darkness on every side. At the far end he could see another figure, another figure of light, although not one so bright as his companion, whom he called master, and it was this who was calling his name.

Turning back toward the Valley of Home, he saw the master of the valley was gone now. In his place, there was someone else, someone he knew well seated at a keyboard and playing a tune which brought back bittersweet memories of another time. The features of the pianist were calm and still as they never were before, but he recognized the black curly hair combed back at the sides, the high cheek bones and narrow face.

Most of all he knew the hands, the long strong fingers running over the keys as lightly and surely as a mountain goat ascending the heights, and he recognized the tune the young man was playing. It was a song from another time, another age. For them it was a time of innocence, innocence of good and evil, and the player was his constant friend and companion, the first ever he lost to Death.

The tune his friend was playing was a favorite of his, one his friend played for him often. It was an old ragtime melody, one the Americans used to sing to in the cantinas they frequented along the border. He felt his lips move as though on their own volition, whispering the words of the soft refrain he could hear this friend long dead now playing. *Way down yonder, Someone beckons to me.*

You're flat! his friend said, laughing and giving him the dazzling grin he knew so well. His teeth were white, brighter than ever, and the eyes looked on him with affection. *You're always flat, but you're still my friend. You always will be.*

As he heard these words, he felt the tears come, running across his cheek and down his neck. Then off in the far distance he heard someone saying, "Look! He's crying." Yet he did not care. For there is no shame, nothing unmanly, in shedding tears for friends and for Home....

"He will live," another voice said, this time much closer by and he opened his eyes, squinting at the fierce light which seemed to be pouring in through the window. Turning his gaze he saw someone in a long white coat frowning at him in concern, and someone else beside him dressed in a uniform.

For a moment he was taken back in time, taken down the decades to a time of war. "Poncho?" he asked. "Is that you? Where am I? Why am I here?"

"Padre," the doctor spoke quietly. "You are in a hospital in Lima. You were injured very badly. The police brought you here. Can you hear me?"

The police. That was who it was in the uniform. Somehow they had captured him, but he had to protect Poncho and the others. He decided to act as if he did not hear, could not understand. "Mother of God," he moaned, shutting his eyes and wincing in pain. Nor was his response entirely an act. He felt as if he had been beaten and left for the buzzards. "Where am I?" he moaned, rolling his eyes back in his head. Then he shamelessly began whispering an Act of Contrition.

The doctor was alarmed, but Captain Molina was not. "Juan Calderon!" he said sternly, waving aside the doctor's glance. "This is Captain Molina of the police in Lima. We have met, you and I. I need to talk to you." There was no response from the old man and the captain continued. "Please, Padre. I need you to talk to me. Rosario's safety depends on it."

Hearing Rosario's name Juan Calderon opened his eyes. "Rosario?" he asked. "Rosario isn't born yet!" He looked around in confusion. "Lima? How did I get to Lima?"

The captain answered gently. "Some of my people brought you here. You were very badly shot when the kidnappers attacked the rectory."

"The rectory?" Juan Calderon asked, truly confused. "At the church? What was I doing in the rectory?"

"You live there," the doctor replied softly. "Don't you remember? You are the priest in Pisco."

Juan Calderon blinked. The others could see comprehension dawn, come to full awareness in his eyes. "Goodness," he said to the captain. "I thought you were one of the Mexican *federales*." Then his face fell as he began to remember. "Rosario!" he cried. "What happened to Rosario?"

"Someone took her from the rectory," the captain replied. "That is why I need to talk with you. I need to know why they would do that."

"To get at Pablo," the old priest replied. He thought a moment. "I beg your pardon, Captain. I am still a little confused. How long have I been here?"

"Four days," the officer answered. "She was taken five days ago and we brought you here right away. It was good for you Sergeant Gomez heard about it right away. Otherwise you might well be dead now." He looked at the doctor, who nodded.

"I can't remember much of what happened," Juan Calderon answered. "All I remember is being very frightened for Rosario. Nothing else." He frowned. "Maybe I remember some gunshots, and her scream, but that's all." He looked at Molina. "You haven't had word?"

The captain shook his head. "I imagine I will soon. Gomez is trying to find out whatever he can and I expect him to report in soon." He stared intently at the padre. "Why would someone want to get at Paul Radford?" he asked.

The old man shrugged and Molina knew he was hiding something. "Maybe because of his work, Captain. I know he was looking for something specific, but I didn't ask what it was. Maybe he found a gold mine or something and someone is trying to force him to tell them where it is."

Molina sifted this through the screen of what he actually knew. It was plausible, but somehow he did not believe the young American was after gold. He said as much.

Juan Calderon shrugged again. "Gold, oil, guano. Who knows what the Americans are after? It's all the same to me and I really didn't ask for details. I was interested in him, not his work."

The captain nodded. This was probably true, he thought. Even so he thought it unlikely that there would be no mention of Radford's work. "I understand, padre," Molina replied quietly, "but I thought he might have said something to you that might help us."

Juan Calderon made a decision. "Well, you know his pack was stolen and he lost some of his notes. We talked about that."

"Ah," the captain replied. "I wasn't aware of that. When did this happen?"

"It was maybe two weeks ago," the old man told him. "It was after he was attacked up in the mountains and he was very distressed. He lost some of his notes but what upset him was losing a very good set of field glasses."

"Not the loss of his notes?" the captain asked. "I would think that would upset him more."

"There was nothing in his notes he said he couldn't remember," Calderon responded. "The glasses were very expensive."

"But the information," Molina objected. "Even if he could remember that, whoever stole it would have it, too."

"He laughed about that," the padre said. "He told me it was customary to use one's own cipher taking notes because they might be stolen. 'Cut hand' I think he called it. And he said he doubted anyone else could read his writing, anyway."

"Did he mention who he thought might have taken it?"

"Besides a common thief?" Calderon asked. Molina nodded and the old man shrugged. "Well, he did say there was a German company looking for the same things. There were also rumors they were bribing his guide."

The moment he said this, Calderon knew he had made a mistake, gone too far mentioning Quito, but there was no going back. "Rumors, padre?" the captain inquired quietly. "What kind of rumors."

"Cantina talk," the priest told him. "You know the sort of thing I mean. People were laughing at the stupid foreigners." It was the best he could do, but Juan Calderon could see his answer did not satisfy the policeman.

"And how did you hear this cantina talk?" the captain wanted to know.

"At the market, of course," the padre told him. "They always repeat last night's cantina talk and that's how I keep up with that is going on in town. When I don't go myself, Rosario brings it to me."

"I see," Molina answered dryly. It was another dead end, he knew, for even though he suspected the priest had a more direct pipeline to the cantina, as a policeman he often relied on the same source of information in Lima. Even addled by a bullet to the head which almost killed him, the old priest was canny and incredibly fast on his feet.

"Tell me about your housekeeper, padre," Molina probed, switching direction. "I understand she and Radford are ... involved. As a man and a woman," he added.

Juan Calderon nodded. After all, it was common knowledge in Pisco and he was sure Gomez had probably passed along the information from their conversation. Though he might have been asking as a man, he was still a policeman, and probably too good a one to be less than honest with his captain. "Yes, Captain. They are quite involved. Radford wishes to marry her."

"So I understand," Molina replied. Once again he sensed there was something he was not being told, but before he could follow the thought he was interrupted.

"Have they talked to you about it, father?" asked another voice spoke from behind him.

Juan Calderon raised his head slightly and saw a tall, handsome man in civilian clothing standing quietly in the corner behind Molina. "Who are you?" the old man asked, masking his surprise. "You look familiar. Have we met?"

"I think we met once," Blieu reminded him smoothly. "I came to the rectory a few weeks ago looking for Paul Radford and you invited me to stay for supper." Molina raised an eyebrows. This was news to him and he felt a touch of anger at the way the Americans were operating. Yet there was nothing he could do about it and his pique never reached his face.

Even so, the old priest saw the anger rise in the policeman's eyes. *Jesus, Joseph and Mary,* he thought. *What have I gotten us into?* "Of course, forgive me," Juan Calderon said, lying boldly, touching the bandage on his head. "I still seem to be a bit confused."

"Actually, you're remarkably coherent," Molina observed dryly, not fooled by the charade. "The lieutenant is being kind enough to help me search for our elusive Mr. Radford."

"I am afraid the embassy forced me onto Captain Molina." Blieu responded. "He's being a much better sport about it than I would be in his shoes." He shrugged, looking at the captain apologetically. "It puts me in an uncomfortable position, too, yet there's not a lot either of us can do but accept it."

The captain nodded, somewhat mollified by Blieu's words. "How does Rosario feel about this?" he asked. "About marriage to the American. Has she spoken to you about it?"

The old man looked distinctly uncomfortable. "Forgive me, captain, but I cannot speak of what I talk about with Rosario. At least, not that sort of thing. I am her priest as well as her employer. What I can tell you from my own observations is that she has been very happy since they met." He smiled. "We eat much better when

Pablo is coming to dinner, especially when she takes him to market with her."

At that moment a starched archangel descended into the room in righteous fury. "What in the world are you doing with my patient, captain?" Sister Ignatius demanded. "I said you could speak with him for a few minutes and it's been over a half hour!"

"It's all right, sister," Juan Calderon tried to intercede.

"I beg your pardon, father," the sister replied with some asperity, "but your jurisdiction is Pisco. I am the one who decides what is and is not all right around here." She turned to Molina and Blieu. "And I am afraid you gentlemen need to leave. Right now."

"It's a matter of life and death, sister," Juan Calderon tried again, but there was no argument with this gentle angel of wrath.

"It is, indeed, father," the good sister said over her shoulder as she herded the men out of the room like a flock of school children. "Your own. Now rest!"

"Yes, sister," murmured Juan Calderon, smiling as he relaxed back into his pillow. *Grace upon grace,* he thought as sleep called him to rest. *The miracles are always there when you need them.* Nor was he thinking of the intervention of the good sister, but of Molina and Gomez and Blieu. The situation was still grave, but he was strangely not fearful for Rosario. For as he drifted into oblivion the words of the fourteenth century mystic, Julian of Norwich, came to mind, words uttered at the height of the Black Death sweeping across the Continent. "All shall be well, he told me," the abbess had written of her mystic vision. "And all manner of things shall be well...."

Rosario liked the place she was being held better than the last place, but she was worried about the guard. After a long, wild ride held down under a blanket in the back seat of the getaway car, she was dragged out of the vehicle like a sack of potatoes and shoved into a dark cellar. Even though there was no light, and the cellar smelled of mildew and tar and rotted vegetables, Rosario was not really afraid until an hour had passed and she heard a soft snuffling in the darkness and felt the furry form move across her foot. *"Madre a Dios!"* she cried pulling her foot back and retreating as far up the stairway as she could before an iron door stopped her. Not even poisonous snakes frightened her as much as rats.

Even so she could hear the snuffling moving closer, and she felt around her desperately for a stick or some weapon she could use to drive the rats away. Suddenly her hand touched a furry body and she jerked it back, electrified with panic. *"No,"* she moaned softly, praying to the Virgin to intercede, for God the Son she carried within her to send the Angel of Death. *"O, Dios! O, Madre a Dios, no."*

A small squeaking sound came from her left, and again she felt the brush of soft fur on her arm. This time she did not pull back. Something was not quite right, and with all the courage she possessed, Rosario reached out slowly and touched the furry body, which responded immediately by pushing against her hand. "Meyouprrrr," it squeaked again, and a small furry head butted her palm.

Rosario laughed, hysterical with relief. "You wicked cat!" she said, petting the kitten even as she scolded it. "You almost scared me to death!"

"Mwarr," demanded the kitten, and through what remained of that long, dark night, it sat quietly on Rosario's lap, purring and gently kneading the rise of life within her abdomen.

When day came, light filtered into the cellar through cracks around the steel door and foundation. While the cellar was still dim, Rosario could see well enough to explore her place of captivity, and it was even more dismal than it smelled in the darkness. It was apparently the cellar of an unused warehouse, and empty crates were stack loosely along the walls. Broken boards littered the dirt floor, and in one dusty corner were the remains of what had been a sack of potatoes. Hungry, Rosario dug among the blackened mess, but the contents were so old the rotted spuds had dried to withered shells filled mostly with mold spores and air. For a long moment she considered trying to eat what was left, but the thought of what this might do to her child prevented her, and settling back against one of the crates as comfortably as she could, Rosario drifted off to sleep with the kitten once again in her lap.

Suddenly the iron door was flung open, blinding Rosario with the brightness of full daylight. At the crash of the door the kitten leapt from her lap, bolting behind a crate where it crouched watching the dark figure of a burly man descend the steps. "Here," he said to Rosario in Spanish, setting down a bucket of water and a bulky sack. "There's food in the sack. But it's all you're going to get today."

Turning to leave, he looked back. "If you need to make water, use the corner," he said gruffly, laughing. Then he slammed down the iron door and Rosario could hear the rattle of a chain and the snap of a lock.

Through the rest of that day and the following night, Rosario sat quietly in the cellar, wondering why she had been taken captive and rarely moving except to stretch cramped muscles. After sharing the food their captor brought, the kitten was content to sleep in her lap much of the time, occasionally opening one eye to see what his new friend was doing. From time to time when it awakened, Rosario teased it with a bit of string until it became bored with the game and began to bathe itself. That done, it would stretch and yawn before curling up for another nap in her lap.

There was little to do but think and it did not take Rosario long to understand that her being taken had something to do with the work Paul Radford was doing for his government, the things he and the padre talked about, and the war. She also realized she might be questioned about this, and resolved to tell her captors as little as she could. Thinking about this, she decided that pretending to be stupid and ignorant was probably her best defense since most people did not look beyond the surface and assumed she was both. Yet she also knew that, given the choice of telling everything she knew and risking the life of the child within her, she would tell. While she knew the padre would forgive her, she could only hope Pablo would, too. Surely, he would understand.

Coming to this decision, there was little else to do, and Rosario began to sing softly, singing to the life within her. When she began, the kitten looked up, blinking its eyes sleepily, then decided all was well in its realm and nodded off again with the soft crooning. After a while, Rosario's own eyes began to grow heavy, and at last she dropped off into a deep sleep, with soft snores replacing her song.

Not long after daylight the next day, her captors came for her. When they did, the kitten was fast asleep within the blanket Rosario wrapped around her against the damp, and since the men did not take time to search her, it was taken along when she was shoved into the back of a black sedan and once again pressed down to the floorboards. Crushed between her breasts, it struggled free and then curled itself quietly in the hollow of her neck and continued its nap. *I wish I could be so calm as this cat,* she thought, and then Rosario smiled despite her predicament as the kitten began to lick her chin. *Angel,* she whispered to the kitten. *You're my little angel sent to teach me to trust.*

About an hour after their ride began, Rosario felt the car turn sharply to the right, bump across something in its path, and come to a stop. Suddenly the blanket was jerked off her head and Rosario was told to get out of the car. "Where did that cat come from?" the guard snarled as she climbed out of the rear seat. He grabbed for the kitten, but Rosario turned back toward the car, defending it with her body. "Give it to me!" the guard commanded, gripping her shoulder so tightly she gasped. "Now!"

"Stop it!" the other man, the European, commanded him. "I told you not to hurt her. Never mind the cat. She can keep it for all I care. Just get her into the house."

The guard glared at the European but obeyed. Jerking his head toward a doorway into the house they were parked beside he said, "In there. Right now!"

Clutching the kitten tightly to her, Rosario crossed from the car to the doorway, glancing around as she did. They were parked in the walled courtyard of a large house, and several feet behind the car she could see massive doors of an entry gate. The doors were fit closely into the framework and shut tight, allowing no view of what might lie outside them. For all she could tell, Rosario thought, she might be in the middle of Lima as easily as on some large estate in the countryside. Nor was there was there anything she could hear from the other side of the doors to tell her which it might be.

The inside of the house was beautiful and well furnished. Although she only got a momentary glimpse of the main rooms as her captors led her to her room, she noticed the place had an air of disuse. There was dust where no good housekeeper would allow dust to gather and while the draperies on most of the windows facing the courtyard were open, some were tightly drawn where direct sunlight might come in and fade the elegant fabric of the furniture. There were no windows to the outside world, nor any other door she could see except the one she entered.

"Here," said the captor leading the way, the European, as he opened a door into a comfortable bedroom. He spoke Spanish with a heavy accent. "You will stay in here except to prepare meals for him and yourself." He nodded to the man behind her. He pointed to a small room to one side. "The toilet is there when you need it and you can use the tub to wash yourself." He looked at her, not unkindly. "You have nothing to fear from us as long as you do not try to escape. If you do there is another place here like the one you were in last night, and we will keep you there. *Verstehen?*"

Rosario nodded, even though the last word was uttered in a tongue she did not understand. The meaning was clear enough. "Thank you," she said, averting her eyes. "Could I have some sand for the kitten, sir? And a small box?"

The second man glared at her, but the slightest hint of a smile touched the European's face. "Of course," he said. Turning to the other man he said, "See to it."

It was clear the rough looking man did not like this, but he nodded. When the German was gone he would simply ignore the instruction and claim forgetfulness if asked about it later. "Do it now while I'm still here," the German told him and the rough man's face flushed. "And bring the lady a drinking cup and a saucer, too, while you're at it."

The second man grunted and turned back down the hall. When he had disappeared, the German said, "I have told him not to harm you, but you better not do anything to offend him. I will look in from time to time, but he's the one you have to be careful with." He shrugged. "I have told him you must not escape and to lock you in the cellar if you try. So for your own sake I would suggest you not try."

Again Rosario nodded. She could see the man clearly although her gaze was averted. He was much younger than she thought at first, perhaps even younger than Pablo. "Thank you, sir," she replied softly. "I will remember your words."

Satisfied, the German nodded and left the room, locking it carefully after himself. Seating herself on the bed, Rosario looked around the room carefully. The first thing she noticed was that the windows all faced the courtyard. They were also tall, reaching almost to the floor to the ceiling, but unlike the windows they passed in other rooms, these were barred.

The second thing she noticed was that she was apparently being kept at the end of the living wing of the house. So while she had an excellent view of the courtyard through the windows, and could see the car which brought her, she could not see the gates very well. This meant that even when these were open to let the car in and out, there was little likelihood she could see anything beyond them.

The thing which puzzled her, however, was the bathroom. While the wealthy of the country used indoor plumbing, a room with its own bath was an unusual luxury, one Rosario herself had never seen or even heard of. So even though it was not all that large, this room must be where the master of the house slept. That would explain the bars on the windows, too, but what did not make sense was for her to be kept in the master's chambers. Unless the master was away and this was the most secure room in the house. But why were they so afraid of her escaping? Unless....

Her thoughts were interrupted by the rough man opening the door and dumping a small box filled with sand onto the floor. "There!" he snarled. "That's for your damned cat." Rosario sensed the man might have liked to say more, but the German was standing right behind him and he simply glared at her and said, "I'll be back when it's time to cook supper." Then he shut the door and once again she heard the lock slide solidly into the mortise as it was turned.

Turning her attention back to the room, Rosario thought about what she could see and what it might mean. It occurred to her rather quickly that they might be holding her with the knowledge of the owner of the house, but it seemed more likely they were not. That would explain the air of disuse. The owner must be away and if they were holding her somewhere without the owner's permission, that meant they would wish to avoid attracting attention. So if she were right, she must be somewhere in at least the outskirts of a settlement, and with a house this large, it was likely she was in Lima. That would explain why they were so afraid of her getting away. Out in the country they could simply hunt her down, a matter of inconvenience, but no real trouble. In Lima, on the other hand, she could find her way to the authorities fairly quickly, and this was driving their fear. For the first time since she had been taken, Rosario began to feel a measure of hope, and she began looking for ways she might attract the attention of the authorities without warning her captors. Even in the company of an angelic kitten, two nights in a cellar was enough.

Thinking of the kitten, Rosario rose from the bed and picked up the box of sand. Placing it in a far corner of the room, she set the kitten in the box gently and watched as it sniffed the sand curiously. Then it began to paw the sand and Rosario nodded. "That's right, chica," she said. "That's what it's for." And feeling very tired and drowsy, Rosario returned to the bed and fell into a deep sleep. More than tired, she was exhausted, worn out from the last two days, and not even thought of the rough man who stood guard on the other side of the heavy door could trouble her rest.

Within the dreamtide, he found himself walking through a bright, sunny glen. How he got there or when, he did not know. Nor why he was here. Somehow it did not matter. In fact, nothing mattered but that he was here, that he was safe here. He knew that as surely and certainly as he knew the sun would rise the next day. Thinking of the sun, he glanced up. He could see the brightness of mid day filtering down through the lush green leaves, but it was not hot. Nor was it cold. The temperature of the air was ... perfect, and he could feel the warm breeze softly playing through the hair on his chest.

Looking down he became aware he was bare of clothing. Not naked. No, somehow the fear which goes with the word "naked" did not exist here. His skin was bare to the elements, and the soles of his feet touched the soft ground in gentle communion, but there was no sense of shame to this. Somehow this seemed right, too, and ... perfect. Nor did it trouble him he might meet others here, might meet them in all his ... glory. The word came to mind effortlessly, even as the "nakedness" slipped away like a bad smell barely remembered.

What an odd word for him to think of. Glory. It was not a word he used much, and never without irony. Only here it was a common word, common as dirt. Here it was just another word, another simple word describing this strange and majestic place. Yes, that was the perfect word, majestic. This place was full of majesty and ... mystery. That was another good word which was somehow meant this place, right Here where he stood. With this thought other simple words, other names for Here came tumbling to mind. Honor. Praise. Splendor. Rejoicing.

Yes, this was the place of rejoicing. As the word came to mind the light, bright sound of a penny whistle drifted to his ears on the wind

153

and he found his feet begin to move, dancing to the reel it played. Again he was surprised, amazed to learn he could dance like this, keeping perfect time to the music as his feet moved over the meadow. When did he learn to do this?

The music began to whirl him faster and faster, over the meadow and down the glen until at last he stood on the brink of a high cliff overlooking a crystal sea. Looking down he could see the waters breaking against huge boulders fallen from the cliff, breaking against the rocks in perfect time to the music, sending spumes of spray high into the air, as if the sea itself was raising its arms in the dance the pipe was calling.

Faster and faster the penny whistle played, filling the air even over the thunder of the surf, yet strangely he felt no weariness. Nor did he feel fear, even though this feet were playing about the stones an inch from the edge where a single misstep would plunge him a hundred or more feet into the sea.

He thought about his lack of fear. Somehow he knew in this place there was nothing in the heavens above nor in the depths of the earth below, nothing before him or behind him or anywhere around him which could harm him. He knew that even if his feet failed, casting him over the edge into the abyss, he would either find he had missed the rocks, or that somehow he had learned to fly.

Yet how did he know this? The question rose and troubled him for a moment, then it passed. Somehow even the question itself had no place here. There was nothing in all which had been, nor all that was, nor all which would be that could harm him. For this was the Land of Joy.

11. Awakenings

"Well, Johannes, Rott tells me you did a good job," Schwartz told the younger man. As usual, he was standing next to the window overlooking the courtyard to the embassy, turned so he could look in either direction. The other two were seated across the large oak table which served as his desk, Rott slouched in one of the leather chairs and Weiss sitting rigidly at attention in another. Turning his gaze to look out the window at the courtyard, Schwartz continued. "The loss of Mueller was unfortunate, but you were not at fault. It was a calculated risk and we had no way of knowing the old man was armed." Giving them a sardonic smile, he added, "The other man, of course, was no loss to us at all. As a matter of fact, the priest saved us some trouble, didn't he?"

Rott grinned, but Johannes looked stricken. "Thank you, sir," he said, "I regret having to shoot the priest but there was really no choice. It was him or me at that point and he had already shot Mueller." He frowned. "I hated leaving that other man but he was already dead and there was no time to waste going back to get him. I hope that doesn't cause any trouble."

Schwartz waved it away with a careless hand. "A minor inconvenience at the most," he assured the young man. "There is no way we can be connected with the affair, and even if there were, we have diplomatic immunity. Including yourself, by the way. We are not required to even talk to the police." He smiled again, "Of, course, it's always better not to be caught. The Secretary hates surprises."

Rott grinned openly at this blatant hypocrisy, remembering a number of instances he and Schwartz were very lucky not to get caught at what they were about. "Always," he said quietly, and he could see the irony was not lost on his superior. "Come on, Manfred, get on with it," he prodded quietly. "Johannes and I have a lot to get done today."

"Yes, of course," Schwartz replied with a slight frown at Rott, more for the breach of formality than for the prodding. The truth was, he depended on Rott to keep him on track at times. Smiling at Weiss, Schwartz picked up a small box from his desk and handed it to the younger man. "The point is, Johan, we are so pleased with your performance that we have recommended you for a field promotion." Holding out a hand, he added, "So congratulations, Lieutenant Weiss. You will still have to attend officer's school when you are assigned back to the Fatherland, but for the time being, enjoy the increase in status if not the increase in pay."

Rott gave Schwartz a sardonic grin, one Weiss could not see. For while it was Weiss' good work which led to the promotion, it was Rott who had insisted on it over Schwartz's objections. "Damn it, listen to me, Manfred," he told his commander. "So long as he stays a private, no one will take orders from him, nor will he really expect them to, and I need him to be able to lead a tactical group."

"So make him a sergeant," Schwartz replied. "You know the minute we promote him to lieutenant, the bastards in Berlin will grab him and order him home to the front."

"He doesn't have the experience to be a sergeant," Rott replied, a bit heated at having to state what, to him, was the obvious. "The men will not respect him."

"And he doesn't have the training or the family background to be an officer," Schwartz snapped back. "How do you expect them to take orders from him as an officer if they won't as a sergeant?"

"Officers are not expected to be experienced," Rott answered in kind. "Especially green ones. A sergeant is supposed to know what he is doing. New lieutenants can get away with being a bit stupid."

Schwartz chuckled, then laughed, remembering some of their own stupidities. "Your point is well taken, my friend, but that doesn't solve the problem with the people in Berlin. Promote Weiss and they'll snatch him up in a minute."

"Not if he's breveted," Rott told him. "Or not if his papers are somewhat delayed. Wait a few weeks before you send them in and then put on his papers that he's an intelligence specialist and is being promoted for military intelligence. Tell them he's needed for specific intelligence operations here." He shrugged. "Hell, tell them anything, Manfred. Use your imagination. Tell them he's having an affair with a senior minister's wife and we need him as a source of information. It doesn't really matter what you tell them. Just get him promoted on paper so I can use him."

"Why don't we just transfer him to intelligence?" Schwartz asked. "That would do it, wouldn't it?"

"Do you really want him out of our control?" Rott asked. "Because that's what you're suggesting. Attach him to intelligence and that bastard Gehlen will have him spying on us. Do you really want that?"

"I see what you mean," the other finally admitted. "Very well, I'll see what I can do. He actually could be a very valuable asset to us here."

Now the bastard's acting like it was all his idea, Rott thought as he watched. *Well, it doesn't matter much anyway. If Weiss messes up it will be Schwartz's neck on the block and not mine.* "What a surprise, eh?" he asked the stunned Weiss as they left the office a while later. "You thought he was going to bite your ass and you ended up with a promotion."

"I really don't deserve it, Rott," Weiss replied. "All I did was what you told me to do. You're the one that deserves the credit."

"No, Johan, you don't understand," Rott explained, unusually patient with the other. "What you did was exactly what I told you to do, and that is exactly what we need in officers. You didn't think things over and arrive at a decision you thought was better. You did what you were told. Continue doing that and you will do well. We're not looking for brilliance but obedience. Understand?"

Weiss nodded his head, suppressing a shudder as he felt a goose walk over his grave. *Sheiss!* he thought. *What have I gotten myself into now?* For he knew, as soldiers in any army know, the higher one climbs the command pole, the more one's backside becomes a target. Yet despite that, it occurred to him that whatever the future might bring working for Rott, it had to be better than serving on the front. As it turned out, he was only partially right.

The first thing Radford saw coming awake was Pico's face. *Why, he looks like an angel,* he thought, taking in the intent black eyes and fierce features of the guide. *A guardian angel. Or maybe an avenging angel.* He tried to reach up and touch the other's face, but the effort of lifting his arm was more than he could do. *Don't leave me,* he implored with his eyes. *Don't leave me, Pico.* Then his vision began to swim, and for a moment the darkness flooded back over him.

"I think he's coming out of it," a familiar voice said from far, far away. It was Pico. "He opened his eyes for a moment. I think he tried to say something."

Radford opened his eyes again, this time keeping them open and blinking against the light of the late afternoon sun. "Where am I?" he whispered.

"Take it easy, fellow,"' another voice answered. This one was unfamiliar. "No hurry. We're glad you're back in the land of the living."

Radford felt his head being lifted. He opened his eyes again to see Pico holding a cup to his lips. "Drink, Pablo," the guide told him. "It is bitter but swallow it quickly. It will make you feel better."

Radford opened his parched lips and drank greedily from the cup, swallowing twice before the awful taste registered on his tongue. "Damn!" he said, turning his head aside and spitting out what was in his mouth. "That tastes awful." Even so, he felt his head clearing and strength coming back into his legs and arms. "What in the hell is that?"

"Something an old *curandero* showed me once," Pico laughed. "A sure cure for hangovers and fevers. Try to drink some more if you can. It will make you feel better."

"It already has," Radford answered, lifting a weak arm and guiding the cup to his lips again. This time he managed three swallows before pushing the cup aside. "God!" he declared. "The cure's worse than the disease!" Shaking his head and looking around, he saw two other men standing behind Pico. One he recognized as Captain Molina from the police in Lima, but the other was an American he had never seen before. At least, he guessed the man was an American by the way his hair was cut. When the man spoke he was certain.

"Jacques Paul," the man said, squatting down so he could hear Radford better. "We haven't met but Denis Blieu sends his compliments. I'm a ... friend of the family."

Friend of the family, Radford thought, rolling the words over in his mind. *That's supposed to mean something. Something about Blieu.* "Good to meet you," Radford smiled, raising a feeble arm. "It's good seeing you, too, Captain. Forgive me for not getting up. I seem to be indisposed."

This brought a chuckle even from the taciturn Captain Molina. "Believe me, the pleasure is mine, Mr. Radford," he answered. "We have been looking very hard for you."

"I can't recall any crimes worth chasing me out here for, Captain," Radford told him dryly. Then the meaning of what he had just said broke through. "Is something wrong?" he asked, suddenly anxious, trying to raise himself up. "Is it my family?"

The look Molina gave him answered his question. "I am afraid so," Molina replied simply. "Not your family back home in America, but your friends here." Quickly and concisely he described the attack on the rectory. "The padre will be all right," he assured Radford when he was done. "He is recovering well. However, we still have not found the housekeeper."

"Rosario," the young man moaned. "Why did they have to take Rosario?"

"I am afraid it was to get to you," Molina answered. "That's what the padre thinks and I agree with him. Someone wants information you have and that is why she was taken."

"What information?" Radford asked, trying desperately to get his mind around the news, and also trying to gain his composure. "Who could want anything I know?" he asked trying to gain time to order his scrambled thoughts. It was a noble effort, but futile.

"I was hoping you could tell us that, Mr. Radford," the captain said dryly. "Juan Calderon seems to think it is the Germans?"

"Screw the Germans!" Radford said trying to get up. "We've go to find Rosario."

"Please, Mr. Radford," captain said, restraining him gently. "You're in no shape to do anything but talk to me right now. I have one of my very best men looking for Rosario, even as we speak. I assure you that if anyone can find her, Gomez will."

Radford lay back but looked stubborn. "Excuse me, if you will, captain," the American said. "I may be able to help."

"Please do," Molina said softly, nodding, moving to one side.

"Paul," said the American. "My name is Jacques Paul. I'm a United States Army captain attached to the embassy here. I work for Denis Blieu. Do you understand."

He's a friend of the family, Radford thought. *I should know what that means.* Then suddenly he did. "Yes," he said, nodding weakly.

"I remember now. You're a friend of the extended family. He told me all about you." The phrase was part of a code Blieu had given him, a code phrase telling him this was someone he could trust, and his reply was another phrase of the same verbal code, one demanding a precise confirmation.

"Only good things, I hope," Jacques Paul replied. Then he completed the sequence. "We're really not that close. I'm a third cousin, on his father's side." Seeing his response register, he went on. "Listen, Paul. A lot has happened since you left town. Captain Molina is working with us and it's time to come to Jesus." He spoke the last phrase in English.

Come to Jesus. Radford remembered that was a code phrase too. But before he could answer, Captain Molina broke in. "'*Come to Jesus*?' What does this mean?" he demanded.

"It means it's time to be completely honest, captain," Radford answered, remembering. "It's an American slang phrase. I'm not sure there is a Spanish equivalent. Maybe '*venga a Dios*'."

"So why don't you tell Captain everything?" Jacques Paul cut in once more. "About the map and the whole works. Everything." He nodded encouragement.

"All right," Radford said, reaching a weak hand for Pico's tonic. This time he could only manage a single swallow, but color began to show in his face as soon as it was down and Pico helped him into a sitting position. "I came here in January, almost four years ago now, working for an oil company and sent to look for mineral deposits. The funny stuff did not begin until a couple of months ago when I was attacked in the mountains. I told you about that."

Molina considered for a moment, then asked gravely, "That's 'come to Jesus'?"

Despite himself, and the gravity of the situation, Radford smiled. "Yes, captain, that's 'come to Jesus' true. As a matter of fact, everything I told you about the attack was true. What I did not mention at the time was a map I found on Quito's body...."

Three days had passed since Rosario last saw the German. During that time she had seen very little of the rough man except when he came for her to fix their meals, and these he ate in a sullen silence, ignoring her presence as completely as he might a piece of furniture.

Not that she wished to change this. She was perfectly comfortable with her own company, though she missed the easy table banter of Pablo and the padre, and she had no desire for conversation with her captor. There was a brooding quality to his silence which worried her, as if there were a vast volcano of anger and resentment boiling just under the surface waiting for the slightest pretext to erupt. So Rosario was very careful to not give him the slightest excuse for offense, and waited quietly in the corner until the man was done to eat her own meal and clean up the dishes quickly and as silently as she could.

The German had showed up twice since she was brought to this house, once the day after he left her with the rough man, and again two days later. Nor was it lost on her that he chose different times of the day to appear, and she suspected it was equally clear to her jailer that the German's primary reason for doing this was to make sure his instructions were being followed. So far they had been, and the rough man had done nothing overt to threaten her in any way.

Even so, Rosario was growing more and more concerned because of the way her captor was drinking. At first it was confined to a bottle or two of beer when the man slipped out for a few minutes in the evening, bringing his goods back to his post before consuming them. Then it had been several bottles consumed one after another as he sat leaned back against the courtyard wall, although the only sign she saw that the liquor was affecting the man was the careful way he walked when he went to relieve himself against the wall on the other side of the entrance doors. Yet for the last two days, his trips to the cantina had become more and more frequent, and the day before, when the man had ordered her to clean up the area of the courtyard where he kept watch, she counted over twenty bottles. Now there were at least a dozen more new ones littering the pavement from the morning's binge.

It occurred to Rosario early on that the man might drink himself into oblivion, and she waited for this, planning her escape. The second day of her captivity her careful fingers had discovered a key, one hidden in the recess of a closet, and it looked as if it fit the door. The next afternoon she had tried it when her captor left for the cantina, and she found the key turned easily in the lock. So hiding it again in the place where she found it, Rosario waited for her opportunity to flee.

Yet somehow the rough man never drank quite enough to pass out, at least for long enough for her to get away, and she observed his drinking with dread, fearing the moment when the alcohol running through his veins overcame his terror of the German. Experience told her this would not be long, given the amount he was consuming, and she had no illusions about what would happen then.

Though it made her sick to think of the rough man on her, in her, violating her, Rosario came to a decision. To protect the child within her, she decided to yield at once, to even to pretend pleasure if she had to do so to save her life. *God, forgive me,* she thought as she came to this decision.

Then she fell to her knees. "God forgive me," she whispered, crossing herself. Yet even as she said this to the empty room, she knew she was not praying for God's forgiveness, or even that of Juan Calderon. No, she was praying for something else, for Paul Radford's understanding of the necessity of her decision. "Dear God," she added quietly. "Please help him to forgive me, too."

Even as she uttered this prayer, she heard the lock turn at the portal and tuned to see the heavy door swing slowly open. The rough man stood there, swaying unsteadily on his feet and squinting at her with eyes turned red from drink, and it was all Rosario could do to keep the terror she felt rising within her from showing. "Is it time for supper already?" she asked as pleasantly as she could.

"Supper?" The question seemed to confuse her captor. Feeling his fat belly with one hand he nodded, "Yeah, woman, I'm hungry. Fix something." Yet as she walked past him he grabbed her by the shoulder painfully and leered. "And when I'm done eating, then we're going to do something else!" He threw back his head and laughed drunkenly.

"Oh," said Rosario, thinking quickly. "Yes, the bottles. We've got to do those. Maybe we better do them first, no?"

"Bottles?" said the rough man, squinting in concentration. "What bottles?"

"The bottles in the courtyard," Rosario answered. "We need to pick them up like we did the day before yesterday. So the German won't know you've gotten a little drunk."

"A little drunk?" laughed the jailer. "I'm not a little drunk! I'm a whole lot drunk! To hell with the German! I don't care if he does know! I don't care if the whole world knows!" Turning clumsily in the passage he laughed again. "So screw the German. If he shows up here I'm going to screw him, just like I'm going to screw you!" Trying to make an obscene thrust with his hips, the rough man almost fell down on the spot.

Had she been clear of the man, Rosario might have made a run for it right then. It was doubtful her captor could have caught up with her, but she decided it was not time. More than likely she would only get one chance to escape, and she had better make that one good. "Ha!" she said, shrugging the man's hand off her shoulder and giving a suggestive wiggle of her derriere as she walked down the hall. Taking a calculated risk, she added. "You better sober up then. Right now all you're good for is screwing yourself into the floor."

The rough man shook his head, confused at this apparent show of spirit. Then Rosario's chance paid off. He laughed again, this time so hard he had to brace himself against the wall before following her into the dining room. "Sit down," she ordered when they arrived there, pointing toward a chair. "I'll get your meal. Then we'll see."

The rough man dropped himself into a chair so violently Rosario heard the wood crack and thought it would break. Then, instead of waiting for his meal as she hoped, the guard grabbed her by the arm and pulled her down onto his lap. "No!" she cried, trying to pull back but the man was too strong.

"What do you mean, 'no', you damned tease!" the man snarled harshly, pulling her tightly against his chest. Yet even as he did, the tortured frame of the chair gave way against their combined weight, and with a loud snap, they fell to the floor.

"I meant the chair is going to break, fool," Rosario responded with all the spirit she could muster, rolling off the man, who seemed to be having a hard time breathing, and dusting herself off. The man waved at her wildly, gasping, and she realized he was winded from the fall and in no shape to give chase. Seizing the opportunity, Rosario flung herself through the door and toward the entrance to the house. This time luck was on her side. She was between the man and the door, and as she flung open the outer door into the courtyard, she found it unlocked.

Hearing something behind her, Rosario glanced over her shoulder to see her captor now up and stumbling through the doorway into the dining room after her. Yet even as he came after her he lurched into a large chair, spilling himself on the floor. Breathing a prayer that the outer gate would be unlocked as well, Rosario turned the heavy door latch and swung open the door. Then she gasped, for her luck had run out. Standing right before her was a European she had never seen before, with another native man like her captor standing just behind him. Yet what captured her attention was not the two men but the dark eye staring into her own, the dark, bleak eye of a gun.

Though he felt much better once the fever had passed, Paul Radford found his strength returning very slowly, and the trip back to Pisco, and then to Lima, was an ordeal. What made it possible to travel in his condition at all was the intervention of Captain Molina who commandeered the personal car and driver of a local official in Ica. Yet even Molina's authority had to be bolstered with the promise of a large rental fee before the official grudgingly agreed. Then the man insisted on having his money in advance, which was impossible, and only Molina's threat of confiscation without compensation moved him to agree.

"What do you mean, confiscation?" the official demanded. "On what grounds?"

"Take your pick," Molina responded, taking out a leather notebook and thumbing through. "I've had my eye on you for years. How about suspicion of smuggling and possession of contraband?"

"Who doesn't smuggle around here?" the fellow sneered, trying to hide his fear behind bravado. "No judge around here would take you seriously, Captain. And no one who has to live around here would dare testify. If they did they would disappear."

"Perhaps," Molina acknowledged. "But either way the vehicle goes to Lima and I go with it. If I were to confiscate it, then the vehicle would be in Lima and you would have the expense of having to send someone to get it back. Plus the time it would take." He shook his head sadly. "You've got no idea how long the paperwork on something like this can drag out. Or the forms I would have to fill out." He threw up his hands. "It could take months."

The official glowered at him but said nothing and Molina smiled. "On the other hand, this way we both profit, and this way we avoid tiresome official action. I give you my word. The money will be paid."

The official's vehicle turned about to be an ancient touring car which had seen better days. Yet it was one of the few serviceable vehicles in town, and it made what would have been a journey of days cross country by foot, into a journey of hours by the primitive roads through the region. Despite this, Radford found the ride a harrowing experience. Part of this was due to his recent illness, but most of it lay in the casual attitude of their driver, who steered the big car over the steep grades with cavalier abandon. The only concession Radford could see their driver ever made to safety was taken at blind switchbacks, where a loud blast on the air horns preceded a quick downshift as the wildman sent them flying into the turns. For all the wear and tear years traveling over roads like this had lent it, he imagined that someone salvaging the vehicle after the driver missed a turn would find the horn button worn beyond salvage and the brakes in factory new condition.

Turning his mind from the gyrations of the car, Radford thought about the decision for him to return to Pisco with Molina. Now he had to admit it was a wise one, but when the subject first came up, he was vehemently opposed, wanting to rest for a day or to and then continue their search. "That's where they'll have her," he protested. "That's where they've taken Rosario."

"Wait a minute," Jacques Paul interrupted. "What are you talking about? That doesn't make any sense. Not a bit." Molina nodded, as did Pico.

"Pablo, I think that's your fever talking," Pico told him. "Why would they take the trouble to bring her all the way up in the mountains? There are hundreds of hiding places much closer to Pisco."

Radford stared at them, uncomprehending. "Look at it from their point of view, Paul" Jacques Paul said. "Taking her anywhere in the countryside would increase their risk of being discovered. The more logical thing to do would be to keep her somewhere in Pisco, or maybe, Lima."

165

Radford said nothing for a few moments, digesting what he had been told. "I guess you're right," he said, speaking slowly Then another thought struck him and his face clouded. "Do you really think she's alive, Captain?" he asked Molina. There was a terrible vulnerability written across his face.

"I don't know," the captain replied gently. "I have been operating on the assumption that the reason they took her was they want something from you and will offer to trade her for what they want. If that is right, and I believe it is, then they would need to keep her alive until they got what they want. Then they might kill her, but they would probably try to kill you too." He looked grave. "You, yourself may be what they want. For what you know and what you can tell them. I think that is most likely, but, of course, I may be wrong."

"And if you are wrong?" Radford asked, and Molina looked uncomfortable. "What then?"

Molina shrugged. "Who knows? Maybe they simply wanted to make it look like they had taken her. If that is true, then I am afraid there is not much chance for her being alive." There was compassion in the captain's eyes. For a moment Radford thought the policeman was about to add something, but he simply shook his head. *If you are a praying man, Mr. Radford,* he thought, *then you better pray.*

"Well, I think your working assumption is correct, Captain," Jacques Paul cut in. "They went to far too much trouble just for show. So don't give up hope, Paul, not yet. The game's a long way from lost. There's every reason to believe Captain Molina is correct."

Radford nodded. "I hope you're right." He shook his head and slumped back to the ground. "I don't know what got me, but it was sure bad stuff. I feel as weak as a kitten."

"Which means you'd be a helluva lot of help on a rescue raid, wouldn't it?" Jacques Paul observed dryly and for the first time, Radford grinned weakly.

"There is that," the young man said. "So how do we do this? I can't make it back to civilization on my own and it's out of your way to pick me up here on your way back. I guess we have to split up."

It didn't take them long to come to the decision that Pico and Jacques Paul would continue to look for the secret base while Molina and Radford returned to Pisco. The police captain did not really like this, but it was the lesser of poor choices, and he agreed. Yet before he did he made Jacques Paul swear he would reveal everything he found once he arrived back in Lima. "I must have your solemn promise on this as an officer of your country," he told him sternly. "I think working with you is in the best interests of my country but I am very much at risk here. You must be absolutely candid with me. Much more than you have so far. Agreed?"

"I give you my most solemn assurance," Jacques Paul agreed. Paul Radford nodded and within the hour he and Captain Molina were on their way.

Eric Rudd was swearing. Not only was he swearing but he was punctuating his words pounding his desk, and Alex White leaned back in his chair and grinned. Finally Rudd slammed the document he had been reading down on his desk and glared at his executive officer. "What are you smirking about?" the Commander demanded.

"I don't think I have ever heard you this creative," White replied with sincere admiration. "Or this forceful, for that matter. I think they must have heard you all the way to the main gate, and I'd bet you set a Navy record for not repeating yourself." He chuckled. "Too bad Denis wasn't here to hear it, too."

"Oh, he'll hear it, all right," Rudd. "The next time I see him Little Boy Blue is going to be blowing his bugle out his ass."

"I'm sure there's a reason you can't raise him," White replied, laughing. "It's not like Denis to just disappear like this without a reason."

"If I find the reason he didn't answer is because he's shagging some skirt," Rudd promised, "I'm going to circumcise him at the ears. Damn it to hell, anyway! Here we are busting our butts to get it all together on this end and I'm told he's even sent Frenchy off on some wild goose chase with the national police. What the hell was he thinking?"

"This is not about Blieu, is it?" White asked.

For a moment White thought he was too soon, for Rudd turned to snap back a blazing retort. Yet his snarl died before the words were out of his mouth. Taking a deep breath, he let it out, then took one more. "Shit!" he sighed, letting it out slowly. "No, it's not. That was just the last straw and that asshole at the embassy didn't help." He pointed at the letter he had just slammed down on the desk. "Self important prick! Who does he think he is writing shit like that to me about one of my best officers?" Then he glared at White. "Don't you dare tell Denis I said that!"

"I wouldn't presume to," White grinned. "His head is big enough already." He frowned. "That was not the only thing, I gather."

"No," Rudd glared. "While you and the guys were out playing fun and games today I got a call on the horn from a couple of congressmen. How they got our number here I don't know, but the Senator is working on it from that end." He frowned. "At least, they claimed to be congressmen and they sounded like it, too. Didn't like it much when I wouldn't answer their questions over an open line. Or when I wouldn't tell them who I was." He shook his head. "It always amazes me how a fool thinks the sun shines out his ass once he's elected to office."

"Or how loose a grasp of reality they have," White agreed. "The Senator is an exception."

"Even the Senator has his moments," Rudd smiled.

White laughed. "I'll never forget the day you asked him how we were supposed to defend his sorry ass with a rusty musket and no powder or shot."

"Nor will I," Rudd chuckled. "But he came around. He came around." He frowned. "You know, Alex, I really am beginning to get worried about Denis and Jacques Paul," he said. "It must have been pretty serious for him to take off without letting us know what was up."

White shrugged. "Well, the transmission was garbled. And we may not have gotten the whole picture. Has the Senator gotten anything through the diplomatic pouch?"

Rudd shook his head. "That's part of the problem. I can't raise the Senator, either. His assistant is giving out that he's fishing somewhere in Florida and can't be reached until next week, but I don't like it. He knows we are in the middle of mounting a major operation and you'd think he'd let us know where to reach him." He shrugged. "I would."

"Yeah, but you're military," White reminded him. "For all his good work on our behalf, the Senator is still a civilian. They don't have the same sense of urgency."

"No shit!" Rudd replied. Then his face changed and White knew a decision was near. "So what do you think, Alex? I think we need to move ahead with this thing or stand down."

The executive nodded. "I agree we need to shit or get off the pot. We've kept things on hold as long as we can and if we keep training much more, our men will lose their edge. I don't like moving ahead without our advance men knowing we're on the way, but I'd say let's go."

The Commander nodded and looked at his watch. "I agree. Final gear check tomorrow at reveille and move out." He grinned. "The weather being what it is between here and there, we better fill them up tonight and not feed them again until we hit on the ground."

12. Discovery

"Well, I'll be damned!" Jacques Paul exclaimed softly. "The sneaky sons-a-bitches!" He continued to peer through the high powered field glasses. "That truck just disappeared into the side of the mountain but thcy have some kind of camouflage rigged to hide the entrance. Whoever came up with this really knew what he was doing." He gave the glasses to Pico who handled them awkwardly before getting them set to his eyes. "See how they disguised the road as a turn-around in a mining camp? I bet those three buildings around it are either phony or set up to hide their radio antennas."

Pico handed the glasses back and pointed off to their right at another high ridge. "Two men up there, just under that big white rock," he whispered, putting a finger to his lips. "Watchers."

Jacques Paul looked through the glasses where Pico had pointed. "Yeah, I see them now," he said quietly." You think they spotted us?"

"No," Pico answered simply. "They can't see the trail we came up from where they are. But there may be others. Maybe on this same ridge."

The other glanced at him in surprise, then looked left and right and nodded. "Further down hill, I'd think," he whispered. "We're still pretty far away." Digging through his rucksack Jacques Paul took out a spiral notebook and an ordinary yellow pencil and started sketching what he could see in the notebook, creating a rough, but accurate map of the area.

Pico watched him for a moment, then whispered, "I'll go to find the other watchers. I'll be back in twenty, maybe thirty minutes." Jacques Paul nodded as he continued outlining the phony mining camp, glancing at his watch and then looking up only to note the position of the buildings and the topography of the area around them, and carefully noting his own position when the map was drawn, as well as the position of the watchers. This took him almost fifteen minutes, and when he was done sketching he took out a compass and noted the direction of magnetic north and the vectors. Satisfied with his work, he checked the time, then carefully wrapped the notebook in oil cloth before replacing it in the rucksack and sat down to wait.

Jacques Paul was reaching for a cigarette when a brown hand clamped his arm. "No!" hissed an urgent whisper in his ears, and even as he started to react, he relaxed. It was Pico. "No smoke," said the guide. "The others are very close." Then he gestured urgently for Jacques Paul to follow and the two men silently made their way back down the path they had followed.

Thirty minutes later, Pico called a halt. "You can smoke now," he said in a quiet normal voice. "We are almost two miles from them now and the wind is blowing from their direction."

"I didn't even think about that," Jacques Paul said, shaking his head. "How far away were they?"

"Fifty yards, maybe sixty," Pico grinned. "There's a better spot to watch from just down the hill from where we stopped."

The other's eyes widened at the news. "Damn!" he said, absently reaching for a cigarette and a match. "We were very lucky we didn't walk right into them." He started to light the cigarette, but paused. "I never thought about someone smelling the smoke. How far can you smell it?"

"With the wind right, a mile away," Pico answered. "Even when they're not smoking, out here I can smell them ten yards away. More if the wind is right. That's how I knew where they were. One of them is a smoker."

This explained a great deal to Jacques Paul. "You mean in the dark you can smell me ten yards away?" he asked. Pico nodded and Jacques Paul replaced the unlit cigarette into its packet. "I think I'd better wait until I get back to town," he said and Pico grinned.

"Unless you want to look around here some more, it won't make any difference. There's a third ridge you couldn't see to your right and there is another set of watchers there, too." Pico looked at him placidly, waiting for an answer.

"No," the officer decided. "I think I have all we need for the moment. I don't see how we can get much more information without going inside or staying here and watching for a long while. To get near the place we'd have to go in at night." He thought a moment. "Is there any way we can check out that site on the coast, too? How long would that take?"

"Four days," Pico replied promptly. "Then three more days to Pisco." He shrugged. "Hard days," he added. "With bad weather it will take more."

"Damn, I hate to go a week without getting this information back," Jacques Paul frowned. "How far are we from Pisco now?"

"We can make it to Pisco by noon the third day, if we start right now," Pico answered. "Unless we head north and get lucky and get a ride. Then two days, maybe less."

Jacques Paul thought a moment. "What's important is getting the information to Denis Blieu at the embassy in Lima. You could take it there and I could go on and check out the other site."

"That's not a good idea," Pico advised, shaking his head.

"Why not?" Jacques Paul demanded, but Pico only stared at the ground. Jacques Paul started to probe, then stopped and chuckled. "I see. You mean that by myself I would have walked into a trap today don't you?"

Pico looked at him and shrugged. "Maybe not."

"No, you're right," the American said. "Out here I don't know the lay of the land. I'm literally a babe in the woods. I don't know what I could expect to find there, anyway, except maybe some more watchers, too. We'll check it out later." He picked up his pack. "Let's head for Pisco."

Yet Pico nodded but didn't move. The other looked at him in question. "What?" he asked.

"Don't you want to smoke now?" the guide asked. "It may be quite a while to our next stop if you want to make good time."

"No," answered his companion, grinning. "I'm beginning to think it's a habit I can't afford. Not if the bastards can smell me coming."

Rosario screamed at the sight of the gun and tried to run back into the house but the native man behind the European shoved past him and grabbed her, flinging her to the floor. "Please!" Rosario cried to the man on top of her. "Don't hurt me. I wasn't trying to run away! He was trying to rape me."

The only response her words drew from the native man were a growl. "Stay down!" he ordered her and rolled to one side. Somewhere above her she heard someone shout, "Put it down!" in English and then another voice, the same in Spanish. Then there was a yell and a scurrying sound followed by a shot, then so quickly by another the explosions sounded almost like one.

"*Madre a Dios,*" Rosario moaned burying her head in her arms. "Don't let them hurt my baby."

"I'll watch him," the European said in curiously accented Spanish. "You check the woman."

A moment later a strong hand reached down and shook her shoulder. "Are you hurt?" a voice asked in Spanish. There was no mistaking the concern in the voice.

Rosario looked up, saw a face she recognized. "Juan!" she cried, grabbing Sergeant Gomez around the neck and throwing him off balance. His pistol clattered against the floor as he put a hand out to keep from falling.

The other man chuckled. "I think she's glad to see us," he said in his curious accent. Then his voice changed to concern. "Are you hurt?" he asked Rosario, helping Gomez up.

Rosario flushed. "No," she said sitting up. Then to Gomez she added, "I'm sorry. I didn't mean to ... I mean ... thank you!" she stammered. Gomez took her by the hand and helped her to her feet.

"You're more than welcome," Gomez replied, looking into her eyes with a startled expression. "I am glad you aren't injured." He seemed reluctant to release Rosario's hand.

"I am, too," the other man said. "Perhaps you don't remember me," he added. "I'm Denis Blieu. I'm a friend of Paul's. From the embassy."

"Pablo!" Rosario cried. "Where is Pablo? We need to warn him."

"We don't know," Blieu told her. "But he's with Pico and we have two other good people looking for him. So don't worry. I'm sure he must be all right."

"Here," Gomez spoke, pulling a chair up for her to sit in. "Why don't you sit for a moment. You've had a bad shock."

Rosario nodded and sat. Then her eyes fell on the rough man lying crumpled against the far wall. Blood was seeping out the front of his shirt and his head was thrown back at an odd angle. "Ai!" cried Rosario, remembering. "The padre! What happened to the padre?"

"The padre's fine," Gomez assured her. "I saw him just yesterday morning at the hospital."

"Complaining like mad, too," Blieu chuckled, "so he can't be too bad off."

Rosario nodded dumbly, trying to take in everything she'd been told. Then she felt her head spinning and heard Blieu shout, "Look out! She's going into shock." After that she felt Gomez's strong hands catch her, lift her gently to rest, cover her with a blanket. As the darkness came over her Rosario thought how good those strong, gentle hands felt holding her up.

Juan Calderon was not simply complaining. He was truly angry. Nor was he reluctant to let the world know it in general, or Sister Carmelita, in particular. "You wicked man," she scolded him after his last tirade. "What kind of priest are you? Priests aren't supposed be like this! What kind of example are you to your flock?"

"Priests aren't supposed to be held prisoner by ugly nuns, either!" the old man snapped back. An instant after he said the words he wished he could call them back, for the good sister threw up her hands and fled the room in tears. "I didn't mean ugly looking, sister," he shouted after her. "I only meant ugly acting. Truly." Yet there was no response. "Jesus, Joseph and Mary!" he sighed, leaning back onto his pillows. Now he'd have to apologize, and the thought aggravated him even more.

"I see you're feeling pretty good, young fellow," a familiar voice greeted him from the doorway. "Good enough to raise hell, anyway."

"Pablo!" the old man cried. "And is that Pico behind you? Goodness, you don't know how glad I am to see a friendly face."

"I gather you don't many friends left here," Radford chuckled, shaking the old man's hand warmly. "Didn't you once tell me never to bite the hand of kindness?"

"Yes, of course," the old man admitted baldly. "But this isn't kindness. This place is worse than being in jail. They boss me around and won't let me do what I need to do."

Radford looked at Pico. "In other words, they won't let him have his way, right?" Pico grinned and nodded as he stepped up to the bed to shake the old man's hand.

"Rosario was right," the guide said. "He must be getting well if he's so being so grumpy."

Juan Calderon put on a hurt face. "Rosario, too!" he cried raising his hands to the heavens. "What is an old man to do?"

Radford laughed. "Well, for starters, why don't you get up out of that bed and get dressed? Your doctor says you can go home." He chuckled. "As a matter of fact, I have the distinct impression they will be glad to see you go." He stepped across the room and opened the closet, but it was empty except for one of Rosario's baskets.

"*Gracias a Dios!*" the padre cried, whipping back the covers and swinging his feet to the floor. He began putting on his shoes, which were already by the bed.

"What are you doing already dressed?" Radford asked. Then a suspicious frown crossed his features. "You were trying to sneak out of here, weren't you?" he demanded. "That's what your cross words with the sister were all about, no?"

Juan Calderon shook his head. "You don't understand," he protested. "She didn't even want me to break wind without asking her permission!" He began to gather up his things in an old suitcase he fished from under the bed.

"If you think she's bad, wait until you get home," Radford laughed, taking the suitcase in one hand and firmly gripping the padre's arm with the other. He was surprised when the old man did not protest his helping. Nor did Juan Calderon object when Pico fell into step on the other side, taking his other. "You'll be lucky if Rosario lets you out of the house for a month!"

"Well, at least I will be in my on bed," the old priest grumbled. "Just a moment," he added as they passed the nurse's station. "I need to have a word with the sister. Alone," he added, gripping Radford's arm and directing him toward the supervisor's office, where he knocked quietly.

Ten minutes later Juan Calderon came out again, much abashed and leaning docilely on the sister's arm. As they left, the sister gave Radford and Pico a smile. "Take care of him," she said softly, kissing the old priest on the cheek.

"Goodness, I think it's true love," Radford murmured as they moved down the hall. Pico laughed and the padre gave him a strange look.

Dinner that evening at the rectory was a fiesta. Under the supervision of Rosario and Sergeant Gomez, repairs to the rectory had been completed the day before, and only a practiced eye could tell where these had been necessary. To celebrate the occasion, Blieu and Jacques Paul had driven the padre back to Pisco in an embassy car, along with Radford and Pico, and two other Americans newly arrived in Lima had driven down in another car with Captain Molina.

"Welcome home, padre," Rosario said happily, kissing him lightly on the cheek as they came in. "Why don't you rest a while in your favorite chair while we finish up?"

"To tell the truth, I'd like to lie down," the old man said. "The ride from Lima was more tiring than I thought it would be."

"Of course," Rosario replied. Then to Paul Radford she said, "Maybe having the fiesta tonight was not a good idea, after all."

"No, it wasn't," Radford agreed. "Why don't we just feed our guests and have it later. Christmas is only three weeks from now."

"No, no," replied Juan Calderon. "We have every reason to be thankful and we are indebted to our guests. No, I just need to rest a while and then we can celebrate. Please," he added, seeing their doubtful looks. "It is time to be joyful." He looked at them. "What day is it?"

"Saturday, padre," Radford answered. "But don't worry about mass tomorrow. The bishop will send someone else to scrve until you're feeling strong enough." He frowned. "We were expecting him by now, but I guess he's been delayed."

"No, I'll do the mass tomorrow," Juan Calderon said. "At least the first one. But that's not what I was asking. What day of the month is it?"

"The sixth, padre," Rosario answered, smiling. "That's why we thought it would be a good day for fiesta. It's the feast of St. Nicholas."

"Of course," the old man smiled. "All the more reason why we should celebrate. And it looks like such a nice night out. We can eat in the courtyard."

By common consent, there was no talk of war that night, and when the guest arrived three hours later, Juan Calderon was in fine form. Throughout their meal he entertained them with funny stories from the Mexican revolution, spicing his history with nuggets of gossip about the frailties of the leaders of the times, and as the party went on he seemed to gain strength. Then Denis Blieu asked if the piano he had seen in the sitting room was in tune and kept them going with his renditions of Scott Joplin's most famous songs. The piano was not that badly out of tune, except for one or two notes, and Blieu made the most of this, playing along flawlessly and pausing just enough before each clinker to call attention to it.

Yet when the party broke up in the early hours of Sunday morning, Juan Calderon was not there to send his guests off to the hotel. Three hours before, he had suddenly grown very tired and asked to be excused, insisting his guests continue with the celebration. Radford suggested they retire back to the courtyard for a nightcap of brandy and cigars, and it was only then the talk turned to the distant war which was never far from mind.

So it was that when the war came to Pisco, Paul Radford was asleep in the arms of Rosario Martinez. He awoke out of a deep sleep when the news burst on the sleepy port like a tidal wave and his first thought was that a revolt was taking place. Shots rang out in the market square, fired by two brothers walking home from their drunken Sabbath celebration, and the church bell took up the alarm as their third brother, who had forgotten to bring his pistol the night before, ran into the unlocked church and began to yank the bell rope vigorously.

Yet even as Radford was pulling on his pants, the bell ceased ringing. Within moments a soft knock came at the door and Juan Calderon stuck his head into the room. "A thousand pardons," he apologized gravely. "The news has just come. It is war. Your country was attacked earlier this morning by the Japanese, but there's no immediate danger."

Even though he had been expecting the news, the old man's words struck Paul Radford like the news of death in the family. "Damn!" he replied, sitting down on the side of the bed and clasping his head between his hands. "They finally did it," he added sadly. "They finally did it." Tears welled into his eyes and Rosario came around the bed quietly, sitting beside him and cradling him like a child.

"I'm afraid so, my friend," the priest said gently. "I'm afraid so. I'm going out to get more news but I think it would be best if you stayed inside until I get back." Radford nodded and the old man closed the door gently behind him. As he did, he heard Rosario saying something, but her words were to her lover and too soft for Juan Calderon to hear.

When Juan Calderon arrived back at the rectory thirty minutes later, Paul and Rosario were in the kitchen talking. Radford was seated at a small table against the wall drinking coffee while Rosario busied herself at the stove. While he was wearing trousers and shoes, the young man had not yet pulled on his shirt and the padre was struck by how gently domestic the two had become with one another. *All that will change now,* he thought. *All that will change because some stupid sons of witches could not be content with what they have and decided it was time to go to war.*

Then he remembered another time, a time when he himself had been one of those *hijos de brujas* who went to war tearing families apart and wrecking the domestic bliss of many scenes exactly like this. Not for the first time, nor the last, Juan Calderon stopped for a moment and whispered an Act of Contrition for all his personal sins against the simple joys of human being.

Though his prayer was brief and uttered within the silence of his heart, Paul Radford sensed his presence and turned toward the padre, a look of concern replacing the tranquillity of the moment before. "How bad is it?" he asked, even before the old man could speak.

"There is little more news than I heard before," Juan Calderon told him. "What I heard is that the Japanese attacked one of your naval bases in the Pacific."

"Pearl Harbor," the younger man said. "It has to be Pearl Harbor. That's all that makes sense. That's headquarters for the Pacific fleet. On Sunday morning, too." His face grew grim as he assessed the possibilities. "This could be very bad, padre," he said. "This could be disastrous if all our ships were in port. When did it happen?"

"I don't know," Calderon replied. "I was preparing for the late mass when that *boracho* began to ring the bell like he was crazy."

"What time is it now?" Radford asked. "It must be getting late."

"It's almost eleven-thirty now," the padre told him. Remembering his duties, he headed for the door. "I have to do mass now, but we can talk when I am done. Oh, yes, I ran into your friend Blieu when I went out. He and the other Americans will be here shortly." Shrugging an apology to Rosario he added, "I asked them to breakfast."

Rosario simply nodded but Radford spoke up. "Can I come, padre?" he asked. "I know I am not Catholic, but I like to if it's all right."

"Of course, my friend," the old priest answered gently. "Of course you can, and you can take communion, too, if you wish."

"I don't want to get you in trouble with your bishop....," Radford began.

Juan Calderon snorted. "I'm always in trouble with him, Pablo. Maybe not with God but always with the bishop. But I won't tell him if you don't, and I can assure you God doesn't mind."

"Thanks, Juan," Radford replied. There were tears in his eyes. Then he looked down at himself and grinned. "I guess I better put on a shirt first."

Rosario blushed and the old man laughed for the first time that morning. "It might be best." Then he laughed over his shoulder as he left the room. "There are still one or two of the faithful who might be scandalized. Or jealous."

There was little humor among the men who gathered in Manfred Schwartz's office at the German embassy late that morning. Aside from Rott and Weiss, and Schwartz himself, there were three other men present. One was the ambassador's personal secretary, another was the commander of the special base in the mountains, and the third was a submarine commander none of the others but Rott had met before. Under normal circumstances, the ambassador would have been present himself, but for some reason he could not be reached until much later in the day. Not knowing the Japanese were about to drag Germany into war with the United States, the ambassador had accepted a shooting invitation in a remote hunting lodge, one without a telephone, and someone had to be sent by car to carry the news.

"Those shit heads!" Rott expostulated. Of all those present, he was the most upset by the news. "Those complete shit heads! What in the world were they thinking? How do they think they can even hope to conquer America?"

"Well, they've taken most of Asia," the commander of the base pointed out. "Now they command the whole Pacific."

"Which means they are stretched thin as a ribbon!" Rott snapped. "Now their reach has exceeded their grasp by a long measure."

179

"Why are you so upset, Jergen?" Schwartz asked. "We knew war with America was coming."

"We knew it was a possibility," Rott corrected him. "But there was a lot of sentiment in America against it. We had a chance of putting it off indefinitely, or if we were going to do it, to pick our own time. Now those honorable shit heads have dragged us into a war we are not ready to meet. We are already fighting on two fronts."

"The Americans are already supplying the Russians and the English," the submarine commander pointed out. "I don't see what difference this makes, Rott. Personally, it means I have a great deal more latitude in choosing my targets."

"War materiel is one thing," Rott responded. "Manpower is another. So is industrial production. Do you have any idea of how many million fully equipped troops the United States can put into the field? As well as supplying their allies?"

There was silence in the room after Rott's challenge. It was Schwartz who finally broke it. "Well, regardless of all that," he said in a calm voice, "the fact is that the United States will very likely be our enemy within a matter of days. What we need to think about here is what effect this may have on what we are doing here, and how we need to respond. I think the starting place is where we are with the building of our hidden bases. Colonel?"

"As far as our construction goes, I would have to agree with Rott," a tall, thin officer answered. "We are well ahead of our time table, and are almost operational now, but we are only about eighty percent completed with the whole project." He shrugged. "Of course, some of what we have on the table is not absolutely necessary."

"When will you be operational?" Rott asked.

"Six weeks," the colonel answered. "Maybe as little as four if our deliveries are not delayed, or as much as eight weeks if they are. This new development may slow things down. Not from our end," he added quickly, "but from the other. We have no control over that."

Rott nodded and thought a moment. The others waited quietly. While he was not the ranking officer in the room, there was no question of his sway on any decisions they might make. His was the position which pulled them all together, and the force of his personality had affected every man there. All had a healthy respect not only for Rott's organizational abilities, but even more for his capacity for sudden violence. He looked at the colonel who had just spoken. "What about the security of the project? Have you had any indication of anyone showing interest in what is going on there?"

The colonel shook his head. "There has been nothing within the sector to indicate it. There have been a few planes over the area in the last three months, but none of them directly over us. Nor have our scouts found any tracks along the trails inside the sector. And Lima seems to accept it as another mining operation, but I believe you would know more about that than I do."

Rott nodded. "How about outside the sector? Have any of your scouts found anything there? Any unexplained activity."

The colonel shrugged. "Signs work both ways. Too many tracks would point to our presence. So except for occasional excursions, I have instructed our scouts to stay within the sector." He shrugged. "At least, within visual sight of the camp."

Rott was quiet. "How long has it been since someone has surveyed the area outside?"

The colonel thought a moment. "Six weeks. Maybe a bit longer. With the warm weather coming on it's about time for another."

"I would think so," Rott remarked dryly. He turned to the submarine commander. "How about in your area, Captain? Any unusual activity?"

The commander shook his head. "Aside from a few fishing boats, my lookouts have not spotted much at all." He shrugged. "These are the same boats which have been there from the beginning and they follow predictable routes. None have shown much interest in the area at all and there have been no aircraft at all in the three weeks."

"There were before?" Rott asked, surprised.

"On two occasions, but those were assessed as training flights gone off course," the commander told him. "The markings were Peruvian military and the pilot seemed to be following the coast to find his way back to Lima." He chuckled. "The watchers reported the handling of the aircraft was rather inept."

A ripple of humor went around the room, but Rott was not smiling. "Why wasn't this reported?" he asked in an ominously quiet voice. The ripple ended abruptly.

"It was," the officer replied. "You were not here so I informed Herr Schwartz."

The former professor nodded to confirm this. "I meant to let you know, Jergen," he said, "but we had more pressing matters at hand and it slipped my mind. It was of no consequence."

Rott disagreed, but let it ride. He would deal with Schwartz later. "Very well. Is there anything of consequence I'm not aware of?" he asked as he looked around the room from man to man, but the others only shook their heads in answer. "All right, then," Rott said. "Keep me informed. If there is nothing else, Herr Schwartz, Johan and I need to take care of a few details right away." He glanced at his watch. "Why don't we take a short recess and meet back here in a half hour?"

"An excellent suggestion," Schwartz agreed. Rott's asperity was not lost on him. "I'll ask the cook to send in something for us to eat while we talk."

There was little humor among the men who gathered around the padre's dining table in Pisco that afternoon, either. All the Americans had returned and Blieu made a special point of making sure Captain Molina was included. "I asked Captain Molina to be present as a representative of his country," Blieu told the others. "Not in an official capacity," he continued quickly as Molina started to object, "but simply to let him know what is going on and to ask his opinion on how certain proposals might be received by his government. I have also asked Father Juan to use the rectory so this meeting remains unofficial. Fair enough?" he asked the captain and the policeman nodded. What was curious to Molina was that Blieu was leading the meeting even though he was not the senior American officer present.

"We are not at war with Germany at this point," Blieu continued, "but we will be in a matter of days. I don't know how it will work, but I imagine Germany will declare war on us once we declare war on Japan. At that point our position here will change since Peru will be a neutral nation at that point. The problem is that Germany has apparently set up two secret bases within this country, one in the mountains and one at sea, but within the territorial waters of Peru. We are not that concerned about the mountain base, but we believe the sea base will be used for submarine operations against shipping coming out of the Panama Canal. Normally we would simply report the existence of the base to the authorities and encourage them to make sure it never becomes operational. As a neutral nation, it would be their duty to do so."

Blieu paused, took a drink of water. "What puts a kink in things is that we know there are certain elements in the national government which are very sympathetic to the Germans." He shrugged. "This is understandable given the large German population here. My concern is that these elements friendly to Germany might successfully thwart any efforts to move against the base, and a number of them are in the official capacities which would make it easy to do so without officially siding with Germany." He looked at Captain Molina. "Is this a fair assessment?"

Molina thought for a moment, then nodded without speaking. Blieu shook his head and continued. "This means that if we are to make any response to the situation, we must do so without overtly violating Peru's sovereignty. My thought is that it would be best to act in a way which would neutralize the German supporters in the government without doing something so outrageous it would cause Peru to break off diplomatic relations with us." He looked at Molina. "Are you comfortable with that, Captain?"

"Within limits," Molina answered noncommittally. "Nothing you have suggested violates the law."

"With that limitation in mind," Blieu said, "that we stay within the framework of the law, we probably need to confer among ourselves and come up with a course of action. What I would suggest is that we reconvene at the embassy this evening and come up with specific plans. What I need to know is if we can count on your keeping what you have learned about the German operations to yourself, Captain? Would doing so put you in an untenable position with your government?"

The policeman thought for a moment. "No," he decided. "At this point I have no real knowledge of these things, only information I have been given. I will have to investigate it, of course, but I am sure there are many other things on my desk which are more pressing at the moment. One of which is catching the culprits behind the shooting of Father Juan. I expect it will be at least two weeks before I can get to the other matter." He smiled. "One must admit, after all, that rumors of secret bases in the middle of nowhere sounds a bit far fetched." Then he frowned. "On the other hand, I think you understand how I would be most offended if my trust were abused."

"Thank you, Captain," Commander Rudd spoke for the first time. "It has been a pleasure meeting you and I appreciate your candor. I give you my personal assurance we will do nothing to embarrass you or your government and Commander Blieu will make every effort to keep you informed."

13. Acts of War

When the following story appeared in the December 22, 1941, issue of a number of American newspapers, only a few of the larger regional papers carried the story at all. Even where it was carried, it was overshadowed by news of American involvement in what had become a world war. The *New York Daily Times* buried it on a back page inside the third section and there were few readers who understood the significance of the story, or that the incident represented the first American victory of World War II.

> ***Lima, Peru (UPI).*** *Peruvian officials are still investigating the strange explosion of an American cargo ship loaded with nitrates in territorial waters about seventy miles south of the fishing village of Pisco. Initial reports indicated a fuel leak into the main guano hold may have resulted in spontaneous combustion, but analysis of the wreckage indicates more than one ship was involved. Two of the bodies recovered in the wreckage were seamen wearing the uniform of the German submarine service, and the rest remain unidentified. Yet all the members of the cargo ship's crew escaped unharmed in life boats before their ship went down. They were recovered by another passing cargo ship two days after the explosion and taken to the port of Callao where they were questioned by officials of the Peruvian National Police.*
>
> *One unidentified police official, who spoke only on the condition of anonymity, has suggested the explosion may have been set off when the American cargo ship collided with a German submarine partially submerged under a rather strong sea, rupturing the fuel tank of the ship and killing the entire German crew. Crew members on the cargo ship report hearing only a single loud crash and two minor explosions before the order was given to abandon ship. Luckily for the crew, their boats were well away from the ship*

*before the main hold exploded, breaking the vessel in
two and sending it to the bottom.*

*Even so, many questions remain unanswered and
the Department of the Navy is investigating whether
the first crash and explosions were caused by a faulty
German torpedo....*

"Well, how does it feel to be an unidentified police official,
Captain?" Denis Blieu asked Molina as he and Paul Radford sat in
Molina's office in Lima. He had just read the news story aloud.

"I imagine it feels like being an unnamed investigator for your
Department of the Navy," Molina told him. "Even so, it is better than
being identified and finding oneself on the ... hot chair?"

"Hot seat," Blieu answered, nodding. "I quite agree. Anonymity
has its, ah, consolations." He took a sip from his cup of tea. "I gather
you are not experiencing any repercussions from the incident, then?"

"Not at all," Molina answered. "My superiors are convinced a
German submarine attacked your cargo ship and somehow got caught
in the explosion or accidentally blew itself up. There seems to be a
great deal of confusion how this might have happened, but there is no
particular pressure to find out."

"Even though it happened in your territorial waters?" Blieu
asked. "I would think that would raise a question of violation of
sovereignty. Perhaps put the Germans in a bad light."

Molina nodded. "Yes, but there is enough ambiguity that it is not
certain this was a violation of our territory. The crew was not picked
up for almost two days and even though the wreckage was in our
waters, it could have drifted there, too." He shrugged.
"Unfortunately, this makes it easy for the *politicos* to ignore the
violation."

"Damn!" the other answered. "The base was within two miles of
shore, and we obviously scored a direct hit. It's a shame it worked
out like this."

"I am curious about two things," Molina told him. "One is how
you found a ship to use so soon. There was not time to bring one
down from the north and no record of one being purchased anywhere
near here. I personally checked."

Blieu looked at the policeman gravely. "Do you really want to know, Captain. I know we agreed to be completely candid, but I would hate to put you in an awkward position."

Molina considered this for a moment, then shrugged. "Perhaps I do not want to know specifics, and certainly not officially. Perhaps you could speculate how it might have happened. I think that would be sufficient, Lieutenant."

Blieu nodded. "The whole thing is rather curious, isn't it? Yet I can think of several possibilities of how a ship might be available on short notice. One is that a ship full of nitrates was going north toward the Panama Canal and was turned around and diverted south. That would seem almost too lucky. Another is that a ship was standing by off shore and was diverted from its original purpose to use here, which seems far more probable." He shrugged. "Another is that an American ship was available at just the right time and had just taken on a load of guano from Chile, but that is definitely too coincidental. The most probable explanation is that things were set in motion to cover a number of possibilities a lot earlier than you might imagine, and that things simply came together at the right moment. Take your pick."

Molina nodded. "Any of the nitrate theories would work with the destruction of two ships. On the other hand, if a policeman thought there was an underwater base destroyed, he would have to think the American ship was filled almost to sinking with dynamite to do such damage."

Blieu nodded. "It could have been loaded to the gills with depth charges which spread over a wide area before exploding, too. This might mean it was one originally scheduled to arrive in Pearl Harbor about now and diverted for a specific purpose."

"That would explain the massive number of fish washing up on the beach," Molina said. "It is very fortunate, perhaps, that where they washed up was a very desolate area."

"Yes, it was, wasn't it?" Blieu agreed. "Imagine them washing up in a populated area. The stink would be incredible." Blieu looked at the captain narrowly. "I gather the degree of destruction was your second question."

"The stink would be unfortunate, indeed," Molina nodded. "But to answer your question, no. The other thing which made me curious was how the base might have been located."

"Captain, I honestly do not know myself," Blieu answered. "Nor do I want to know. I think perhaps it is better not to know certain specifics."

"Perhaps," Molina replied. "Or perhaps not. I don't know. What I do know is that things have not changed much here. Despite the incident there remains the same dilemma as before."

The other frowned. "You were serious when you said the indecent could be easily ignored in official circles, weren't you?"

"Yes," the captain answered sadly. "What must be demonstrated is a flagrant violation of our national sovereignty. Just how that might be done at this point, I can only imagine."

"I see," Blieu said quietly. He sat quietly for a moment, thinking. "What if one could establish that the Germans had built a secret military base within your country, that would be sufficient, right?"

"Yes, it would probably take something that outrageous," Molina replied. "At this point, however, I would have to have something more substantial than rumors to initiate an investigation. There would have to be solid evidence in my hands before I could act."

"What sort of evidence would your need?" Blieu asked. "We can get photographs. Maybe we can intercept their radio signals, but we'd certainly have to break whatever code they're using. The point is, all of this will take a lot of time."

Paul Radford spoke up for the first time. "I think you are making things more complicated than they need to be," he said to Blieu. Turning to Molina he asked, "Captain, what if you yourself came up with such evidence in your investigation of another crime? Wouldn't that be enough?"

"Yes, it would, but what other crime would I be investigating?" the captain responded.

Radford grinned. "Why, Captain, have you forgotten so soon? I was attacked by bandits up in the mountains several weeks ago and you have done nothing about it. Not that I am complaining," he added quickly. "You've had a great number of things on your list, but surely a bandit gang is worth looking into."

Molina game him an ironic smile. "As I remember, Mr. Radford, you were confused as to the exact place where it happened."

"Yes, sir," Radford told him. "However, over the last couple of weeks I've been going over maps of the area. I think I know exactly where it was and I believe Pico and I were not far from there when I got sick this last trip out."

"Ah," said Molina, nodding. "I see. Well, perhaps I will have to look into it, after all."

"We would be glad to help," Blieu interjected.

Molina gave him a puzzled look. "What are you suggesting, Lieutenant?"

"Well, if there is a criminal gang up there you may need some firepower," Blieu explained. "As it happens, we have a special security team guarding the embassy and I would be glad to arrange for them to help you out."

"I don't think so," Molina shook his head. "That could get us into sticky water."

Blieu blinked at the metaphor, but recovered without laughing. "Please, Captain, hear me out. The commander was saying just the other day his men were getting stale hanging around the embassy. He's planning to take them out on a training exercise, anyway. Why not do him a favor and take him with you? Would that be in order?"

"They are soldiers, Blieu, not policemen," the other answered. "That's the problem. They are foreign soldiers. This is an internal police matter."

"What if they were military police?" Blue countered. "What if we were engaged in a joint training exercise. Would that make a difference?"

Molina reflected for a moment, then nodded. "It might, but a formal request would have to come from your ambassador to my minister. The problem is this will take more time than we may have."

"Would it hurt to try?"

"I suppose not," Molina answered. "But it would have to be clearly understood that your men were under my direct command and that of Sergeant Gomez. Just like before." He was far from convinced.

Blieu jumped at the chance before the policeman could back away. "Agreed," he said. "The request will be on your minister's desk before the day is out. How should I word it to ease things along?"

Molina leaned back in his chair and was quiet for a couple of minutes. Then he began to speak while Blieu took notes. Ten minutes later the Lieutenant and Radford were on their way to the embassy, and an hour later Foreign Officer Rea found himself on his way to the Minister of Justice with a special request from the United States of America. Along with the request was an envelope containing five thousand dollars in cash intended to "compensate the government of Peru for any expenses which might arise." Rea's instructions on the exact phrasing of this in Spanish were quite explicit. There must be no intimation of a bribe being offered, only compensation from one sovereign state to another. What the official chose to do with the money, of course, was his business.

The next day a courier arrived at the American embassy bearing a written invitation from the Minister of Justice. The language was flowery but the message was simple. The security team from the embassy was invited to participate in a training exercise with the Peruvian National Police, at a time and place to be arranged to their mutual convenience. To arrange this, would the leader of the security team be so kind as to get in touch with Captain Molina of the Peruvian National Police?

The raid on the mountain base took place under the conditions Captain Molina had dictated. The only change was the decision to leave Sergeant Gomez in Pisco, where he could not only keep an eye on Juan Calderon and Rosario, but could also give the impression the police were about their normal duties. Radford suggested it might be better if Gomez stayed at the rectory rather than the police station and was surprised when Juan Calderon spoke against this. Molina agreed with the old priest and Gomez assured the young man he would keep a particularly careful watch.

Since there were three watch posts, and possibly more, it was decided the raid would take place just before first light. "That is when the human body is at it's lowest ebb," Commander Rudd explained, and that is when the guards will be least alert. They'll probably have a change of guard right after dawn so we need to get in an hour before that."

There was some debate whether or not to take out the watch posts first, but Molina overruled that. "We would have to split up our team too much for that," he said. "Since their are only eight of us, and who knows how many of them, we will take out the post Pico found first. Then two men can remain there to cover our line of retreat. I suspect we may find other watchers closer to the base."

"I imagine we will, Captain," Alex White spoke up. "What worries me is going in not knowing what may be there. They may have trip wires and mines set up."

"I don't think so," Jacques Paul broke in. "Their whole strategy is based on secrecy. There's too much chance of a trip wire mine being set off by wild animals or even someone wandering by. That would call attention to the place."

"Why don't we just follow the road in?" Paul Radford asked. "The one the trucks use. I know it sounds dumb, but we're supposed to be a police unit. Isn't that the way a police force would go in?" He looked at Molina, who nodded but said nothing.

"Yeah, but that's where other watchers are more likely to be," Rudd told him. "We might as well send them a telegram that we're coming."

"Well, maybe that's what we should do," Alex White suggested. Seeing the look on his boss' face he laughed. "No, I ain't gone bonkers, sir. Let me tell you what I have in mind." He quickly outlined a very simple plan and when he was done the others nodded.

"It just might work," Rudd said. "But I think Captain Molina has to make the call here. It's his neck on the block along with Radford's." He looked at the policeman.

"I don't think there's that much risk," Molina answered. "I am not just a policeman, I am a captain of the police and if anything happened to me they know it would be investigated. Particularly if I have a foreign national with me. The last thing they want to do is to call attention to themselves or antagonize my government."

"I don't know, Captain," Gomez said. "The foreign national is a citizen of an enemy. After losing their submarine base they may be getting desperate."

"And desperate people do desperate things," Molina nodded, finishing the thought. "Even so, it is better than discovering a trip wire the wrong way. I believe if he is under my protection it will be all right."

"If you were investigating bandits, wouldn't you have a couple of soldiers with you?" Rudd asked. "Don't you have someone you trust?"

"Under normal circumstances, yes," Molina told him. "However, Gomez is the only one who I trust completely. And this is a very delicate situation."

"I have a suggestion," Jacques Paul broke in, and within minutes strategy was revised.

"As long as they don't shoot us right off we ought to be all right," Molina said when they were done. He stretched and looked at his watch. "When can your team be ready, Commander?"

"An hour ago," Rudd assured him. "I put them on alert before I came here."

"Excellent!" said Molina. He wrote down some simple directions and an address. "This place is easy to find. Meet me there in an hour and we'll get started." He looked at Radford. "For appearances I think you should travel with me. Pico can travel with the rest of the team."

"All right," murmured Captain Molina. "Here we go. Slow down and stop twenty feet from them." It was two days later and two armed men had just stepped out of the brush into their path, rifles cradled in their arms. Corporal Jack Yellowhawk, USMC, was driving the Peruvian Army truck and Radford was seated between Molina and the driver. Slouched on benches in the back of the truck were two other Marines from the Special Action Group, armed with Thompson submachine guns and Colt .45 automatic side arms, and everyone but Radford was dressed in police fatigues.

Captain Molina stood upright in the open top cab of the truck as it rolled to a stop and the two troops in back swung out of the truck, unslinging their machine guns and taking cover on either side of the road. The two armed men started bringing their rifles to bear, but Molina shouted, "Police! Put down your weapons!"

The two men looked at each other, then complied, stepping back from their weapons. Corporal Yellowhawk came out from behind the door where he was crouched, weapon in hand, and gathered up the rifles. Radford noticed he was careful not to get in the line of fire of either of the Marines behind him.

"Hey, sir," one of the men shouted in heavily accented Spanish. "We meant you no harm. We're just here to guard the road."

Molina climbed down from the truck and beckoned for Radford to follow. "Do either of these men look familiar?" he asked the American in Spanish, stopping in front of the men, but Radford shook his head. Turning to the men Molina demanded, "What's up here that's worth guarding?"

"A mining operation, sir," said the man who had spoken before. "There has been some trouble with things being stolen."

"Ah," said Molina, who looked at the other man. "What's the matter with you?" he demanded.

"Please, sir, he doesn't speak Spanish," the first man replied. "We are foreigners."

"Foreigners! Let me see your papers!" Molina demanded, and the first man translated for the second. When he did he spoke German. Both reached for their breast pockets and pulled out identical documents. From where Radford stood, the documents looked like passports, or perhaps identity cards, but he couldn't tell if they were military or not.

Molina scanned the documents. "So you are German citizens," he said. "I take it you are civilians and not military people." He stared at them hard.

"Yes, sir," the first man said, looking uncomfortable. "We work for the mining company. Right now we are not needed so we were told to watch the road."

Molina nodded even though he knew the first statement was a lie. These men moved like soldiers and not civilians, particularly in the way they handled their arms. But he kept his knowledge to himself. "I see. How far is it up to the mine? I need to talk to the owner or the manager."

"He is not here right now, sir," the German told him. "Most of the others have gone into Lima and I guess I'm the one in charge." He translated for his companion, who nodded.

"Well, I'd like to see it anyway," Molina. "How far is it?"

"About one or two kilometers, I'd guess," the other told him. "The road winds around quite a bit. But there's really not much to see. Just two or three buildings and the shaft entrance." It was evident he did not want Molina investigating further, but there was not much he could do to prevent it.

"Well, your companion can stay here with my men," Molina insisted. "You come with me to show us the way and translate."

There was nothing to do but comply. The man spoke briefly to the other German, who tried to argue, but Molina cut them off. "Tell him not to try to contact the camp," he said suspiciously. "Something is not right here."

"Oh, no, sir, everything is in order," the first man protested. "It's just that we were given our orders and he is afraid of being discharged. And if you show up without us calling ahead, someone may shoot at you without knowing who you are."

"Tell him I will settle things with your boss," Molina said. "Well, you call ahead and tell them I will be coming that way shortly."

"What shall I tell them you are looking for, sir?" the guard wanted to know. "They will ask me."

"There have been reports of bandits operating out of this area," Molina told him. "We are looking for them." He looked at the sun, which was about to disappear over the horizon, and frowned. "It's getting close to dark," he said to Radford, who nodded.

"I was just thinking that," the younger man said. He had spotted the brief reflection from a mirror on the distant ridge, too. It was their signal that Rudd and company had taken the scout post Pico found and had them in sight. "It will be too dark for me to pick out land marks. Why don't we head for camp and come back tomorrow morning? Then we can check out the area beyond the mine, too. I really think that's where we need to look."

"That would be much better," the guard told them. His relief was evident. "Perhaps the *jefe* will be back by tomorrow afternoon and you can talk to him, too, if you wish."

Molina's frown deepened, but he seemed to be thinking it over. Then he nodded and walked back to the truck. He signaled the corporal, who holstered his automatic and laid the men's rifles on the ground. When he started the truck, the two flankers climbed in the back as he turned it around. "Expect us before mid-afternoon," Molina said to the guards as he climbed into the truck and the driver gunned the engine. "I will want to talk with your *jefe*."

"What about our papers, sir?" the first man called after then.

"I'll return your passports when I see you tomorrow," Molina shouted back over the roar of the truck's engine. "Ask me then."

Four hours later, Yellowhawk and one of the marines took the guards by surprise. Molina was glad to see these guards were different men than he had spoken to that afternoon. Nor was he surprised to find out they, too, held German passports. One of them was even carrying a military identification, too. "He's not on the embassy list," Molina whispered to the others. "So we are in the clear going in. Tie them up so they can't make a sound."

The second tier of guards was more difficult to find and the raiding party almost stumbled into a deadly trap. What alerted them was the smell of cigarette smoke, but even then the warning almost came too late. Only quick action by the three Marines prevented an ambush and silenced the guards before they sounded the alarm.

"There may be a third perimeter of pickets, too, sir," Yellowhawk told Molina quietly. "If it was me that's what I'd do."

"What about dogs?" Radford asked. To him the night sounded unnaturally quiet.

"Not likely," Molina told him. "They make too much noise, even when there is nothing to see." He glanced at the dial of his luminous watch. "We're still ahead of schedule, so go slowly."

Their caution was rewarded. Though there was no third perimeter of guards, there was a strand of barbed wire attached to a series of tin cans on either side of the road and Radford almost blundered into it before one of the Marines grabbed his arm and hissed a warning. From where they were standing they could see the opening in the camouflage netting which concealed the entrance to the base from the air. *More than likely*, Radford thought, *there are other guards there.*

A moment later the flare of a match to one side of the entrance confirmed his suspicion as the light evening breeze brought the rich, pungent smell of cigarette smoke. Suddenly Radford found himself consumed with a desire to smoke. It was all he could do to fight down the urge.

A moment later someone emerged from one of the darkened buildings and walked directly to the spot where the match flared. Sounds of an urgent, hushed conversation came to them on the wind before the glow of the cigarette blinked out and the shadow returned to the darkened building. *Someone just got his ass chewed,* Radford thought, smiling. *And for exactly the right reason.*

Then it occurred to him someone needed to take out the sergeant of the guard before anything else and he turned to look toward Yellowhawk. The same thought had apparently struck the corporal, and Radford could barely make him out moving toward the building where the shadow had returned. Paul Radford nodded to himself. *I'm glad he's on our side.*

Then Radford's attention was captured by Molina patting him on the arm. The captain held up two fingers and a thrill of tension spread through the young man's body. Two minutes. Rudd had made it, too, then, and the attack was about to begin.

Two minutes. One hundred and twenty seconds. The time crawled by so slowly Radford was sure something had gone wrong when one of the Marines slapped him on the boot. "Now!" the man hissed and they scrambled to their feet, charging toward the entrance of the camouflage. Even under the cover of darkness, Radford felt naked in the face of hostile fire. He found himself hoping whoever was to supposed to take out the guards had done their job.

Then they were under the camouflage and still no alarm had been given. Four other figures joined them in the darkness. Silently they crouched by the entrance of peering into the dim light coming from deep within the tunnel. Then one of the shadows gave a signal and two sappers began placing high explosives charges at the mouth of the tunnel.

"What are you doing?" Molina asked in a hoarse whisper.

"Shutting this sucker down just like we planned," Rudd answered. "Why? Don't you have enough evidence yet?"

Whatever answer Molina may have intended to make was drowned out by the staccato chatter of a machine gun raking the entrance to the tunnel. "Police!" Rudd shouted in Spanish as the members of the team scrambled for what little shelter there was. "Police! Stop your fire!" Yet the only response was a burst of machine gun fire in his direction. "Police!" Rudd shouted once again in the silence which followed, but the machine gun showered the ground above him, targeting his voice.

"That's evidence enough," Molina shouted, his voice filled with anger. "Take them out!"

Suddenly two explosions rocked the ground, almost simultaneous. One took out the building the shadow had emerged from, flattening the building next to it and igniting both. The other was not as loud, but silenced the machine gun.

"Good work, Delgado," Rudd murmured. "The bastard must have been in a pill box."

"To the rear!" a voice cried in English and Radford turned to see a dozen armed men running up the tunnel toward them. Flipping the switch of his Thompson to full automatic, Radford sprayed the tunnel and saw three men go down before the charge was broken. The others fell to the ground and started firing toward him. Bullets screamed off the rocks over his head.

"Keep them pinned down," Rudd ordered him. "We'll fall back and cover you. Ricochet!"

Turning his weapon toward the rocky side of the tunnel half the distance between himself and the men, Radford began firing short bursts, moving his aim along the wall as he did. Suddenly the metallic scream of ricochets was punctuated by a scream of human pain. One of his bursts had found a target.

"Move back, Radford!" Rudd ordered from behind him and he rolled to one side of the tunnel, crab crawling his way backwards and keeping as low as possible. Overhead he could hear the nasty snap of rounds going into the entrance to the tunnel.

Suddenly someone grabbed him in the ankle and jerked him back, pulling him into the shelter of a large mound of earth. "Fire in the hole!" he heard Yellowhawk cry out, and the man who had pulled him to safety pushed him down. A moment later an enormous explosion made the ground beneath him heave, and Radford found himself showered with debris.

"Damn, corporal," Rudd said in the silence which followed. "How much explosive did you use?"

"Not that much, sir," Yellowhawk said. "They must have had the entrance mined themselves."

"Shit!" said White. "That means we better get the hell out of here. If they mined the entrance like that, I bet the bastards have a hidden escape hatch somewhere else."

"I quite agree," Molina said, speaking up for the first time. "I certainly have evidence of a flagrant violation of our borders." He shook his head. "Machine guns!" he murmured, almost to himself. "How did they think they could get away with machine guns!"

"Would the gun they used help your case, sir?" the corporal asked.

"A military machine gun?" Molina replied. "That would be very hard evidence to deny."

"Back in a flash, sir," the corporal grinned and within a minute he was handing the policeman the twisted remains of what had been a precision instrument of death. "Not much left, is there?" he remarked. "But there ain't much denying it's German." Clearly marked on what had been part of the metal housing was the deep imprint of a swastika.

"Good work, corporal," said Molina. "Now I think we better leave."

The events in the days after that were a blur for Paul Radford. Rather than returning to Pisco, he was sent directly to Lima to make a statement. At Molina's insistence, he stayed over instead of leaving when that was done, and the embassy gave him the small room in the carriage house formerly used by one of their staff. While he was puzzled by this, and anxious to return to Rosario and Juan Calderon, he understood that Molina had his reasons and waited as patiently as he could. Writing Rosario and Juan Calderon, he promised to be there as soon as he could and hopefully in time to celebrate the traditional Christmas on January 6.

However, this was not to be. One complication followed another, and at the end of the first week Molina came to see him. "I believe you had better stay here for a while, my friend," the policeman advised him. "At least until things get sorted out. There are certain factions of the government who are trying to distort your role in the affair. The suggestion has been even made that you be arrested for the murder of the guide Quito."

"What?" said Radford. "I don't believe this. I was the one attacked, Captain. I came to you as soon as I could. The only delay was checking with the embassy to find out who I needed to report it to."

"I know that and you know that," the policeman replied. "Yet there are those who are determined to doubt it, and to raise doubt in the mind of others."

"I have a witness," Radford replied. "Pico was there and saw the whole thing."

"These same people would point out Pico is the village drunk," Molina reminded him. "They say he is more an accomplice than a witness." He shook his head. "You don't understand how angry these people are, Mr. Radford. Your presence was the catalyst that precipitated a crisis which laid all their plans to waste. They cannot reach Blieu and the others because of diplomatic status, but they can reach you if you leave the embassy."

"What about Pico?" Radford asked. "Isn't he in danger, too?"

"Not like you," the captain answered. "To them he is a minor player, of no significance. They might strike at him if they found him with you. However, Pico has been absent since the incident and it is very unlikely they will seek him out or even bother with him after a certain time has passed."

This was bitter news. Among other things it meant Radford could not go on working for his company and at Rudd's suggestion, he wrote them to let them know the Navy had placed him on active status. He also requested permission for Juan Calderon and Rosario to visit him at the embassy, but wiser heads advised against it. "That would put them in an awkward position, Paul," Alex White told him bluntly. "The last thing you want to do is for the people who want you to become interested in them."

"What do you mean?" Radford asked. "They already tried to get at me through her."

"That was the Germans," Blieu reminded him. "Who Alex is referring to is the people behind the Germans in the government. That is who Molina is concerned about. As long as your friends can appear as unwitting accomplices, Molina can protect them."

Radford did not like it, but there was nothing he could do about it. So he made himself useful and the time went by more quickly than he would have imagined. During the first days in residence he helped Blieu put together a report for the Senator and his colleagues, and after that he became Blieu's de facto secretary after the rest of the Special Action Group returned to the United States.

While the purpose of the mountain base remained a mystery, there was no question it was a military operation. The raiders recovered several military identification cards from the Germans killed in the raid, and these, with the wreckage of the machine gun salvaged by Corporal Yellowhawk were instrumental in shifting the balance of power in the national government. As a result, Peru joined with twenty other American nations convened in Brazil and on January 15, 1942, formally broke off diplomatic relations with the Axis nations. Even so, no formal declaration of war would be made by Peru until 1945 when the government wanted to join the newly formed United Nations.

Then on February 2, 1942, six weeks after the raid on the secret base, Paul Radford was quietly smuggled out of the country. Nor was he allowed to say goodbye. "You can write them from home," he was told. "But if you do, remember it could get them in trouble. Molina, too." Despite his protests, Denis Blieu was adamant about this and it took Paul Radford many years to completely forgive the man, even knowing he was completely right.

14. Casualties of War

The letter followed Paul Radford for over a year before it caught up with him, and it had been written some time before that. When it finally did he was stationed at the other end of the earth, trying to keep warm and keeping watch on the Russians across the Bering Straight while they kept an eye on him. The Navy, in all its wisdom, looked at his record and learned he was fluent in Spanish, German and Quecha, and decided they needed an intelligence officer in Nome, Alaska. Just why this decision was made was a mystery, unless the Navy expected an invasion spearheaded by Andeans.

At the same time, his military records mysteriously showed him on convalescent leave at home in Texas. So the letter was forwarded there, where it lay on the mantel of his parents' house while they waited word of his whereabouts. They knew he was alive from the heavily censored letters which arrived from time to time, but they had no idea where he was stationed or what he was doing. When Radford's father began beating official bushes for information about his son, a call came one day from the Senator. All he would tell Radford's parents was that Paul was alive and well and as safe as one could hope, but he emphasized to Mr. Radford that further inquiries might endanger his son. "I cannot tell you why this is the case, sir," the Senator said. "Your son is involved in very important work in the war effort. What that is I cannot tell you, but I can tell you this. Calling undue attention to him could certainly put him at risk."

The Radfords could do little else but wait and it was almost six months later before they saw their son again. So glad were they to see him, the letter remain forgotten until three days after Paul arrived. It was his mother who remembered it and she brought it to him on the verandah. "I'm sorry, Paul," she said. "I almost forgot. This came for you some time back but we didn't know where your were. I hope it isn't anything important. We thought about opening it to see but decided not to. It looks official."

"No," Radford laughed, seeing the familiar embassy envelope Blieu used to keep in touch. "It's just a friend from down south. I guess the Navy still has him poking around down there." Setting the letter aside for later reading, he forgot all about it until he was unpacking his bags back in Alaska. Seeing it, he poured himself a cup of coffee and settled back to enjoy Blieu's good natured bitching. The man's letters were often the bright spot in a dull and colorless week, and Radford wondered why it had not been sent to the right address. Surely Blieu knew where he was.

Opening the letter, he discovered it was not a letter from Blieu. There was a brief note from one of the people at the embassy telling him Captain Molina had brought by the enclosed envelope and had requested it be sent to Radford. Looking at the envelope he saw his name written in a fine Spencerian hand and recognized it as Juan Calderon's writing. Opening the envelope with trembling hands, he began to read the letter it held. *Dear Pablo,* it began and Radford felt tears coming to his eyes.

> *Today it seems an eternity has passed since your presence graced our lives here in Pisco. I understand the need for your silence, as Rosario does, and there are times the heaviness of your absence is almost overwhelming. Yet both of us appreciate what you are doing to protect us. Several times I tried to get your people in Lima to allow me to call or to work out a way of communication but always I was denied. Nor would anyone there accept the letters I wanted to leave, and even Captain Molina was reluctant to deliver this one. Yet there are two things I must tell you, and he finally agreed.*
>
> *The first is that you have a beautiful daughter now. You had left the country when she came into the world and Rosario named her Azul. I don't know the significance of the name, but she told me you would understand, and that is what I named her in the parish records when she was baptized. You are recorded as her father.*

The tears flooded down Radford's cheeks when he read this and he was forced to stop and wipe his eyes before he could continue reading. Then he smiled when he thought of how his mother would react to the news she was a grandmother. Once she gets over the initial shock, he thought, she'll love Rosario and Azul. Still smiling he picked up the letter to continue.

> *The other thing I have to tell you is painful. When she had waited for you for a year, Rosario came to me with a decision. Nor could I fault it. Since you and she were never officially married, she decided that for the well being of your child, and for her own sake, she would accept the proposal of marriage offered by Sergeant Juan Gomez.*
>
> *Pablo, I understand her decision. I am not long for this world and Rosario had no one in the world but me before you came along. On her own, she would have waited for you to the end of time, I believe, but you gave her a child without giving her or the child the protection of the law of her country or yours. And when your country took you away from us, there was no word, ever. Even though we knew you could not write for fear of placing us in danger, no one would tell us if you were alive or dead. Not even Blieu, and he was soon transferred south to Chile.*
>
> *My friend, I hope with all my soul you can find it in your heart to forgive Rosario for the hard choice she felt she had to make. And I hope you will forgive me for honoring that choice by uniting Juan and Rosario in marriage. There is no better father your child could have in your absence than Juan, and he has accepted her completely as his own.*

There was more written than this, but it slipped unread from Paul Radford's fingers as he began to weep. An officer passing by in the hallway heard him and looked in. "What's the matter, son?" the gravely voice asked. "Bad news from home?"

Radford looked up and saw it was the admiral who had spoken and who was now looking at him with concern. Forgetting all military etiquette he simply nodded and said, "Yes, sir. The very worst. I just lost my wife and my daughter."

"Jesus," the admiral said gently. "I'm sorry son. What took them from you?"

"The war, sir," Radford answered, pulling himself together. "The war and the frigging politicians who caused it. That's who took them."

"Easy, son," the admiral said. "I know you've had a shock, but that kind of talk can get you in deep trouble."

"With all due respect to you, personally, sir," Radford responded, his voice unnaturally calm, "I don't care. They took the one thing I care most about. And if you had me taken out and shot, sir, I'd consider it a favor."

The admiral looked at him thoughtfully. "I don't think you really mean that, son, but if you do, I have a better way to die."

"I'm listening, sir," Radford replied, getting to his feet and snapping a belated salute.

"Not now, son," the Admiral told him, returning the salute. "If you feel the same way next week come in and see me. It is very unlikely whoever takes the mission will ever come back."

"Thank you, sir," Radford told him. "I'll see you next week."

The admiral nodded and started to turn away. Then he turned back. "You're not up for Section 8 are you, Lieutenant? I don't need a loose cannon on my deck."

"Check my record, admiral," came the reply. "I won't disappoint you."

The admiral nodded. "As you were." *Jesus,* he thought as he walked away, thinking of Radford's icy calm. *I'd hate to have that young man after me.*

Some months after this, BUPERS, the Bureau of Personnel, discovered it needed someone fluent in Spanish and Quecha and sorted through its records. The list of available personnel was very short and one Lieutenant Paul Radford was the name at the top of their list. Within hours after his file was pulled, Paul Radford found himself on the way back to Washington. After close to two years of haggling on the part of Rudd and White, he was being assigned to the Special Advisory Group.

When they met, Denis Blieu was stunned by the change in his friend, and even Jacques Paul was taken aback. "It is like his body is present, but there's no one at home," he remarked to Blieu after they were done. "I don't know exactly what happened to him in Alaska but he sure has changed."

"To be very honest, he worries me," White said. "There's something very wrong there. I wonder if we ought to use him at all. He's too damned cold. He could go off the deep end."

Rudd nodded. "I know. The last thing we need is a loose canon on the deck in South America. On the other hand, I busted my butt to get him reassigned. What are we going to do with him if we don't send him to keep an eye on Haya and his commies? Who else can we get? We don't have a lot of time." He looked at Jacques Paul. "What do you think, Jock? You think you can work with him?"

The other shrugged. "Well, he hasn't done anything to tell me otherwise. He certainly handled himself well in that firefight and there is nothing but good marks in his record. Not many people would volunteer for the assignments he took in Alaska, and the admiral there bitched like hell loosing him. He also put Radford up for three silver stars. I'd guess whatever is eating at him is something very personal. Maybe the change will do him good. I'd say let's go with him."

"What about you, Denis?" Rudd inquired. "It's your call, too. You won't be working with him directly but he could affect your operations if he goes bad."

Blieu shook his head. "I don't know what to say, Eric. The file says nothing but good about him and he's done good work for us before. He's a also personal friend, but I don't know. We wouldn't be doing him any favors dumping him into a mess he can't handle."

"Oh, I can handle it, all right," came a quiet voice from the doorway. Paul Radford stood there watching them, a faintly mocking smile on his lips. "I came back to ask Denis something. Why are you talking about me behind my back?" he asked, as if he were inquiring about the weather. "Why don't you just ask me face to face?"

"You've changed, Paul," Blieu told him. "We don't understand the change and it worries us."

Radford shrugged. "I've had some personal problems," he told them. "Now they're under control and they haven't affected my work. What's the deal with Haya? What's he done now?"

"You know him?" Jacques Paul asked.

"We argued politics over beer one night in Lima," Radford answered. "I didn't agree with him but I respect him. He's very sharp. Probably very dangerous, too." The sound of his voice as he spoke was disembodied as an echo. "So if that's who you're thinking of linking me up with, there's rapport." He looked around the room. "Unless, of course, you think I'm unfit." He shrugged and sat down. "Personally, I don't give a shit either way," he added, lighting a cigarette. There was no defiance in his tone, just a simple statement of fact. "I'd just as soon go back to Alaska. At least I'm wanted there."

There was quiet for a long time. Finally Rudd spoke. "What I need to know, Paul, is very simple. Can I can trust you?"

"I don't know, Commander," Radford answered quietly. "I don't trust many people myself these days. I guess you can trust me to be who I am, what the hell ever that is." He grinned and took a drag on his cigarette, looked at them calmly. "The main thing is, I do know the guy. I respect him, too."

"You wouldn't mind going back to Peru?" Jacques Paul asked.

For a moment there was a passing shadow of something in Radford's eyes, but when he spoke it was in the same quiet tone. "No. The heat should be off by now and I can keep a low profile." There was silence and he looked around the groom. "Look, Commander," he said. "I'm not going to screw things up. What the hell. Winter's coming. Chasing bananas sure beats the hell out of freezing my nuts off in Nome, all right?" A ghost of a smile played around the edges of his mouth. Radford chuckled and the others laughed, the tension broken.

"That's more like it," Rudd said. "That's the guy I used to know. All right then. You're our man. Alex can make some coffee and we'll go over what we have in the files." He glanced at his watch. "Take five for a piss call an we'll hit it."

As the men left the room Jacques Paul nodded to himself, frowning to mask his growing sense of excitement. *Very good, Paul Radford,* he thought. *You did that very well, my friend, and nobody noticed. But I did. Maybe I don't know what's eating you but I know why you want to go back to Peru. You want to die and Alaska couldn't kill you. But sooner or later I will find out what makes you tick and when I do I'll use it to make you the best assassin this country's ever known.*

Yet when the captain looked up he found Radford watching him with a canny, knowing look. As their eyes met, the corner of the younger man's mouth curled up into the same light, ironic smile. *Not this time, Jacques Paul,* it seemed to say. *Not this time.*

Joel B. Reed

About the Author

Joel B. Reed is the author of eight novels, a number of nonfiction works, and two collections of poetry. Two of his novels have been published with 1stBooks, *The Journal of Martin Quinn* (1999) and *Lakota Spring* (2002). He is also an avid photographer and storyteller, and makes his home in southern Minnesota.

Printed in the United States
1174800003B/238-294